Penguin Books
Spanish Stirrup

John Prebble was born in Middlesex in 1915 but spent his boyhood in Saskatchewan, Canada. A journalist since 1934, he is also a novelist, film-writer, and the author of several highly praised dramatized documentaries for B.B.C. television and radio. During the war he served six years in the ranks with the Royal Artillery, from which experience he wrote his successful war novel, *The Edge of Darkness*. His other books include *Where the Sea Breaks*, *The Buffalo Soldiers*, which won an award in the United States for the best historical novel of the American West, and *Culloden*, a subject he became interested in when he was a boy in a predominantly Scottish township in Canada. *Culloden* was published in 1961 and *Glencoe* in the spring of 1966. All these books are available in Penguins. His latest book is *The Lion in the North* (Penguin, 1971).

John Prebble

Spanish Stirrup

and other stories

Penguin Books

Penguin Books Ltd,
Harmondsworth, Middlesex, England
Penguin Books Inc.,
7110 Ambassador Road, Baltimore, Maryland 21207, U.S.A.
Penguin Books Australia Ltd,
Ringwood, Victoria, Australia
Penguin Books Canada Ltd,
41 Steelcase Road West, Markham, Ontario, Canada
Penguin Books (N.Z.) Ltd,
182–190 Wairau Road, Auckland 10, New Zealand

This collection first published by Martin Secker & Warburg 1973
Four stories in this volume first published in 1958 under the title of
My Great-Aunt Appearing Day
'The Long Hate' first published in England 1973
Published in Penguin Books 1975

Made and printed in Great Britain by
Hazell Watson & Viney Ltd
Aylesbury, Bucks
Set in Linotype Pilgrim

For my Father
John William Prebble
whose great-aunt was the
original Appearing Day

Contents

My Great-Aunt Appearing Day

I was thirteen when I first heard of my great-aunt Appearing Day.

Late one afternoon, shortly after my birthday, my father discovered me at play with a crude bow and arrow I had fashioned for myself. For some minutes he watched me from the kitchen door, his hands thrust into the front pockets of his check trousers, his eyes squinting against the sun. Then he called me to him abruptly, and when I came he took the toy from my hands. I waited, expecting a rebuke, but instead he slipped the bow back into my hand and said, 'Your great-aunt would like that.' Then he looked down at me with the warm and gentle smile of a man enjoying some secret humour.

Because he was a man who liked to make the most of the little dramas of life he did not tell me immediately of my great-aunt, but chose to be mysterious. I cannot blame him for this. Being postmaster to a small Kentish village offered him little other excitement, and the story of Joshua Tanner and Appearing Day deserved the touch of theatre he gave to it. When he had returned the bow he took one hand from his pocket and gently fingered his watch-fob. 'Come with me, boy,' he said at last, 'I'd like to show you something.'

We walked through the kitchen, through the dusty little post office to the street beyond. He kept his hands in his pockets and walked with great strides that outpaced mine, so that I hopped and skipped along behind him. We went up the street to the Norman church, and when we reached the gate he stopped and played with his watch-fob again, watching me to see how I was responding to this mystery. 'Where would it be, now,' he said, winking slily to let me see that he knew all the time. My curiosity began to generate heat.

'Of course!' he said, and slapped his thigh, 'It's over there beneath the cypresses.'

So off we went again, across the churchyard, threading our way past the little hummocks of old graves, until we reached a lonely spot, almost overgrown with meadow-sweet and traveller's joy. I looked at it with some disappointment.

My father took a stick and carefully beat down the grass about the grave, and then he scratched the moss from the face of the stone. 'Can you read it?' he asked, looking over his shoulder at me. I could not, and I said that I could not, with some truculence, for I had expected more excitement than this. He straightened his back. 'Well then, I shall have to read it for you.' He traced the stick along the inscription on the stone, line by line. 'Here lies ...' he said.

Here lies
JOSHUA TANNER
of this parish
Late Major of the United States Army
and his beloved wife
APPEARING DAY
a daughter of the Cheyenne, sister of the Arapaho
and a devout Christian
Joined in death October 14, 1894
'Nothing lives long, except the earth and the mountains'

When my father had finished reading he repeated the words *a daughter of the Cheyenne, sister of the Arapaho*. There was sadness in his voice, although he was smiling. Then once more he said the words *Cheyenne* and *Arapaho*, and made them sound like notes of some barbaric music. With his hands he gently moved the grass over the grave and threw the stick into the corner of the graveyard. He turned to face me. 'Well, what do you think of that?'

What was I to think, except that in this overgrown spot, twenty years before, had been buried two of my distant relatives? I considered this a very poor secret, and the expression on my face must have shown this, for my father's emotions suddenly exploded, blowing his hands out of those tight pockets and flinging them wide from his shoulders.

'An Indian, my boy!' he shouted triumphantly, 'A daughter

of the Cheyenne. A real Indian buried here in Kent, and she was your great-aunt.' He placed his hand on my shoulder and the wonder of it came to me slowly. When he saw that my imagination was beginning to catch fire he whirled me about and set off smartly across the churchyard, through the creaking gate, down the village street. I trotted behind him, full of questions which were primarily concerned with whether this did or did not make me something of an Indian too.

Into the house again we marched, my father strutting as if he were following a military band. Past my mother, up the stairs, up the attic steps until, finally and out of breath, we were beneath the rafters of the roof. My father stood in the centre of the attic and particles of dust glittered about him in the sunlight.

'It's here, somewhere,' he said, returning to his game of mystery, 'If only I could remember where.'

Then he attacked the great confusion of jumble, throwing boxes and bundles behind him, stirring up more dust until we were both coughing. At last, beneath everything else, he found a small cabin trunk, barred with brass and with a vaulted roof.

'This was Uncle Josh's,' he said as he threw back the lid. There was little enough inside, a few books that looked like ledgers, a wide-skirted coat and a broad belt, some woollen socks and a pair of old moleskin trousers. There was also a brown-paper parcel which my father opened carefully.

It contained a large, empty knife-sheath made of soft leather and decorated with white and red beads. It, too, was old, and the thongs at the bottom of it crumbled in my father's fingers. 'That was Little Dog's, I imagine,' he said, laying it on the floor. 'And this, this was your great-aunt Appearing Day.'

He held towards me a small, faded photograph in an oval frame. Emerging not too distinctly from a dusky cloud was a plump little woman in a black dress covered with jet at the shoulders and throat. Her face was round and seemed to have no eyebrows, but she was smiling with a placid gentleness. Her black hair was long, parted in the middle and lying on her breast in two plaits. She looked like a gypsy, not the Indian of my imagination. There was not even one feather in her straight, shining hair.

But this was she, my great-aunt Appearing Day, a daughter of the Cheyenne, sister of the Arapaho. It seemed too great a title for so ordinary a face.

'There was a devil of a to-do about burying her in the churchyard, I remember,' said my father. 'Particularly over the inscription which Uncle Josh said should go on the headstone when he died. But he produced some scrap of paper which said the old lady had been baptized.' He took the photograph from my hands, smiled at it affectionately, and wrapped it carefully in the paper again.

My father told me something of Josh Tanner's story, some of it there in the attic that afternoon, filling in the details as he remembered them during the following years. When I was able to read the writing in the ledgers, half diary, half business accounts, I learnt a little more. I don't think my father ever caught the real spirit of the story. His picture of an Indian had been formed in his boyhood, when Colonel Cody toured England. But he told me enough for me to understand.

Years later I met an old man sitting on the veranda of a clapboard house in Butte. He said that he had known my great-uncle. Certainly he had been at Laramie during the Treaty Talks. Reporters often went to him for memories of the frontier days. I suspect that he often repaired his memory with his imagination, yet it was largely because of what he was able to tell me, there in Butte many years ago now, that I believe this to be as much the story of Little Dog and American Horse, as it is the story of my great-uncle Joshua Tanner and my great-aunt Appearing Day.

*

Josh Tanner was thirty-eight when he rode from St Joseph to the fork of the North Platte at Laramie Creek. He was then, as he was to be all his life, a handsome man. His hair was long in the extravagant fashion set by Custer, curling over the collar of his coat, and to groom it he carried a mother-of-pearl comb inside a vest-pocket. He was proud of his hair and the curve of his high nose. He wore high boots like a Texan *vaquero*, but his black felt hat and flowered vest made him look like a riverboat gambler.

The horse he rode was a livery stable mount that he had bought in Atchison, Kansas, and the journey across the plains had almost finished it.

He must have been sighted before he reached the fork, for a trooper rode out from the fort, splashed across the creek and asked him his business. The soldier was dusty and nervous. He was young, and probably he had never imagined that there could be as many Indians as those who had set up their villages about Fort Laramie for the Treaty Talks. Some of his nervousness was in his voice, pitching it on a high note as he held his horse on short rein and shouted to Josh.

Josh took some papers from his pocket and waved them at the boy, but the trooper did not take them. He backed his horse and spat the dust from his mouth, saying the colonel would have to read that there, for he could not read at all.

Josh shrugged his shoulders. He did not think that the Army, worried enough by the gathering Sioux and Cheyenne nations, would be interested in him. But he turned his horse down to the fort, and the soldier followed.

On either side of the Platte, and particularly along the shallower waters of the creek, there were enough Indians to try the nerves of any soldier fresh from the East. There were the lodges of several thousand Sioux and Northern Cheyenne. The creek was full of women, children and dogs; screaming, laughing, barking. Smoke from lodge fires threaded through the cottonwood groves. Young men drove herds of ponies to water. Some of the further villages stretched on to the sandhills.

Josh took his eyes from the villages and looked to the north, where the distant Black Hills were darkening. 'There they are,' he said to himself, but aloud.

The trooper clattered up to him. 'How's that, sir?'

Josh nodded toward the lodges. 'Never seen so many, have you, boy?'

The soldier flushed. He pulled at his cap-peak and waved his hand towards the fort. Josh smiled, swung one leg up to his saddle and let his tired horse choose its own pace. Laramie had long since ceased to be a defensive fort. It was not even as Josh remembered it from before the War. The palisades were still there, and the great blockhouse at the gateway, still marked by the old red horse of the American Fur Company. But a city of tents and huts, the office of the stage line, a gambling show, the camps of waiting miners, spilled away from the walls until they mingled with the Sioux villages.

The Colonel, when the trooper took Josh to him, looked up wearily and nodded. He stared at Josh's black coat and flowered vest. He was a middle-aged man, thinned and browned by plains life, and what hair he had was white. He sat at a camp desk, before a map of the Territory, and his cap and sword made a costumier's set-piece before him. Behind him a capless sergeant looked at Josh with disgust.

The Colonel flapped a hand through Josh's papers without interest. '*Major* Tanner?'

'Courtesy title more or less, Colonel. I did some buffalo killing for the Army during the War.'

'You're English,' said the Colonel with distaste.

Since this was less of a question than an observation Josh did not reply. The Colonel pulled at his chin, and then wiped his hand across his cheeks, listening critically to a bugle-note fluting beyond the post. 'What are you here for, Mr. Tanner?'

'It says there, Colonel. I represent a group of businessmen in the East. They're interested in the Black Hills country.'

'Who isn't since gold was struck?' The Colonel pushed his tongue hard against his cheek and now looked at Josh without disguising his dislike. 'That's still Sioux and Cheyenne country, Mr Tanner. There are too many white men there already, and illegally from the Indians' point of view. There are 15,000 miners waiting at Custer for these Talks to end. Having people like you around can be a handicap, Mr Tanner.'

'It won't be Indian country will it, Colonel, not when the Commissioners get the treaty signed? What stretch of desert are the Sioux and the Cheyenne getting in exchange?'

The cavalryman sat upright and looked beyond Josh's shoulder, his pale eyes suddenly without expression. 'My instructions are to see that civilians do not prejudice the Talks. I'll waste no time nursing prospectors or gamblers.'

'I'm neither, Colonel.' Josh slapped the dust from his hat against his knee. 'You might say I prospect for towns, though.

Where there's gold there's a city very soon. The businessmen I represent wish to stake claims in real estate.'

'Admirable public spirit,' said the Colonel wearily.

An orderly came in and brushed a hand against his forehead. 'With the Colonel's permission, sir. One of the Cheyenne chiefs, Broken Hand. He's outside, sir.'

'All right.' The Colonel dismissed Josh. 'Oblige me, Mr Tanner, by keeping to this post until the Talks are over.' He stood up, put on his cap and buckled on his sabre. He held his gauntlets in one hand and waited behind the desk. He fell unconsciously into the pose which the situation demanded – the commander of four companies of cavalry undisturbed by the knowledge that he was surrounded by three thousand Indians.

Josh left. Outside the wind was rolling tumbleweed through the open gateway and across the square. At the bottom of the steps a mounted Indian waited in the dust. He was an old man and his face seemed woven from deep wrinkles and old scars. He wore no paint and his grey hair was gathered into a knot at the back of his skull and held there by the wingbone of a war-eagle. A trooper's yellow bandana was tied about his throat and his shoulders were covered by a blanket. His long legs hung straight on either side of the saddle, the braids of his moccasins touching the earth. He looked tired. He looked, thought Josh, like the Eastern papers often pictured the savage Indian.

Behind him were a few of his people, young men daubed with vermilion, decorated with turkey feathers. They stared about them with curiosity and insolence. At the old man's bridle was a girl. She carried Broken Hand's white shield, his medicine bag and his long, feathered lance.

The door of the office banged and the sergeant came out. He shouted for a Pawnee interpreter, and then he said 'All right!' to the old man and jerked his thumb over his shoulder.

The Cheyenne slipped from the saddle gracefully, gathered his blanket about him and walked up the steps as if there were nobody in the fort but himself and his people. When he left, the other Indians squatted patiently in the dust, half-closing their eyes. Their arms shone with grease, and the turkey-feathers on their rumps dipped in the dust. The girl remained on her feet by the horse.

Josh's curiosity in them passed. His mouth was dry and dust itched on his skin. From the sutler's store there came the thin, giggling music of a guitar, and he walked towards it, pulling the bridle of his horse. As he passed the Indians he was aware that the girl had turned her head to look at him. He stopped and looked at her, struck by the grace of her figure against the horse's flank. Then he walked on.

Magruder, the sutler, was a big man with a chest of thick, red hair. He was talking of gold, waving heavy hands in the air as if to form the words that came clumsily from his lips. He was talking of gold and he was saying that because there was gold in the Black Hills there was another reason for exterminating all Indians. He told the idlers and the loungers that he had always hated Indians, long before Custer's expedition found gold in the Black Hills. He pointed to a corner of the store where, eight years before, Red Cloud had signed the treaty that gave the Black Hills to the Sioux in perpetuity. It would have been better to have shot Red Cloud then.

When Josh asked him if he had a room or a bed Magruder stared at him carefully, studying the coat and the flowered vest as the Colonel had done. Then he waved his hand towards a door at the end of the store, and said that his daughter attended to such things.

Josh, expecting a girl who would be the daughter of her father, was unprepared for the woman who answered his knock. She was perhaps three or four years younger than he, but her face was younger still, and her dark, widely-spaced eyes were preoccupied with some inner and speculating amusement. Her pale skin, the plain white dress, made her look like an unfinished water-colour.

Josh adopted a defensive gallantry with all women who were not the red-faced, heavy-armed wives of settlers. 'I hesitate to trouble you, ma'am. I could put my blanket on the ground outside the fort like the others, I suppose, but after a month of that I would appreciate the luxury of a bed, or at least a roof over me.'

'We have no room,' she said cautiously. 'This is a sutler's store. There's a hotel of some kind, I'm told, among the tents below.'

'I know, ma'am, I have seen it, as no doubt you have. It will embarrass neither of us if we don't speak of it again.' He smiled at her, and suddenly she returned the smile. 'A shelf in the store, maybe, after it closes?'

She laughed. 'The store is never closed, except to the troopers at night. There's a small room, if you're set on it.' She placed the tip of her tongue in the corner of her mouth. 'If you're not too much of a gentleman. It's full of hides and flour.'

'May I see it, Miss Magruder?'

She showed him the room, a narrow box thick with flour and lit by a small, high window. She folded her arms and watched him now with open amusement as he dropped his blanket and saddle-bags and began to pace the room in silent appraisal. 'You've come from the East?' she said, suddenly wistful.

'From Saint Jo, ma'am, and further East still.' He turned to her on his heel. 'You're from there, yourself?'

She looked at him with what he thought was suspicion. 'My mother was,' she said and she left him. He shrugged his shoulders, lay down on the hides, pushed his hat over his eyes and went gratefully to sleep. Above him the flies quarrelled on the curtain of flour dust across the window.

*

Josh had longer to wait at Laramie than he had expected. The Treaty Talks went slowly. Sometimes they were held in the square, in the red glare of the sun, sometimes in the shadow of the south wall. The Indian leaders sat in a half-moon of savage colour, facing the Commissioners who sat on chairs behind a table, clapping their hands against the flies, or holding them down on their papers against the wind. They were sober, well-covered men in black suits, dogmatic in argument, rich in rhetoric, full of faith in the Colonel's four companies of cavalry.

But what they had to say was funnelled through the halting words of a Pawnee interpreter who was despised by the Cheyenne and the Sioux, and who, in his turn, despised the Commissioners in their high hats and elastic-sided boots. The Indians bargained shrewdly, and their young men walked away from each council carrying presents of cloth, blankets, and skillets. The warriors rode their ponies across the plain outside the fort, trailing bolts of brilliant calico through the dust. Sometimes naked children stood before the embarrassed Commissioners, sucking their fingers while flies crawled over their bodies. There was something comic and yet something dignified each day, and Josh was amused and entertained for a while.

The Indians were in no hurry, and they enjoyed themselves. The Government had sent meat from the cow country in Kansas and Texas so that buffalo hunts might not take the chiefs from the council. The slaughtered cattle hung like red banners in the streets of the villages.

Young Cheyenne and young Sioux strutted through the fort, painted and feathered. There was an ugly moment when a nervous trooper fired his carbine at a Cheyenne Dog Soldier who prowled too near the horse-lines at dusk, but even this ended in laughter when it was discovered that the trooper had killed a horse rather than the Indian. The Indians had nothing to lose by the delay, this was their land they were being asked to leave, land granted to them by previous Treaty so long as grass grew. The Commissioners sweated and grumbled in the heat, searched their minds for new arguments and new threats, and asked the Colonel for yet another drill parade to amuse them. He complied with obvious irritation.

Josh was soon bored. He played euchre with the enlisted men at the sutler's store. He played monte in Old Bedlam, the officers' club. As the days passed more and more gold-seekers came in from Kansas and Missouri, and there were also cowhands from as far south as the Neuces looking for new range country. The tents outside the fort grew into a brawling city. The stage-line became rich, and so did some of the Indians. Still the Commissioners sweated, and the lines about the Colonel's mouth tightened with impatience. He overcame some of his earlier hostility when he discovered that Josh was not a professional gambler, that he could speak some Cheyenne and that he understood the sign-language of the plains. He asked for Josh's help at the councils, 'unofficially, you understand, Mr Tanner.'

Broken Hand worried the Colonel. The Old Man Chief of the Cheyenne sat silently at each day's talks, beating at the flies with an eagle-wing fan, his old body as red and as sterile as the sand between his feet. The same slender girl stood behind him always with his shield and lance. When the day was over he left the council without taking the presents that had been spread before him.

'That's a bad Indian, Mr Tanner,' said the Colonel for the third time.

'I don't know, Colonel. Would you sell New England for a few blankets?'

A fat little Commissioner with sandy hair protested hotly. 'You have an uncommon sympathy for them, sir! Their habits are disgustingly immoral, any white man knows that. That, that young girl ...'

Josh interrupted him coldly. 'The chastity of Cheyenne women is renowned on the plains. The girl is Broken Hand's daughter.'

The Commissioner frowned. 'Well, then, sir, what about this? Yesterday I saw an Indian wearing a necklace *of human fingers*! What about that, sir?'

Josh laughed, held up his hands and drew the right forefinger quickly across the left forefinger.

'Are you mocking me, sir? What does that mean?'

'No, Mr Simmons, I'm not. That's sign-language for the Cheyennes. The other tribes call them Cut Fingers. Once they always preserved the fingers of the enemies they killed. As ritual trophies, you understand.'

Simmons wiped the sweat from his forehead with a large handkerchief. 'Abominable savages!'

Josh shrugged his shoulders. 'It's a point of view, Mr Simmons. The Cheyennes never beat their children or their women, and they believe that white men who do so are barbarians. They also believe that a man's word should be honoured. They thought that when this country was given to them and the Sioux for as long as grass grew and water ran it meant for ever. It's as I say, Mr Simmons, just a point of view.'

Simmons turned his back abruptly. 'Can't we force Broken Hand to go south, Colonel?'

'Force him? How?' The Colonel did not look at the Commissioner. 'He's a bad influence. But damn it, sir, hasn't this country had enough fighting?'

Simmons looked unhappy. 'I did not mean force of arms.'

'What did you mean, sir?'

'Why, Colonel, *food*!' The Commissioner opened his hands to show how simple the solution was. 'These savages are slowly starving, yet they would rather kill each other and us than work the land. But they'll do anything if they are dependent on us for food. Sooner or later you soldiers will have to accept Washington's view that it is cheaper to feed lazy Indians than fight them.'

The Colonel thrust his heel into the earth and steadied his body on it. He bit his lower lip gently. 'I'm aware, sir, that considerable fortunes have been made in the East by men who have secured contracts to supply the reservations. Sooner or later, in your own words, Mr Simmons, sir, Washington may have to accept the view that the plains Indians are subjects of this Republic in armed insurrection.'

'Now, Colonel, you must leave politics to us.'

'Glad to, sir. I see your colleagues have gone to their quarters. I shall be happy to see you at dinner.'

They watched the little Commissioner climbing the slope to the fort. Josh caught the Colonel's eye and smiled.

The Colonel's shoulders stiffened. 'My views amuse you, perhaps?'

'Yours is another point of view, Colonel. But I was wondering how little Simmons thinks an Indian should be allowed to eat in return for good behaviour. And I was wondering whether the thought that he is a subject of the Union has ever occurred to Broken Hand.'

'You have some other solution, of course, Mr Tanner?'

'I've no solution, Colonel. There's a certain inevitability in this situation. The Indians will accept defeat when they are convinced that it is their destiny. I suspect Broken Hand is already convinced, what worries him is that some of his young men are not.'

'Your concern for them does you credit, Mr Tanner, though your employers might not agree with me.' The Colonel straightened his back and marched up to the fort, his sabre held tightly to his body by his left hand, his long legs jerking forward.

In the gritting wind that blew day after day Josh lost most of his pleasure in the colour and the excitement of the Treaty Talks. He became impatient with the young shavetails in Old Bedlam who explained to him again and again that Custer, had he not been killed by the Sioux, would have handled these Indians more effectively. It was their lack of faith in their old Colonel, rather than their boyish judgment, that irritated Josh, and he could no longer listen to them.

Eventually he avoided their company and chose instead that of Ann Magruder. He turned to her first in curiosity. It was difficult to believe that she was Magruder's daughter, and he decided that her mother must have been singularly lacking in judgement when she made her choice of husband. The sutler himself seemed to be in awe of his daughter's cool and untroubled complacency. Now and then the younger officers attempted to squire her, but were repulsed by her gentle mockery, her refusal to disguise the fact that she was amused rather than impressed by their gallantry.

Josh rode with her in the mornings when she could spare the time, and he admired her complete mastery of the horse he rented for her. He was intrigued, but more often faintly irritated by her efforts to take command of his mind. She had a little library of books and she lent him a volume now and then. These he pretended to read.

She told him that she was keeping a journal of her life on the plains, 'all the manifold and extraordinary things one sees here in the West.' He dredged his memory for experiences of his own that might be put down in this journal. He complimented her gravely on her foresight, for such a volume, he said, would be of great interest to Easterners could it be published. She told him that a Boston publisher had indeed expressed an interest in such a book.

Away from the fort her self-confidence made Josh feel like a child. For him to have touched her hand would have seemed a boorish presumption, yet there were times when she placed her own fingers on his arm as she spoke to him. He was vaguely alarmed by this intimacy.

She preferred to ride to the top of the bluff where she could look down on the Cheyenne villages and see the arrogant warriors stalking along the banks of the Platte, the boys and young women splashing in the creek. Josh suspected that she chose this spot because there she could enjoy the colour of the scene without having to endure the stench of it. She asked her careful, detailed questions, and she stored away his answers in her mind.

The bugle marked the hours of the day in the cavalry post. At dawn a jingling patrol rode out towards the mountains, a column of blue, yellow and steel, threading through the mist. It returned at dusk, leather creaking, men slumped in the saddle. Still the Commissioners and the chiefs bargained, and the Pawnee scouts began to yawn insolently in the faces of the Sioux and the Cheyennes. But one by one the chiefs made the agreement sign with their hands and surrendered. At night the drums throbbed with pleasure or anger over the terms given. Only Broken Hand's silent intransigence remained unchanged.

On the ninth day after his arrival at Laramie Josh rode as usual to the bluff with Ann Magruder, dismounted there and sat with her. They were watching the gaudy colour below them when the noise of hooves startled them. A group of Cheyennes topped the bluff in a flurry of dust.

There were five of them, all young, all Dog Soldiers, members of that elite warrior society which had lodges in both the Sioux and the Cheyenne nations. They halted and they scowled. Their leader was a young dandy. His broad face was lighter in colour than the others, and his hair, which hung loose and unbraided on his shoulders, was a dark brown rather than black. The tail of a prairie-cock fluttered at the back of his skull. Pendants of shells drooped from the lobes of his ears, his deerskin leggings were decorated with silver. He was more than six feet in height, lithe and elegant. Josh heard Ann Magruder draw her breath quickly between her teeth, and he suspected that this was more from admiration than fear.

A dragoon's sabre was tied to the warrior's wooden saddle, and an otter-skin quiver hung below his left armpit, but he carried a rifle. From the centre of his shield, where it rested on the flank of his horse, there radiated a star of scarlet feathers.

'Mr Tanner . . .' said Ann Magruder.

He turned to her. 'Please behave quite naturally, Miss Magruder. There's no reason to be afraid.'

She frowned. 'I am not afraid, Mr Tanner. I merely wished to ask why his horse's ears are split in that cruel manner.'

Josh smiled, thinking of the journal. 'It means that it is the young man's buffalo pony, the best he has.'

'Thank you, Mr Tanner.' The words were too precise, their tone too casual, and he thought *she is afraid, after all.*

Another warrior, almost as elegant as the first, heeled his pony forward and halted it. He, too, was strung with pendant shells and painted with vermilion. But he wore a breech-clout instead of leggings, and he carried a lance, not a rifle. The sun glistened on the taut muscles of his legs.

The first Dog Soldier slipped from his horse and stared at Josh with a mixture of boyish insolence and adult nobility. The silver dollars on his leggings jingled as he walked, and he strutted to increase their music. The second warrior dismounted and joined him. Then all the others alighted and squatted in the shade of their ponies.

'What do they want, Mr Tanner?'

Josh shrugged his shoulders. He was asking himself the same question. The two warriors walked to within a yard of him and sneered gallantly. He looked cautiously at the distance between the bluff and the fort, and then he looked back at the Cheyennes and nodded gravely.

'I am Little Dog,' said the first, 'This is my friend American Horse.' Then he walked across to Josh's horse, felt its neck and legs, examined the saddle appreciatively. He breathed into the animal's nostrils, put his hand on the bridle and slowly the horse was forced down on its knees.

Little Dog stood back and grinned. He pointed to the horse and said something quickly at which the others threw back their heads and laughed.

The Cheyenne turned to Josh angrily. 'I am Little Dog.'

'I am Josh Tanner.'

Little Dog sneered at Ann Magruder, dilating his nostrils. He seemed proud of his ability to do this, for he repeated it several times. Then he picked up Josh's hat from the ground, put it on his head, forward over his brows so that the crest of feathers stuck up behind it. His companions grinned, and pounded their fists into their palms approvingly. Encouraged by their amusement the Cheyenne changed his lithe carriage into a heavy, swinging mockery of a white man's walk.

'Mr Tanner . . .' said Ann Magruder, and this time there was a tremble in her voice.

'They are hoping I will lose my temper, Miss Magruder.' He pulled a cigar from his pocket and lit it. He hoped that at least one officer in the fort was sufficiently interested in his work to turn his field-glass this way.

Suddenly Little Dog flung the hat into the dust and stood with his feet astride, hands on his hips. The silver dollars tinkled pleasantly. Josh smiled tolerantly, picked up his hat, brushed it on his thigh, and put it on his head.

'Please let me help you mount, Miss Magruder, but calmly.' Her hand quivered when she placed it in his. He then pulled himself slowly into his own saddle and turned his horse towards the fort. The Cheyennes leapt on their ponies and whirled about them astonishingly. Little Dog spun the sabre in an arc of light, looking out of the corner of his eyes to Josh.

Ann Magruder bit her lip. 'Where did he get that terrible weapon, Mr Tanner?'

'Some Cheyennes under Two Moon were at the Big Horn massacre, my dear,' said Josh with a gentleness that surprised her. 'Perhaps the boy was one of them. But it's not a thing the Indians would use themselves. He's boasting.'

By the ford of the Platte Josh halted his pony and held her bridle too. The horses began to drink. Josh took the mother-of-pearl comb from his vest-pocket and began to comb his hair slowly, whistling gently to himself. He watched the Indian youths. They stared and then they grinned. Little Dog trotted his pony to Josh's thigh and placed a hand on the white man's shoulder. He smiled pleasantly and then rode away furiously, swinging the sabre above his head. His friends tugged their ponies about and rode after him, yelling.

Josh took out his handkerchief and wiped his forehead. He saw that Ann Magruder's lips were white.

'I congratulate you, Miss Magruder.'

'It was most interesting,' she said, and turned her face towards the fort.

He could not resist the impulse. 'If there is any question about them,' he said, 'Anything for your journal, I mean. Please ask me.'

He thought she smiled. 'Thank you, Josh.'

Only later did he realize that she had used his given name for the first time, and the remembrance made him uneasy.

That evening one of the Pawnee scouts came to the sutler's store and said that a Cheyenne brave was at the gate asking for *Pe-Han'-ska*. Josh was standing on the *ramada* of the store with Ann Magruder, and when the name slipped ironically from the thick lips of the Pawnee he grinned.

'Why does he call you that, Mr Tanner?'

'It means Long Hair,' said Josh, and his hand went involuntarily to the nape of his neck. 'It's what the Sioux called Custer. The Cheyenne is laughing at me.'

She laughed too, and placed her hand impulsively on his arm. He left her abruptly, walking across the square with his hands in his pockets, a cigar gripped in the corner of his mouth again. She watched him go, smiling again at the arrogance of his walk. He reminded her, she thought, of the actors she had seen in third-rate companies touring the East, and instantly she was ashamed of the comparison.

When Josh reached the gate he found the sentry standing with his feet astride, his carbine across his chest, facing a shadowy horseman. This was Little Dog, and he grinned down out of the darkness at Josh, like a boy calling on another for play. He put out his hand and Josh grasped it with pleasure. Little Dog explained that Josh would be welcome in Broken Hand's village.

He was not alone. There was a girl standing by the flank of his pony. Little Dog looked down at her with pride.

'She is Appearing Day,' he said.

It was the girl, Josh remembered, who held Broken Hand's lance and shield at the councils. She stared at Josh boldly. There were two darts of vermilion on her cheeks. Her face was round, her complexion clear of the smallpox that disfigured so many Indian women, and she held her body upright inside her white smock. The moccasins on her feet were gaily beaded, and a dog snarled and teased at the long tassels that trailed from their heels.

'You will come?' said Little Dog.

Josh nodded, and the Cheyenne turned his horse about and walked it back to his village. Before she left, Appearing Day smiled at Josh.

Josh heard the rustle of Ann Magruder's skirt beside him, and he turned to face her. 'I came to see the sort of man who is not afraid to laugh at you. Wasn't that the young savage we saw this morning?' She slipped her hand naturally through his arm as they walked back. 'That was a pretty girl with him, Josh. It's strange how attractive some of these women can be.'

And she could not understand why this remark seemed to anger him.

*

While the Commissioners argued in the shadows of the fort, and a resigned lassitude fell over all other activities, the friendship of the Cheyennes became, to Josh's mind, the only reality of his life at Laramie. Even the morning rides with Ann Magruder lost their novelty, and he felt too tired to fence with her unspoken humour.

Little Dog and American Horse made no subtle demands on his emotions. They welcomed him with great, sonorous shouts of '*Ha!*' whenever he rode down to their village. They chewed his cigars, they wore his felt hat, and they mocked him kindly. They boasted of their horsemanship to him, but politely applauded his own. They displayed the Crow scalps on the shoulders of their blankets in the manner a white boy would exhibit a prairie-dog skin. They drank in his tolerant admiration, and they brought him a horse which they had stolen from the Crows, and which he had some difficulty in refusing.

Through them he met Broken Hand, an eroded rock among the shifting dust of the perplexed Cheyennes, a quiet, dignified old man whose mind was a compound of harsh realism and primitive mysticism. Because he was an Old Man Chief of the Cheyennes he was permitted no troubles, no problems of his own. He could be the conscience, the heart, the mind and the voice of his people only. This was something, Josh knew, that the Commissioners did not understand. They believed that they were faced by an intractable old man who acted from quixotic and personal motives. They blustered when he reminded them that eight years before the Black Hills had been granted to the Sioux and the Cheyennes in perpetuity. They considered this a frivolous and impertinent objection. Even the tired Colonel was once near to agreeing when Simmons suggested that Broken Hand should be sent in irons to Florida.

Josh suspected that Broken Hand was willing enough to accept a new treaty and take his people south to the arid lands along the Canadian River, not because he believed that such a new treaty was a just one but because he knew that there was no alternative. So long as the thoughts and happiness of the Cheyennes were held to the headwaters of the Yellowstone and the Powder, however, Broken Hand was bound by his office to speak and argue his nation's cause.

One by one the Sioux villages were breaking up and departing for their reservations in the Dakotas. Still the Cheyennes remained in their village along Laramie Creek. The stage from the East brought Josh an angry letter from Kansas, in which he was sharply reminded of his contract and its required fulfilment within specified dates. He answered it with bald irony, saying he had not yet been able to convince the Cheyennes of the white man's need to build cities on their traditional hunting grounds.

One morning Little Dog came to the fort to invite Josh to the Cheyenne village that evening. The young man was sullen and short-tempered, speaking down his nose and looking about the fort with bitter eyes. Appearing Day was with him again, brown and slender in her white smock. Having delivered his invitation Little Dog kicked the ribs of his horse, the dollars ringing on his legs, the cock's feather fluttering in his hair, and he rode away without answering Josh's pleasantries. The girl looked at Josh, smiled gently, and slipped down the hill. He watched her go with regret.

He saw her again that night when he rode up to Broken Hand's lodge. She came and took his bridle, and led the horse away once he dismounted. The firelight shone on the shields and the lances hanging from rods before each lodge. The darkness was splashed by the flames and by the scarlet of the hanging feathers.

Josh entered the lodge. It was full of old headmen, crouched about the fire in their robes, mumbling and grimacing, their faces like malleable masks. There was a rustle behind Josh, and Appearing Day spread a blanket for him beside Broken Hand. He squatted on it, resting his elbows on his knees and nodding to the old men. Little Dog sneered proudly at the entrance flap of the lodge.

Broken Hand sat before the sacred Buffalo Mask and the Red Shield. 'This is my daughter Appearing Day,' he said to Josh, 'Little Dog's father has bought her in marriage for his son.'

Josh gravely nodded his compliments to the young Dog Soldier and the boy grinned back through the smoke.

The girl brought the long pipe, filled it with tobacco and willow-bark, and it was passed round the lodge until the air was almost opaque with smoke. She brought bowls of boiled cow-meat and the old men ate noisily, sucking their fingers and grumbling in querulous argument. But before they ate they waited for Broken Hand to make the ritual offering of the meat to the earth and the sky, to the north, the east, the south and the west. For Josh's benefit the old men boasted like children of the exploits of their youth, of great battles with the Pawnee, the Comanche and the Kiowa in the south. They flung up withered arms and opened toothless mouths. They wrangled, and they laughed broadly, but Broken Hand said nothing.

Across the Dakota plains a thunderstorm broke and shuddered the lodge poles. The old men shook their heads and read portents into the noise. Josh felt that his head was bursting, and he found it hard to follow the wandering conversation of the old men, and hard to understand why he had been invited to this council. Then a headman began to speak of the treaty talks. His words were uttered with great dignity and he accompanied them with swift movements of his thin hands. Little Dog bent his head to listen, and when he approved of what he heard he shouted '*Ha!*' in agreement.

At last the old men stopped talking among themselves and turned their heads towards Broken Hand. Josh watched their faces across the fire, the runnels on the cheeks and foreheads, the smudged paint, the senile remains of past glory, and for a moment he thought he understood Little Dog's contempt for the old men of the tribe. Their lives had been full, but their lives were over, and what had been the joy of their youth was no longer possible for the young men of their nation.

Broken Hand stood up and pulled his blanket about his waist so that it skirted his legs. There were grunts of approval from the old men and they rocked their bodies. Broken Hand spoke slowly, and as he spoke Josh understood why he had been invited. It was Broken Hand's wish for him to carry word of this council to the Commissioners and the Colonel.

Sitting at his feet Josh could not see the Old Man Chief's face, but he watched the effect of the words on the expression of Little Dog. The young Cheyenne frowned, thrust out his lower lip and worked unspoken words about his mouth with distaste. His chest rose and fell and his nostrils dilated scornfully.

'This year,' said Broken Hand, 'we killed buffalo bulls on the plain between the two great rivers, but we saw few cows and few calves. In the days of my youth Pte grazed in two mighty herds between the Shining Mountains and the Great River. In my father's youth they were one herd and we the Tisi-Tsi-Istas, the Shahi-Yenna, were always full of buffalo meat. But now the buffalo are passing and we must decide whether it is our destiny to pass with them.'

He spoke of the white men, calling them spiders, as was the Cheyenne way. 'When the spiders fought among themselves in their great war thousand of buffalo were killed in the passing of one moon so that their soldiers might eat.' Josh shifted uneasily at the recollection of his own part in this historic slaughter of animals. 'Soon there will be no more of them. If we stay in the Black Hills we shall have to fight the white soldiers with empty bellies. There will be no buffalo for our young men to eat.'

There were grunts of grudging agreement from the old men, an odd, singing murmuring. But Little Dog frowned.

'The Lakotas and the Blue Sky People, our cousins, have touched the pen of the treaties and they go south and north to lands promised them by the spider, where they will be given meat. Already our hunting lodges in the Black Hills, given to us so long as grass grows and water flows, have been taken by the spiders. There is no honour in what they have done, but it is done. If we do not do what they further say we shall wither and die. This you know.'

No one spoke, but Little Dog drew in his breath with a hiss.

'Our warriors are brave,' an old man said at last, his voice crackling irritably. 'They fought with Two Moon on the Greasy Grass and killed the white soldiers.'

'Ha!' Little Dog's voice was a great shout.

'This is true,' said Broken Hand, 'but now there are many more white soldiers in this country than when we fought the Long Hair. When my grandfather was young, about the age when boys are given their names, our homes were beyond the Great River, and the plains were between us and the Shining Mountains. But the spider drove the Chippewa towards the mountains. The Chippewa drove the Lakota, and before them we moved too, until plains were between us and the rising sun. Where now can we move? The white men's wagons have taken the place of the antelope. His women wear the buffalo robes that would have warmed us in the winter. It is my advice that we accept their counsel and take the land they offer, and keep locked in our hearts our bitterness. Our young men are brave ...'

'Ha!' said Little Dog proudly.

'But they are few, and already we have wrapped too many in the red blanket. The wisdom of the old men must now take the place of the young man's rifle.'

'I will not die where the spider chooses,' shouted Little Dog.

An old man hawked. It was Little Dog's father. He said 'Children do not chatter at their fathers' council.'

Broken Hand made the sign of disagreement. 'Our customs are changing. He has the right to speak. He has also the duty to listen.' He sat down.

The old men were silent. Behind him Josh heard the soft movements of the girl, and Appearing Day's slender arm passed between him and Broken Hand, taking the cold pipe. The Old Man Chief leant towards Josh and said gravely. 'Outside, Tanner, you may find it easier to breathe. You will take word of this council?'

'I shall speak of it,' said Josh. He rose and left. The village was drifting into sleep. Dogs snarled and quarrelled by the dying fires. As Josh stood there the lodge curtain flapped and Little Dog came out. They heard the mumbling of the old men and Josh saw the fierce pride in the Dog Soldier's angry face.

Little Dog said 'The old men listen to Broken Hand who has grown soft, and in the end the young men will be guided by the old. The Tisi-Tsi-Istas will be led away to the south, Tanner, where your people have chosen, and we shall starve, and grow soft, and be murdered by the wolves among the Apache and the Comanche. Our girls will become the paid women of the soldiers to earn food for their fathers, and our young men will pretend that it is not happening. This is what your people will do, Tanner.'

'It does not please me, Little Dog.'

'My father listens to Broken Hand.'

'But you, Little Dog?'

'I shall not leave here. Nor will American Horse.'

'The soldiers will kill you,' said Josh sadly. 'Perhaps it will not be as you imagine in the south.'

'It will be worse,' said Little Dog. 'Your people do not wish us to live, but they will not kill us in battle like men.'

'The soldiers will kill you, Little Dog,' said Josh again.

'Only the young die willingly. To grow old is to love life too much. Appearing Day is waiting with your horse, Tanner.'

The boy went. Josh walked slowly through the village to the pony herd. The girl was holding the bridle of his horse, and in the darkness she looked like a white shadow. When Josh took the reins she did not slip away, giggling shyly like most Indian girls, but remained, and looked up into his face. The sadness he had felt inside the lodge returned to him as he saw her. 'You are Appearing Day,' he said.

She nodded. 'You are very beautiful,' he said. 'Will you go with your people?'

'I will go with my husband.'

'That is proper,' he said, and then suddenly bent forward and took the girl's chin in his hand. The flesh of her cheeks was soft, but the line of her jaw was hard. She did not withdraw her head from his hand, but stared up at him, frowning. He kissed her on the forehead and then, shamed by what he had done and annoyed because he could think of no reason for it, he mounted, turned his horse, and urged it at a trot towards the fort.

He had reached the bluff before he was aware that he was being followed. He stopped and turned in his saddle, listening to the soft fall of a pony's unshod hooves, a faint musical jingling. Little Dog came up to him slowly, out of the darkness into a patch of moonlight by a fallen cottonwood. He was weaponless except for a knife at his waist, and when he saw Josh waiting he placed his hand on its hilt and filled his chest with air.

Josh let his right hand slip inside his coat, to the pistol under his arm-pit. 'What does Little Dog want?'

The Cheyenne did not reply. He moved his pony forward until his left leg locked itself below Josh's right stirrup. He needed only to swing his foot upward to unsaddle Josh. When this happened, Josh knew, the Cheyenne would lean forward and strike with the knife.

'What does Little Dog want?' he asked again. 'Will he destroy our friendship?'

Little Dog hissed between his teeth and then said 'My father has given six horses so that I may marry Appearing Day.'

'It's a good price,' said Josh tactfully, 'but the girl is worth more.'

'Tanner is a friend to the People of Red Talk?'

'I am proud of their friendship.' Josh stepped his horse forward, but the Dog Soldier moved forward too, his foot pressed against Josh's stirrup.

'You would make Appearing Day a paid woman.'

'You are a fool!' said Josh angrily, 'What you saw was a kindness, no more.' His palm began to sweat under his arm-pit, and as he tested the weight of the pistol he knew that he would not be able to draw it in time.

The young man's knife came out of its sheath and the moonlight washed the blade. Little Dog let it hang loosely in his palm. 'Every day old men have listened to promises and taken worthless presents in exchange for our land. We honour our women, Tanner, we do not sell them.'

'Put your knife away!' said Josh suddenly in English.

Little Dog grinned out of the darkness and raised his hand. He played with the weapon and poised it on a level with Josh's chest. Both of them heard the music of harness, the noise of iron hooves at the foot of the bluff.

'*Hallo, there!*' It was a patrol returning to the fort.

Little Dog released Josh's stirrup and turned into the darkness. He rode away at speed and, with the noise, a trooper left the patrol and plunged up the hill.

'Hallo, soldier!' said Josh, 'Glad to see you.'

The lieutenant, Josh recognized him as a West Pointer called Fraser, looked at him curiously when he rode down.

'Who was the brave, Mr Tanner?'

'A friend, lieutenant. One of Broken Hand's young men.'

'*Broken Hand!*' said Fraser with disgust. As they rode back to the fort he chattered gaily about the chances of another Indian war. He hoped that the great plains fighting was not over. His ideal was Sheridan, his hero was Custer. 'Indians are all the same, Mr Tanner,' he argued brightly, 'It's foolish to expect them to have a white man's attitude towards a treaty. Don't you agree?'

'I agree,' said Josh.

About the fort the camp-fires were winking before the tents, but the square inside was dark, only a fan of yellow light breaking across one corner from the sutler's store. Josh looked and saw a glow behind the curtains of Ann Magruder's room, and unconsciously he shrugged his shoulders. He dismounted as the patrol swung wearily into line, and the young lieutenant's voice rang out clearly.

There was an oil-lamp shining inside the Colonel's office, and Josh saw the round shadow of Simmons' head against the blind. A Pawnee scout, humped in a blanket, grunted as he passed. He was halfway across the square when he heard footsteps padding after him, and his name called. It was an orderly.

'The Colonel's compliments, sir, and he'd like a word.'

Josh returned reluctantly. He was tired, and he was angry with himself for allowing his friendship with Little Dog to be so foolishly destroyed. The Colonel was sitting at his field-desk, his blouse open, a cigar between his teeth. Simmons sat on a chair before him, sweating as usual, and balancing his round hat on his knees.

The Colonel smiled at Josh pleasantly. He thrust a hand into his waist-band and crossed his legs over a chair, indicating that this was to be an informal talk. 'You've been to Broken Hand's village, Mr Tanner.'

'If you wish, Colonel, I'll tell you where I'm going before I go. Don't send your Pawnees to trail me.'

The Colonel smiled indulgently. 'There was no offence meant, Mr Tanner. I have no objection to your visiting the Cheyennes, but we heard that the old men were holding a big council tonight, and guessed that maybe you'd have news of it.'

'I've news of it,' said Josh.

The little Commissioner wiped his face. 'We'd like to hear it, sir. It seems to me this old savage is prejudicing the future of his whole tribe.'

Josh looked at the Colonel whose face was blandly non-committal. 'Washington owes you an apology, Mr Simmons,' said Josh.

'I beg your pardon, sir?'

'You should have been told something of the people with whom you are treating.'

'I still don't follow you, Mr Tanner.'

'Then you'll forgive me if I appear to be instructing you in your business. There'll be little of the Cheyennes' political system left by the time we have pacified them, Mr Simmons, but I think some knowledge of it will have an archaic interest to your friends back East when you return.'

Simmons tugged at his shirt-coat irritably. 'Political system? Are you talking of Indians and politics, sir?'

Josh slowly lit a cigar and studied the end of it, conscious of the fact that his action must appear insolent, and relishing the thought. 'Every few years,' he said at last, 'the Cheyenne bands used to elect a council of forty chiefs. This council selected four or five wise men who were then known as Old Man Chiefs. They were the advisers, the statesmen, if you like, of the nation. They were the elected representatives of all the Cheyennes, under obligation to talk, think and act on behalf of their people only. Broken Hand is an Old Man Chief, Mr Simmons. When you listen to him you are listening to the heart of the Cheyenne nation.'

Simmons blew out his cheeks in doubt. 'That seems a highly

involved system for a savage and uneducated people, Mr Tanner.'

Josh shrugged his shoulders. 'Colonel?'

The cavalryman took his boots from the chair. 'Sociology was not studied at the Academy in my day, Mr Tanner. But is Broken Hand going to sign? He's wasted enough of our time.'

'I think so. Tomorrow, perhaps. Maybe the day after. But prepare to waste more time. You're going to have trouble from the young men. From two of them anyway. Little Dog and American Horse.'

'Who are they?'

'Two young Dog Soldiers. They figure to die up here, rather than along the Canadian.'

'Thank you, Mr Tanner.'

'It's your problem, Colonel.'

Outside, Josh looked at the sky, stretched his shoulders and yawned. The night was cool and kind after the sun-drenched day, and in its shadows even the fort had a bleak and harsh beauty. The Pawnee had gone from the steps. The gates of the fort were closed, and Josh could see the head of a sentry as the trooper leant on the palisade and stared westward to the dark mountains. The man was singing softly, and the tenor sweetness of his voice drifted pleasantly through the air.

Josh did not hear steps behind him, but he sensed a danger suddenly, and half-turned to meet it. A taut arm gripped his neck and forced his chin upward, arching and exposing his chest. Another arm, ending in a fisted knife, came in a swoop towards him. He caught at the wrist desperately and felt the blade cut his fore-arm. He struggled, and in the moonlight, for a moment above him, he saw Little Dog's gallant crest of feathers.

'*You fool!*' he gasped in English, but that was all he had the breath to say as the arm about his throat tightened and a leg curled about his right knee. The Cheyenne said nothing. His head held against the Indian's broad chest, Josh could hear the steady beat of Little Dog's heart. He exerted all his strength to force his body forward. Together they fell from the steps and rolled in the dust. The office door squealed, heavy boots banged on the boards of the *ramada*. Suddenly the weight left Josh's body, tearing itself away and leaving a beaded knife-sheath in his hand.

He looked up from the ground and saw the Colonel standing above him in a heroic if slightly comic pose, right arm extended, pistol pointed. The gun fired once.

'Sentry!'

Josh pushed himself up on his elbow and stared towards the gate. From the blockhouse there was a stab of orange and another report as the sentry fired his carbine at the parade. Josh saw Little Dog running swiftly, body crouched. He heard the excited music of the silver dollars, and then a mounted trooper rode out of the shadows and hurled his horse at the Cheyenne. The boy rolled over on the ground and lay still.

The Colonel helped Josh to his feet. 'Are you hurt, Mr Tanner?'

'A small gash. It's nothing.' He grinned ruefully at the Colonel. 'That was Little Dog, by the way.'

The sergeant came running. 'Johnny White Iron is dead, Colonel, sir. That brave knifed him.'

The Colonel put his feet astride and said angrily. 'How'd that Indian get in here.'

'He came over your wall, Colonel,' said Josh. 'Did you think it couldn't be done?'

'Thank you, Mr Tanner,' said the Colonel stiffly, 'Get the surgeon to dress your arm.' He turned away and then faced about abruptly. 'What the hell was all that about, anyway?'

'Little Dog's confused about something.'

'God damn his confusion when it comes to murdering one of my Pawnee scouts! You'll ride down to Broken Hand with me in the morning, Mr Tanner, and tell him I'm going to hang that savage!'

'With or without trial, Colonel?'

'I'm in no mood for your humour, sir. On this post you're my responsibility and under my orders.'

'Broken Hand will not let you hang the boy.'

'Get your arm dressed, Mr Tanner. It's bleeding on my *ramada*. Good-night!'

But the soldiers did not keep Little Dog for long. Two hours after midnight, while the sentry shivered in the blockhouse against the wind, American Horse climbed over the south palisade near the swivel gun. He walked across the parade on light feet, and he stunned the stockade guard with an axe-haft. He released Little Dog and they clasped arms silently and grinned with delight. They walked back across the parade, climbed the palisade, paused there for a moment and yelled their mockery.

The silence of the fort broke into a yell of '*Corporal of the guard!*' Then there came a yelping of dogs, a shouting, and a useless banging of carbines along the walls. Little Dog and American Horse rode down to the Cheyenne village calling in derision.

*

Josh rode to Broken Hand's village in the morning with the Colonel and half a company of troopers. The Cheyenne lodges were now all that were left along the creek. The other bands had gone, the last of them in the night, and the dust from their pony-drags was still lying along the southern horizon. Broken Hand's young men were screaming like schoolboys about the edge of the water, and they jeered at the approaching soldiers.

As he splashed through the creek Josh studied the women who were gathered in a tight and silent knot beyond the young men. He looked for Appearing Day, but she was not there.

The Colonel halted his horse before Broken Hand's lodge, with a bugler on his right hand and Josh on his left, the regimental guidon snapping above his head in the wind. He pulled off a gauntlet and laid it along his thigh. Broken Hand parted the leather curtains and came into the sunlight, blinking gently, one hand skirting a black and red blanket about his waist. He said '*A-hau!* Peace be with you.'

'Tell him, Mr Tanner, if you please!'

'Get your scout to do it, Colonel,' said Josh in distaste.

The Colonel compressed his lips, but he did not argue. He called up the Pawnee, a dark stunted Indian in a blue soldier's coat. Josh listened uneasily as the voices of the Cheyenne and the Pawnee slipped into soft and musical debate, while their hands parted the air between them.

Young Cheyennes rode in and halted their ponies in a halfmoon about the soldiers. 'Mr Fraser!' said the Colonel calmly,

'Face your rear files about, if you please.' Then there was no other noise but the sound of Broken Hand and the Pawnee, the rattle of a bridle as a horse shook its head against the flies. The sun was hot, and sweat itched on Josh's cheeks.

At last the scout turned to the Colonel, but before he could speak Josh broke in impatiently. 'It's no good, Colonel. Broken Hand says the boys have gone off into the hills. You've got two outlaw Dog Soldiers to worry about, but you're lucky. Broken Hand says the rest of his people will accept the treaty.'

The Colonel bit his moustache. 'Thank you, Mr Tanner. But I don't propose to send men into the hills. Tell the Old Man Chief he must bring the boys in, dead or alive.'

'Colonel, no Cheyenne may kill another.'

'Damn your concern for their customs, sir!' The Colonel pulled on his gauntlet, and then his face reddened. 'My apologies, Mr Tanner.' He wheeled his horse about and raised his hand.

Josh did not ride back with the soldiers. He remained before Broken Hand's lodge until they had gone, and then he dismounted and walked over to the old man. 'Little Dog is young, as you said, my uncle. His blood is hot, but he is foolish. The soldiers will kill him.'

The Old Man Chief looked at Josh sadly, but he did not answer. He tightened the blanket about his waist, and turned his back. Josh remounted and rode back to Laramie.

Ann Magruder met him at the door of the store, her cheeks red. She caught at his arm. 'I didn't think the girl had any right to come, Josh, but she seemed to think you wanted her here.'

'What girl?'

'That Indian girl. My father said you'd be angry. Then he laughed and said perhaps you wanted it this way.' She slowly locked her fingers in the skirt of her dress. 'Josh, you didn't send for her, did you?'

He left her and went through the store into the small room. The Cheyenne girl, seated on his blankets with her hands folded, stood up as he came in. Her teeth were white as she smiled at him. Her blue-black hair was braided over her deerskin smock, and her belt was studded with white and yellow beads. She did not speak, but when he held out his hand she placed hers in it and smiled at him again.

The door was flung open by Magruder who stared at them both, the thick, red matting on his chest rising and falling. 'Get that squaw out of here, Mr Tanner.'

'Shut your mouth, Magruder.'

The sutler loosened the knuckles of his fingers against the palm of each hand, and then he pushed into the room, reaching for the girl. Josh hit him on the side of the jaw, and the big man fell over. He struck the flour sacks and one of them burst, spilling a white fall over his head. Josh took him by the shirt-collar and pulled him to his feet. Magruder shook himself free, pushed past his daughter into the store, calling for a knife or a gun.

Josh said 'Miss Magruder, look after her, please.' And he went into the store. Magruder was pulling himself along the shelves awkwardly, shaking his head against the pain in his jaw. He looked at Josh and then he stumbled out on to the parade. The flour on his hair, his staggering walk, made him look like an old man. Josh shrugged his shoulders when he saw that the sutler was making for the Colonel's office. He lit a cigar, put his hands in his pockets and leant against the hitching-rail, waiting.

The Colonel came out on to the *ramada*, buttoning his blouse at the throat, tightening his belt and pulling his cap forward as he strode across to Josh. *'Mr Tanner . . . !'*

'Yes, Colonel?'

'Just how you conduct your private life, Mr Tanner, is no concern of mine, and I don't fight Magruder's quarrels. But I want to know this, has the girl anything to do with Little Dog?'

'He was going to marry her.'

The Colonel showed his teeth as he bit his lower lip. 'I should have kicked you out of this territory.'

'Colonel . . . !'

'Hear me out! Your stupidity has already cost me one dead scout and a wounded trooper. Now I've got to risk other men's lives bringing in those two Cheyennes. I've a mind to put you under arrest, sir!'

'That's your privilege, Colonel. But you'd have had to fight Little Dog whatever the girl did.'

The Colonel turned on his heel. *'Sergeant!'*

'Sir?'

'Mr Tanner will not leave this post without permission from me.' He turned to Josh. 'Be so good to let the sergeant have your saddle. When Broken Hand brings in those boys you may leave, and I shall be happy to be rid of you.'

'Colonel,' said Josh wearily, 'I find it hard to understand you. Maybe I don't understand Broken Hand either, but I know he won't bring in Little Dog for us to hang him. He'll sign the treaty and he'll take his people south, but he'll not turn policeman for you.'

The Colonel said 'Sergeant, I want a file of men to take the girl back to her village.'

Josh caught the Colonel's arm. 'She hasn't a village any more,' he said, 'Because of what she's done she's abandoned her people and they've forgotten her. Let her stay.'

The Colonel paused and then shrugged his shoulders. 'Very well,' he said. At his elbow Magruder began to splutter indignantly, and the Colonel wheeled on him furiously. 'One more gripe from you, Magruder, and I'll put your store off limits!'

Josh returned to the Cheyenne girl. She was sitting on his bed and when he entered she stood up again. He looked at her gently and then he took her chin in his hand. He pulled a handkerchief from his pocket and wiped the two darts of vermilion from her cheeks. Then he sat before her on the flour sacks, his hands on his knees.

'Appearing Day,' he said, searching for words in Cheyenne that would not hurt her. 'You have been foolish. You were Little Dog's woman and you should not have come here.' Yet he knew that he did not wish her to go. He felt in his pocket and brought out the mother-of-pearl comb, and he placed it in her hand. The girl lifted his fingers and laid them along her cheek.

For the rest of the day Josh loafed in Old Bedlam, biting an unlit cigar and outstaring the young officers.

Everybody on the post was waiting for dusk with a curiosity that was touched by apprehension. No one really expected Broken Hand to bring in Little Dog and American Horse, not even the Colonel now, but there was much speculation and a few wagers on what the Old Man Chief would do. The hollow that held the Cheyenne village seemed to be a crucible of some explosive material, awaiting only the blow of a pestle. None of the Indian women went to the creek that afternoon, and the dogs sat idly on its bank, scratching at fleas. Smoke drifted between the lodge poles.

When the sun dropped below the mountains and flung their shadows far across the Platte, the Colonel came out of his office and looked towards the gate. He held his body erect, the fingers of his left hand tapping at his thigh. There he stood for some minutes and at last he dispatched an unwilling scout to the Cheyenne village for news. The Pawnee returned an hour later, grinning with contempt. Broken Hand, he said, would be at the fort in the morning to sign the treaty on behalf of his people. The scout had not seen Little Dog or American Horse, but he said that before the lodges of their fathers were staked two fine horses painted for war on their faces, their chests and their flanks. The brother and sister of American Horse were already in mourning, their cheeks daubed with white clay, and locks of hair cut from their foreheads.

Appearing Day slept in Josh's room that night, and he laid his own bed-roll beneath the shelves of the store. Before he went to bed he stood in the doorway, smoking a last cigar, listening to the bugler breaking the night's silence into sad fragments of music. Down in the Cheyenne village a dog answered the call with a long, mournful howl.

Josh turned at a rustling behind him. He saw Ann Magruder. She was wearing a dress that merged into the darkness, and it was as if he could see her pale face and bare, folded arms only. He stood aside to allow her to come out, threw his cigar into the dust and thrust his hands down into his pockets. The sky was clear, pricked by stars, and he turned his eyes from them to look at the woman's profile. It was cleanly cut in the moonlight, and he wondered why its sudden beauty did not excite him.

She stood motionless, her hands clasped, and when she spoke it was without emotion. 'Josh, will the Cheyenne boys be captured tomorrow?'

'No,' he said, 'I believe they will be killed.'

'Why? Couldn't they escape?'

'They could escape, but they wish to die. In a way I think

they are wiser than old Broken Hand. It takes great courage and wisdom to choose death sometimes.'

'It seems a pity,' she said, and he felt that she was phrasing sentences again for her journal. 'That boy Little Dog was such a magnificent savage, so splendidly barbaric.'

'Don't pity them,' said Josh, in sudden resentment. 'Would you rather they rotted to death along the Canadian?'

'That isn't the alternative, is it? Cannot they become farmers and useful citizens?'

He was suddenly tired and could not answer her. There was a silence for some time, until she said, 'She's a pretty little thing.'

'Why do you sneer at her?'

She answered impatiently. 'I am not sneering. But what will you do with her? She's an Indian girl, after all.'

'Yes,' he said bitterly, 'she's an Indian girl after all. You know, I once read that the Spanish conquerors of Mexico argued for years on whether the Indian should be considered an animal or some sub-human species. Our own attitude is not always much better, Miss Magruder.'

He thought she laughed. 'Sometimes your erudition surprises me, where did you learn that?'

'Appearing Day is Little Dog's woman,' he said, ignoring her question. 'His father paid a good marriage price in buffalo ponies. It is a great tribute to the girl. Horses mean much to the plains Indians. All in all there is much good in their way of life.'

'It's not a life to admire,' she said severely. 'There are other simple lives more elevating. I must lend you a book, by Mr Thoreau.'

He smiled, and although his face was in darkness she knew that he was smiling, and was angered by it. 'What will you do with the girl?'

He resented the way she was forcing his thoughts to a decision. 'I could take her home.'

'Where is home? You never told me.'

'England,' he said shortly. 'It's getting cold. May I fetch you a shawl?'

'No,' she said, 'I will retire now. Good-night.'

'Miss Magruder ...' She turned in the door. He saw the white oval of her face.

'Yes?'

'You've been kind to the girl. I must thank you for that.'

She paused, as if she wished to say that he misunderstood her. Then he heard the rustle of her dress again and the doorway was empty.

*

In the morning Broken Hand came in to the fort with his head-men and with a fluttering escort of warriors without weapons. The news that the Cheyenne was coming in brought most of the miners and homesteaders up from the camps, and they lounged about the gate, or gathered in tight, arguing knots. Broken Hand rode on to the parade through two lines of troopers.

He had dressed himself as finely as possible. The wing-bone that held his hair was decorated with three war-eagle's feathers. His face was painted. He wore a deer-skin jacket, and a red and black blanket about his waist. His pony was draped in a blanket, too, its hooves painted scarlet. Behind the Old Man Chief three warriors held aloft on a tripod the insignia of his rank and prowess – his bull-hide shield trimmed with ermine, his medicine-bag, his bow and quiver, his pipe and his lance. Two girls walked beside his horse to show that he came in peace.

The Colonel stood behind a little table that had been set up outside his office and covered with a horse-blanket. He was in full regimentals, and he saluted Broken Hand with gravity.

A Pawnee interpreter hastily gabbled through the Colonel's address of welcome, and when Broken Hand replied the wind took up his slow, deep voice and carried it across the parade to where Josh was standing. The Old Man Chief spoke modestly of the courage and bravery of his own people. He explained that he was old and that he was tired, but these were not the reasons why he had come. He had not allowed his own weaknesses, of spirit or body, to influence his judgement. It was not permitted him to speak or think of anything but his people's good. This he wished the Colonel to understand.

By his execrable English the Pawnee broke down the dignity

and power of the old Cheyenne's words. Slily, cunningly making it seem as if Broken Hand were appealing for mercy. Josh dropped his cigar into the dust and crushed it angrily with his heel.

Gripping the pen in his fist like a knife, Broken Hand wrote the only words he knew in English, the only words he could write, his name. He looked at the crooked writing and smiled indulgently. Then, beside his signature, he drew his mark, an Indian in a war-bonnet astride a galloping pony, and above it a hand holding a broken stick.

The Colonel eased his neck in his collar. Behind him the Commissioners smiled, stroked their beards and nodded. When Broken Hand stepped back from the table the old Cheyenne men sighed and scratched their arm-pits, but the young warriors said nothing. They stared at the troopers with open faces.

'Mr Tanner!'

Josh walked across the parade, stepped through the ranks of soldiers and faced the Colonel. 'Mr Tanner, I know this Pawnee is a liar and a bad man for this job. Would you oblige me by telling Broken Hand that while we're pleased he has signed the treaty and that his people now wish to live in peace on lands assigned them, there's still this unresolved business of Little Dog and American Horse.'

'You know the answer you'll get, Colonel.'

'Maybe. But it's got to be said.'

Josh shrugged his shoulders. He spoke to Broken Hand slowly. The Old Man Chief did not look at him, but kept his eyes fixed on the Colonel's face. When he spoke again it was with passion, and his hand cut the air before him. His eyes were hard, and now and then he was interrupted by grunts from the old men, or by a harsh cry of '*Ha!*' from one of the young warriors.

'What has he said, Mr Tanner?'

'Cheyenne's not a simple language, Colonel. The old man's using words that are strange to me ...'

'What has he said?'

'If you want the boys you must bring them in yourself. They will not run away, but they will not surrender. They're in the hills, and they're waiting to fight you.'

'*Fight us?*'

'They say if you do not go out and fight them, they'll come down and fight you here in the fort.'

'And where,' said the Colonel sarcastically, 'would they like us to meet them?'

'Take your soldiers into the hills, Colonel. I imagine they'll pick their own rendezvous.'

'And lead us into an ambush?'

Josh was angry. 'If Broken Hand meant to trick you he wouldn't have signed the treaty.'

'All right, Mr Tanner, tell the old man we'll bring them in and hang them.'

But Josh did not tell Broken Hand this. He said, 'The commander of the pony-soldiers has heard you and understood, my uncle, and he shares your grief.'

The Pawnee scout snickered, and put his hand over his mouth, looking insolently at the Cheyennes.

Now Broken Hand looked at Josh for the first time. He put out his hand, and when it was grasped he said, 'I have given the horses back to Little Dog's father and he has understood. The girl has come to you, Tanner, and she is no longer of our people. But she has been taught well, and you will have no reason to complain of her.'

Then the Old Man Chief mounted his pony and rode out of the fort. A squadron of troopers escorted him back to his village.

Josh stood on the parade watching the Indians go, and he did not know that Ann Magruder was beside him until she spoke. 'What did he say to you, Josh?'

He pulled off his hat and faced her. He knew he would shock her. 'That the girl is now mine. Where is she?'

She bit her lip gently. 'She's in the store. She watched it all from my window. She watched her father all the time. Indians don't cry, do they?'

'Oh, yes,' he said, 'They can cry, but I doubt if she would before you.'

'Will you go with the soldiers to capture Little Dog?'

He smiled at her. 'I shall go.'

'Look after yourself.' She placed a hand gently on his arm and looked at him uncertainly. 'Will it be dangerous?'

'Only for Little Dog and American Horse. If the Colonel is still afraid of an ambush he may take two companies. We shall all be safe.'

She left him, walking across the parade with her flowered dress lifted from the dust. At the steps of the store she turned and smiled.

That afternoon and evening the Cheyennes feasted and danced along the banks of the creeks. They were in good humour and showed no resentment when one of the Pawnee scouts got drunk and rode to the bluff, standing there and shouting in a high voice, challenging a Cheyenne warrior to come out and fight him. He was brought back to the fort by two troopers, and the Cheyenne women stood on the water's edge and jeered at him.

As Josh had expected, the Colonel decided to take two companies into the hills the following morning. Simmons, eager for an exciting story to take back East, asked the Colonel for permission to accompany the soldiers. The Colonel agreed reluctantly, and his reluctance was even more marked when Josh made the same request.

'I would have thought you'd have been happier away from it, Mr Tanner.'

Josh raised his shoulders. 'My motives are unimportant, Colonel. But I'd appreciate it.'

The Colonel stood up behind his desk and bit at his moustache. 'We leave at nine, Mr Tanner. I shall be happy to have you ride with me at the head of the column.' But he did not look happy.

*

The Cheyennes began to dismantle their village as soon as the sun rose above the rim of the Dakota plains. When Josh went to the gate to watch them most of the lodges were now skeletons of poles. The women worked, and the young men sat by the dying fires, silently, holding the bridles of their ponies, resting their rifles across their knees. Soon there was nothing along the creek but a confusion of lodge poles, kettles, and snarling dogs. Away to the south a group of boys already had the pony-herd in motion.

When the band moved, policed by Dog Soldiers, the sun glinted on lance-points and rifle barrels, and the wind fluttered among the feathers. They were few, not more than three hundred men, women and children, and they moved slowly away towards the mountains. When the bugler sounded assembly from the fort the Indians halted, and waited on the bluff for the troopers to appear.

The Colonel looked at them unhappily. 'I don't like that,' he said. He swung about in his saddle. 'Mr Fraser, send your scout over to Broken Hand and find out what the old devil's aiming to do.'

A Pawnee urged his horse down the creek and swung up the bluff until he reached the Cheyennes. The Indians closed about him like a pool swallowing a stone, and there was no movement until the band broke into another ripple and the Pawnee raced back to the fort. He pulled up before the Colonel and he grinned. 'They will come to watch their young men die.'

The Colonel bit his moustache and stared doubtfully at the waiting Cheyennes. Then he stood in his stirrups, raised one hand and brought it forward. The companies moved out.

The stage from the East was in. Its passengers stood about the gate behind a rampart of carpet-bags, wide-eyed, astonished and delighted to find that the West was honouring its reputation for colour, drama and excitement. Miners who were glad that the long Treaty Talks had ended, and that a new Eldorado awaited them in the north, cheered the troopers enthusiastically. Women and children from Suds' Row and the Officers' Lines ran along beside the column, holding the stirrup-irons. A smiling, nodding group of Commissioners raised their hats politely to Mr Simmons, and then raised them again for the company guidons.

From the mining camp a cloud of horsemen galloped suddenly in pursuit of the column, drifters, gamblers, miners, cow-hands, strapped about with guns, shouting joyously, anxious to share in the fun.

'Mr Fraser!' The young lieutenant swung out of the column and rode up to the Colonel. 'Get that rabble back to camp. Tell them that if any unauthorized person follows us I'll have him sent East for trial.'

The lieutenant dispersed the yelping band, and they rode back, firing guns into the air.

Among the women at the gate Josh saw Ann Magruder, the wind blowing her fair hair across her calm, untroubled face. She was not alone. Appearing Day was with her, smiling like a child, and no longer in her deer-skin smock. She was wearing a white dress which Ann Magruder had given her. It was too long, and it fell in folds about her ankles. Her black hair had been unbraided and pinned in a blue-black cluster at the nape of her neck. Her dark skin, against the white dress, was lustrous. Josh placed a hand on his horse's rump and looked back at her in sadness until the bobbing caps of the following troopers hid her from view. He faced about with a troubled and unresolved mind.

The two companies rode all day towards the Laramie Hills, and Broken Hand's band followed them, on the other side of the creek, sometimes hidden by the bluffs, sometimes appearing in a flutter of feathers and scarlet blankets. The barking and snarling of their dogs, the singing of their warriors and the cries of their children could be heard above the water-run and the creaking of the troopers' harness.

The Colonel called for a song once or twice, as if he wished to answer the enthusiasm of the Cheyennes with something as marked and as determined. The voices of the men leaped willingly enough across four or five stanzas, but then died away. Simmons, bouncing uncomfortably on his Morgan, sweated irritably. Early in the day he chatted to the Colonel, and to Josh, but with the falling of the sun, and the needling heat of it on their backs, he subsided into a surly silence.

The column followed the valley of the creek until at last, two hours before sunset, it turned west again into a narrow glen where the creek rolled sharply over steep rock-falls. The left side of the valley was a steep wall of stratified rock, rich in colour. The right rose up slowly, green and smooth, like the side of an amphitheatre, crowned at the top by a dark crest of pine.

Broken Hand's band was now on the same side of the creek as the column, trailing a mile behind, the young men skirmishing on its flanks. When the valley was reached they began to whoop with delight. Josh looked back at them and he said to the Colonel. 'I imagine we're there now.'

The Colonel eased himself wearily in the saddle and took out his field-glass. He studied the pines at the top of the ridge. Before he lowered the glass two young men rode out of the trees, paused for a moment, and then came down.

The Colonel shouted, and the troopers faced into line, a turning, straightening movement of blue and yellow, steel and leather. Far behind, Broken Hand's band was suddenly silent. There was silence all along the valley except for the drumming of the ponies' hooves coming down the hill. Eight hundred yards from the cavalry the two young Indians halted, raised their rifles, and called.

A great cry of welcome and admiration broke from the waiting Cheyennes.

Little Dog and American Horse were mounted on the finest ponies. American Horse rode a paint, and he wore a war-bonnet that dropped a tail of brilliant red, black and white feathers on the pony's rump. Little Dog wore his crest of prairie-cock's feathers in a high roach of hair. The hair was further plaited over each shoulder and studded with shining discs. The face, forehead and cheeks of each young man were banded with paint, and the chests, flanks, and bellies of their ponies were also painted.

'Mr Fraser!'

The lieutenant came up the line and saluted the Colonel. He, at least, thought Josh, looked as if he were enjoying himself. His riding boots shone, and a yellow silk bandana was tied about his brown throat, his campaign hat pulled down gallantly over one eye. He let his horse curvet until the look on the colonel's face stopped him.

'Sir?' he said.

'Take your first two files up the hill, Mr Fraser, and bring those hostiles down.' The Colonel relaxed in his saddle, but he looked down the valley, and he stared unhappily at Broken Hand's waiting band.

The lieutenant swung away with his troopers, and galloped up the rise. A thickening blue shadow was creeping up the valley from the east and the grass was a vivid green beneath the sweating flanks of the horses. As they raced towards the Cheyennes two of the troopers began to yip excitedly. Fraser raised a gauntleted hand and waved it.

'Damn the boy!' said the Colonel.

Suddenly American Horse and Little Dog broke apart, swung together, swerved away from a collision with the troopers and then spun about them, taunting. The soldiers halted. The lieutenant stood in his stirrups, leaning forward and when he placed a hand on his pistol holster the Colonel drew in his breath sharply. 'If that young fool fires I'll have his shoulder-straps!'

For some seconds the Cheyenne boys played with the troopers, isolating them one by one, whirling about them, and then withdrawing to laugh. They mocked laughter, they placed their hands on their bellies and bent over their ponies' necks. From down the valley came the excited and approving shouts of Broken Hand's band.

'*Bugler!* Sound recall.'

The bugle shot silver notes at the black wall of the valley, splintering echoes along the rocks. The lieutenant returned. His face was red with embarrassment, the flap of his pistol holster was unbuttoned and his hand rested upon it. He opened his mouth. '*Sir . . . !*'

'All right, Mr Fraser,' said the Colonel.

'A magnificent spectacle!' Simmons mopped his forehead with his handkerchief and replaced his hat. 'Truly magnificent!'

The Colonel looked at the Commissioner. 'Just so,' he said. 'But they'll stop playing in a minute. Unless we get this over quickly we'll have the whole tribe upon us.'

Little Dog and American Horse now rode to within five hundred yards of the cavalry line and taunted the soldiers obscenely. They swung round on their blanket saddles and elevated their buttocks. They parted, trotted gently apart, turned again, rejoined each other and halted their ponies flank to flank. American Horse's war bonnet blew out in a great crown. He yelled, and Little Dog took up the derisive cry.

Suddenly they rode at a gallop towards the troopers. Little Dog fired first, resting the barrel of his rifle across his left arm. Then American Horse fired.

The little balls of smoke puffed before them, and about them as they rode through. Simmons' horse coughed suddenly and slipped forward on its knees. The Commissioner rolled gently from the saddle and lay on his back, staring up at the Colonel with surprise. A trooper, three files from Josh, swung his shoulder back suddenly as if it had been violently pushed and he cried out. Little Dog shouted and flung the rifle from his body by the lever. A spot of light jerked past his head as the cartridge was ejected, and then he fired again. Further down the line another horse squealed and rolled its rider on the ground. Josh pulled his rifle from its scabbard and rested it across his saddle-tree.

The Colonel shouted. 'You first files, bring those men down!'

The troopers had their carbines out, and they fired almost simultaneously. At the discharge Little Dog reined in his pony, turned it, and raced along the line parallel with the troopers. He swung down on the far side of the pony until only his heel could be seen.

American Horse slipped from his blanket and rolled in the grass. Then he was still. His pony trotted in an aimless circle until, halting, it began to crop the grass. A long moan came from Broken Hand's band.

'Sergeant! Give Mr Simmons your horse and get back to the ambulance.'

The fat Commissioner climbed into the saddle, rubbing his leg. 'Upon my soul!' he said, and then again, 'Upon my soul! But you got one of them, I see, Colonel.'

'We could scarcely miss,' said the Colonel drily. He looked across to Josh. 'Well, Mr Tanner?'

Josh shrugged his shoulders. He put the rifle back into its scabbard.

Little Dog did not look at the body of his friend. He rode to within two hundred yards of the waiting troopers and faced them, the stock of his rifle resting on his hip, the wind moving the feathers of his crest. Then he turned his pony into a gallop along the line again. He fired three times. A trooper slipped silently from his saddle, and a bullet clipped the hat-feather of a Pawnee scout. The Pawnee yelled angrily and heeled his pony towards Little Dog, but Lieutenant Fraser caught his bridle and pulled him back.

'Bring him down,' said the Colonel wearily.

There was a desultory snapping of carbines along the lines of troopers, and Little Dog swayed once on his blanket. His pony dropped into a trot. The Cheyenne was bleeding from the waist. The blood ran down the flanks of his pony and dripped from the silver dollars on his leggings, but he held himself erect. He turned his pony slowly at the end of the line and urged it towards the centre again. There he halted and faced the soldiers. He began to sing.

Simmons jerked nervously. 'What's that, Major Tanner? What's he saying now?'

'That's his death-song, Mr Simmons,' said Josh sadly, and he listened. 'He is saying that nothing lives long except the earth and the mountains. He is saying that he has lived only a short while but is not sorry to die. He asks his people to remember him, and he grieves to think they must go on living.'

'Indeed?' said Simmons.

'Indeed,' said Josh.

Little Dog sang on, and when his throaty, monotonous song was over he raised his arm above his head and kicked the ribs of his pony, crying '*Hopo-hookahey!*' He rode straight at the centre of the cavalry line, and he fired once only.

Five soldiers fired in reply. One, perhaps all, hit Little Dog, for his body described a half-curve in the air and then straightened. His rifle dropped to the ground twenty-five yards from the line, and then he burst on the troopers and passed through them.

Josh swung in the saddle to watch the Cheyenne boy pass through. He saw the prairie-cock's feathers shaking above the white campaign-hats, saw a brown, bangled arm high in the air. Little Dog stayed astride his pony for thirty yards once he had gone through the cavalry line, and then he fell from it. The pony, relieved of the weight, flung back its heels, and cantered on to the creek. There it drank. Little Dog's blood was mixed with the paint on its flanks.

The Colonel sent a trooper across to make sure that the Cheyenne was dead, and then he raised his gauntlet and called.

The two companies turned through a quarter of a circle that brought them to a halt facing Broken Hand's band. There they remained, stretched in a blue line up the hill.

The Cheyennes did not move forward. Some of the young men broke away and rode about the band, their long hair flying, and a few sang their war-songs, but they did not move towards the cavalry.

At last the troopers turned into column and rode up to the brow of the hill, turning eastwards there, widely skirting the Cheyennes. Down below them, in the shadow of the rocks, some of the women were already setting up lodge-poles. Dogs began to quarrel. In a little group, alone, sat the brother and sister of American Horse.

Josh looked back. The body of American Horse lay high on the sunlit part of the hill, where the grass seemed its greenest, his war-bonnet a clump of white, black and scarlet. Below, in the blue shadows by the creek, Little Dog lay where he had broken through the line. Between them were the bodies of the troopers' horses, stripped of their harness.

'Picturesque, isn't it, Major Tanner?' said Simmons. Josh did not reply. He heard the breath whistle angrily between the Colonel's teeth.

A surgeon in a white duster reported. 'No bones broken, Colonel, sir,' he said in a voice thickly Irish. 'Our boys have clean wounds.'

The Colonel nodded. He looked across to Josh, without attempting to disguise the relief in his face. 'Think we've seen the last of the Indian wars, Mr Tanner?'

'There's never been an Indian war we could not have avoided, Colonel.'

Simmons edged his horse between them. He had recovered his buoyancy. 'I wouldn't have missed that. Upon my soul, a spectacle!'

The Colonel ignored him. 'We'll ride beyond dark,' he said. He smiled a little at Josh. 'You see I haven't your implicit trust in Broken Hand.'

Half an hour later he turned to Josh, and his voice was soft as he spoke. 'I didn't like that affair at all, Mr Tanner. It's not soldiering. You understand me?'

'I understand you, Colonel.'

The column reached Laramie at noon the following day. The trooper who had been hit in the shoulder developed fever in the night, and he lay in the surgeon's ambulance screaming a bawdy song. There were no Indians left between the fork of the Platte and Laramie Creek, only the black scars of their fires. Already the miners, drifters and homesteaders were streaming north towards the Black Hills. The Colonel looked at them and pushed his tongue gently into his cheek. 'Seems like they'll be building their cities without your help, Mr Tanner.'

Women ran out of the fort to greet the column. With skirts lifted they passed down the line looking for their men, walking back with hands on the stirrups and eyes uplifted. The guard came out and fell in by the gate. A bugle triumphed stridently. The Commissioners were there too, standing on their toes, looking enviously at Simmons who thrust out his chest and stared down his nose at them.

His back weak, his mouth dry with salty distaste, his thighs aching from knee to groin, Josh left the soldiers at the gate and rode over the parade to the sutler's store. There he uncinched his saddle and took it on his shoulders.

When he looked up he saw Ann Magruder in the doorway, an uncertain smile on her lips. He looked beyond her as if she were a stranger, and she stepped away.

There was Appearing Day. The white dress had been shortened to fit the girl now. Her hair was braided into a crown above her forehead. But there were moccasins on her feet still, decorated with yellow and blue beads.

Josh held out his hand to her, and she took it, slipping her fingers between his. He let the saddle slip to the boards and he drew the girl to his side.

*

In Boston, in 1886, there was published a small octavo volume entitled *Days at Fort Laramie, A Young Gentlewoman's Impressions of Life on the Great Plains*. It did not carry the name of the author, but when I came across it I found this reference to my great-uncle:

Among the gentlemen from the East who were present at Fort Laramie for the Treaty Talks between the Commissioners and representatives of the savage and untamed tribes of the Sioux, the Cheyenne and the Arapaho, was a Mr Joshua Tanner. He was a picturesque character as was evidenced in many diverse ways. He had led a life of considerable vicissitudes, and he had much sympathy for the aboriginal inhabitants of the Great Plains. I have particular reason to commend this gentleman's resourcefulness, for while riding with him one morning we were violently challenged by a band of armed savages belonging, I was given to understand, to the Cheyenne peoples. Mr Tanner's good sense and understanding of their way of life saved us from injury.

Perhaps my great-uncle Josh helped the businessmen of Kansas to grow rich by building their short-lived cities in the Black Hills, but he was not rich when he returned to England. He brought with him a dark, slender girl in a wide dress of rustling bombasine. He came to stay with my grandmother at Folkestone, and my father told me that Appearing Day sat quietly in the corner of the kitchen all the time, her back as straight as the chair's, saying nothing.

My father had a vivid recollection of his Uncle Josh leaning against the mantelpiece (on which he had placed his great pistol), tucking a thumb into the pocket of his flowered waistcoat, and grinning tolerantly while my grandmother said that she would have no savages in her house.

As if my great-uncle, having passed a tumultuous climax in his life, was now content with an ordinary, unexciting existence, he took Appearing Day to a cottage near Ashford. When a branch line of the railway was cut through from Canterbury he worked as a foreman with the gangs. He was immensely popular, a tall, greying, handsome man who swaggered a little in his moleskin trousers.

He was liked wherever he went, and on Sundays he would walk to church with Mrs Tanner, a dark, shy woman clinging to his arm.

The villagers called my great-aunt Appearing Day 'Josh Tanner's gypsy woman.' But never to his face.

The Regulator

The drifters came an hour after dawn. Walter James and his boy heard the nervous beat of hooves down by the corral, and then a man's laugh, an insanely mirthless sound that scratched unpleasantly on the morning air.

Walter put down the skilly of beans and wiped his hands slowly on his hips. He looked at the Henry rifle that hung on a peg by the door. He looked at it cautiously, moving his eyes only so that his son might not catch the glance and wonder at the reason for it. He knew that most men who recognized that laugh would expect him to take down the rifle and use it.

He looked away from the gun. He said flatly 'Somebody come calling, son. You stay here.' But the boy was already bounding into the sunlight outside.

Walter James looked once more at the rifle and then he went out too. Three men sat their ponies near the sunflower patch, their bodies fallen into that hunched unconcern that comes on a man after a hard ride. When he saw them Walter took his son's shoulder in a hard grip, and he said 'You stay quiet, boy. Mind what your Paw says, you stay quiet.'

One of the riders was a thin, yellow man who wore a Rebel cavalry cap, although the war had been over for years. There was a fat Mexican in a striped poncho. His face was wet with sweat beneath the brim of his needle-crowned sombrero. The third rider was a half-breed with plaited hair. Behind them a riderless horse leant over a crooked fore-leg, dirty white lather on its neck and flanks.

A fourth man was inside the corral, passing his hands over Walter's blue roan. He said something, and the man in the Rebel cap laughed again.

Walter stared at the fourth man and knew that this was worse than he expected. This man was big, and he wore a hickory shirt and a cowhide vest. His black felt hat had a punched-in crown and a snakeskin band. Every movement of his powerful body was like an evil answer to a threat, and as he moved the sun shone on his hand-gun. He wore it strapped to his right thigh, and the holster had been cut away below the trigger-guard.

The Mexican looked up to the house and called *'Olé!'* He pulled his rifle from its scabbard and pumped it, resting it on his saddle-horn.

'Paw . . . ?' said Billy.

Walter pushed his hand down on the boy's shoulder and said nothing.

The man in the black hat climbed over the fence and spoke to the breed who dismounted and began to unsaddle the fourth horse. Then the others came up to the house, the big man grinning as he walked through the dust, but with his humourless eyes fixed on Walter's face. The Mexican had a handful of sunflower seeds and he pushed them into his mouth, chewing noisily. His right hand pointed the rifle straight at Walter James.

The big man stopped about four yards from the step, still grinning, a hand hooked in his belt above the gun. His lips were wet and red beneath black stubble. 'You're Walt James,' he said. 'I know you. You know me?'

Walter kept his body still. 'Everybody hereabouts knows you. You're Johnny Owens.' He nodded at the rider in the Rebel cap. 'He's your brother Virgil. The others I don't know, but I guess the Law wants them too.'

They laughed. The Mexican spat a mouthful of seed-husks at Walter's feet.

'That's right,' said Johnny Owens. He jerked his left thumb at the Mexican. 'This here's Cholla.' He ignored the half-breed. 'You think maybe you're the Law?'

Virgil Owens heeled his horse to the left, shifting in the saddle so that his gun-hand was free. In the sudden silence Walter could hear the quickened breathing of his son.

'No,' he said soberly. 'No, I ain't the Law. I'm just homesteading here.'

'No, you ain't the Law. Sure you ain't,' said Virgil, and he pointed at the apron that was still tied about Walter's waist. He looked at the Mexican. '*Olé*, Cholla,' he said, '*Olé la señora!*'

The Mexican kissed his finger-tips and his belly shook with laughter.

Walter looked down at his son. Below the straw-yellow hair a dark flush coloured the boy's neck.

'You've got a gun, maybe?' said Johnny Owens.

'There's an old Henry on the wall inside.'

'Go get it, Virgil.'

The thin man slid from the saddle and walked into the house. Walter wondered if he would look in Mary's settle where there was a shell-belt with a Navy Colt in the holster. But Virgil came out with the rifle only, and Johnny Owens casually smashed it on the chopping-block.

'Who else you got here, James?'

'There's no one else. Just me and the boy. He's only twelve, Owens.' And Walter wondered why he thought this appeal would mean anything.

Owens looked at Billy. 'Where's your Maw?'

'She's dead,' said Walter James quickly, and was surprised to find that it was still not easy to say after all this time. 'She died a year last fall. I told you, there's just me and the boy.'

Virgil Owens leant his back against the hitching-rail and said lazily. 'Heard you was in the war, James.'

'Seventh Michigan,' said Walter.

'Georgia Volunteers,' said Virgil, as if exchanging pleasantries, and then 'Beats me how the Yankees won with yellow-bellies like you.'

The drifters looked at Walter curiously, waiting to see the effect of this taunt. Walter felt the twist of his son's body beneath his hand and knew, without looking, that the boy's face was upturned on him.

Virgil laughed, and the Mexican spat the last of the seed-husks on Walter's boot-toe.

'We got no call to stay,' said Johnny Owens, 'You understand me?'

'I heard the Regulators were looking for you.'

Johnny Owens grinned. 'They're looking,' he said. 'They're homesteading, too, so we ain't worried. I'm trading my horse for that roan of yours. That's a fair trade, you say?'

'If you want it that way.'

Owens nodded, still grinning. 'You're an accommodating man, James.' Then the grin left his face. 'See what food they got inside, Virgil.'

The thin man went into the house again. When he returned he was carrying a bag of flour, some bacon and a sack of coffee. He was eating some of the beans that had been in the skilly. He was also carrying the Navy Colt, and Walter felt a rush of anger at the thought of Virgil Owens' hands pawing among Mary's things.

Virgil said 'Lookut what the Yankee forgot, Johnny. That's downright dishonest, Johnny. Ain't it Johnny?'

Johnny Owens looked at the gun, stepped forward, measured the blow and hit Walter across the face with the back of his hand. As Walter went back with the blow, his hand released his son's shoulder. Billy squealed with anger and flung himself at Johnny Owens, his yellow head down to butt, his arms flailing. Virgil caught him by the neckband of his shirt and pulled him into the air.

'Spunky kid,' said Virgil, loose-lipped in his insane laugh. 'Sure he's yours, James?' He threw Billy back to Walter.

The half-breed came up with the roan, and Johnny Owens swung himself on to it. For a moment he stared down at Walter, his hand resting on his gun, and the other drifters looked at him, as if they knew what was going to happen because it had happened before. The Mexican was grinning, and Virgil chewed the side of his mouth. Then Johnny Owens shrugged, kicked his heels into the roan, and the four men rode down to the draw and away to the southwest.

Walter watched them until the dust was gone. He wiped the salt blood from his lips and looked at it where it smeared the back of his hand. 'Go get some kindling, son,' he said.

The boy went obediently, but with his head down and his feet dragging. He stopped at the corner of the barn and stood there, and Walter waited for him to turn, willing him to turn and look back, but Billy did not turn. Walter walked into the house and sat in the rocker with his hands between his knees. Mary's clothes had been dragged from the settle and spilled on the floor. The anger in Walter's throat choked him. He went down on his knees and gathered the clothes gently, the cotton prints and the ginghams, returning them to the settle, putting away with each a recollected memory of the woman who had once worn them. She would have found some way of explaining to the boy why his father had acted that way before the Owens. If there could be an explanation, that is, that Walter was sure was the right and true one.

He went over to the basin and threw cold water on his face, washing the blood from his mouth. Feeling came back into his lips, and with it the pain. He looked at his reflection in the splinter of mirror-glass by the towel, young-old and thin, grey in the long black hair at the temples. For a moment in his mind the reflection was replaced by the picture of a younger face, one that had stared back at him often enough five years before, self-assured and challenging beneath a Union-blue cap. It occurred to him that this was the face Billy had seen whenever he looked at his father, until this morning. And he knew that there was no explanation that could restore that picture.

He left the house and went to the barn. Billy was sitting there, staring out across the plain, and his face was dirty where he had rubbed at the tears, but he was not crying now. Even more than was usual, the colour of his hair reminded Walter of Mary.

'Billy? Billy, you all right, boy?'

When his son did not answer Walter put out a hand. Billy flinched away from it.

'All right,' said Walter James, much troubled. 'It's all right, Billy. You just sit there.' And he went back to the house.

The sun was well past noon when the Regulators arrived. There were fifteen or twenty of them, mostly neighbours who held sections across the river, and Walter thought it strange to see them wearing guns. Old Man Prescott was leading them, sitting upright, with his long legs straight and thrust forward in wooden stirrups, and his grey hair coming out in spikes from beneath his dirty hat. He looked down from the saddle at Walter James, and bit his yellow moustache. 'Get a horse and gun, Walt. We're going after the Owens boys.'

'I guess you are,' said Walter. 'They stopped by here this

morning. Took my roan and left a spent horse that's no good to itself or a man now. It ought to be shot. I'd be obliged for the loan of a gun, Mr Prescott. The Owens took mine.'

'They stopped by here,' said one of the riders, 'and you're still living?'

'We're both still living. Me and my boy. I'd like the loan of that gun, Mr Prescott, before you leave.'

Old Man Prescott wiped the back of his hand across his moustache, bringing the movement up sharply at the end. 'Then you coming along?' he asked.

'No,' said Walter, 'There's just me and the boy. I'm not leaving him.'

One of the Regulators laughed. 'What happened to your face, Walt? Somebody hit you?'

Old Man Prescott turned in the saddle slowly and stared at the speaker. 'Shut your face,' he said easily. Then he looked back at Walter and said softly 'You signed the articles, Walt. We remember that.'

'That was before Mary died. The boy's only got me now.'

Nobody spoke. The horses moved uneasily, stirred up dust and sneezed in it.

'It won't look good, Walt,' said Old Man Prescott at last. 'You remember what you signed? *We the undersigned uniting ourselves in a party for the laudable purpose of arresting thieves and murderers do pledge ourselves on our sacred honour to ...*'

'The words are in my mind, Mr Prescott,' said Walter.

'You took an oath, Walt.'

'I got the boy to think of, Mr Prescott.'

The old man wiped his moustache again, and then suddenly leant down, his saddle creaking. 'Give me your hand, boy.' He pulled Billy up before him, and the boy straddled the horse, his hands gripping the horn and his eyes looking away from his father. His cheeks were red beneath the pale hair.

'Put the boy down, Mr Prescott.'

'You know why the Regulators was formed, Walt.' Old Man Prescott spoke gently, as if it meant a lot to him to be understood. 'On account of men like the Owens, and no Law being in this county to handle them.'

'I know that.'

'You signed, Walt, along of the rest of us. There's all of us with folks at home. If you won't leave the boy we'll take him along. You got another horse?'

'I got a pony out on graze. They didn't see it.'

'You get it. We'll wait.' The old man looked at Walter and there was no anger, no condemnation in his expression, just patient confidence.

For a moment Walter held that gaze, and then he turned and went into the house. When he came out he was wearing his old Army blouse, faded, except on the sleeves where the chevrons had been. He saw Billy stare at it, open his mouth, and then turn his head away. Old Man Prescott gave Walter a pistol and he went to the corral and shot the drifter's horse. When he came back, riding the pony, the gun was stuck into his waistband. He pulled up beside Old Man Prescott.

He said 'It ain't right to take the boy, Mr Prescott.'

'There's no choice.'

Walter stood in his stirrups, his body inclined forward. Then he settled in the saddle and his voice was harsh. 'Anything happens to the boy, Mr Prescott, and I'll hold you for it.'

'You got that privilege,' said Old Man Prescott easily, 'But ain't nothing going to happen to him. Let's ride.'

But Walter held Prescott's bridle. He spoke to his son. 'Billy, you want to ride with me?'

The boy shook his head, his mouth puckered.

'Let's ride,' said Old Man Prescott again, and he turned his horse to the southwest, with the others curving after him.

They rode until dusk, dismounting and walking their horses for ten minutes in every hour. The Cherokee tracker, Joe Grey Shirt, rode with Old Man Prescott, bending from the saddle, or getting down now and then to touch the trail with his finger. Each time he grinned. But the trail was leading to the border, and the going was slow.

Once Old Man Prescott looked back to where Walter James rode at the tail, his feet below the belly of his pony, his back straight like a cavalryman's. Old Man Prescott pulled out and waited until Walter came up. He said 'You want to ride with your Paw now, Billy?'

'No,' said the boy.

Old Man Prescott said nothing more, but he looked across at Walter, chewed the side of his mouth, and then pushed his horse forward again.

They camped out that night in an arroyo thirty miles from the border. It was a dry camp because Joe Grey Shirt said that the drifters were not more than two hours ahead. Old Man Prescott grunted and said 'We'll catch up tomorrow.' Joe Grey Shirt went out later, on foot, and he came back after three hours, grinning more than usual. He said that the drifters were camped six or seven miles on, nearer than he had thought, but they had not unsaddled. Some of the Regulators wanted to ride on them, but Old Man Prescott looked at them with contempt. 'And lose them as soon as they hear us? And there ain't no sense in risking the boy.' His chuckle was sardonic. 'You get to shooting in the dark and some of you'll do yourselves an injury.'

The men stirred resentfully. One said 'Why'd you bring the boy? We could've done this without him and his Paw.'

'Walter signed the articles,' said Old Man Prescott.

The boy lay that night with his head and shoulders on the old man's saddle. When he was asleep Walter covered him with a blanket, and crouched beside him, watching the still face in the moonlight. Walter sat there for an hour until at last he went over to where Old Man Prescott was sitting with his back against the crumbling bank of the arroyo, sucking a cold pipe. They were both silent for a while, and then Walter said 'What I meant about holding you for it if the boy was hurt, Mr Prescott. I'd be obliged if you forgot that.'

Old Man Prescott took the pipe from his mouth and pushed it inside his shirt. He said nothing.

'What're you thinking of this, Mr Prescott?'

'I'm thinking of them Owens boys,' said the old man. 'A homesteader below the rim crossed them a couple of days ago when they rode in on him, just like they rode in on you. He was a big hero that homesteader. He tried to take a gun to them. They shot up his family before they killed him.'

'I had that in mind.'

'I figure you did,' said Old Man Prescott.

'You think it was that and nothing else?'

The Old Man moved a little in the moonlight. 'No, I guess you was afraid, too. My boy was with you in the War, Walt . . .' He stopped, and at last went on slowly. 'You did nothing nobody else wouldn't do.'

'The homesteader didn't. The one you said.'

'He's dead,' said the old man in sudden anger. 'And his boy, too. A boy of Billy's age I heard. He's dead, on account of his father being a hero.'

'Billy won't see it that way.'

'He might,' said Old Man Prescott, 'When he's a man and gotten himself a son.'

'That's a long way off.'

'It is. You want he should ride with you in the morning?'

Walter stood up. 'I guess he'll ride where he's a mind to. I'm grateful to you, Mr Prescott.'

'Good-night, Walt.'

The trail was broken by the river the next morning, an hour after the drifter's camp was passed, and Old Man Prescott split the Regulators into four parties to ride the banks. He took the south bank with Joe Grey Shirt and Walter and two of the others, and they rode up it to the west. Four miles on, the Cherokee moved into mid-stream where a sand-bank cleared the water and there he found some horse-droppings. He nodded.

'They're getting careless,' said Old Man Prescott.

Another mile and there were hoof-marks in the mud where the drifters had come out on the south bank. The old man called the other party over and they all rode at a trot to the southwest. They were bunched up now, standing slightly in the stirrups, their faces set. Walter rode half a length behind Old Man Prescott, watching the bobbing banner of Billy's fair hair. The heat was thick and it pricked the riders beneath their shirts. Old Man Prescott had tied his bandana about Billy's nose and throat holding the boy's body to his.

The trail led southwards to the mouth of a canyon, rising up there to the rocky shale where it was lost. The Regulators came suddenly upon bodies lying, and the leading horses shied. One of the riders went back over the cantle of his saddle into the dust.

'Get up!' said Old Man Prescott bitterly. He looked up at the wheeling buzzard and then down at the bodies. The bodies of

two men and two horses. Walter could scarcely recognize what the buzzards had left of his roan. The Mexican and the half-breed had been shot in the back and had bled to death. The blood was black in the dust.

Old Man Prescott put his hand over Billy's eyes. 'Ho, Joe Grey Shirt!' he called.

The Cherokee grinned pleasantly. He pointed up the canyon and shook his head.

The old man looked approvingly at the canyon walls, the angry rocks, and the yellow candlesticks of the *cholla*. He almost smiled. 'Box canyon,' he said, 'Men should know the country they run through.'

Then he chewed his thumb, looking at the bodies and working out the story aloud. Johnny and Virgil had been riding the dead horses, he said, and broken their legs most likely in bad country like this. He had never known a bad man who thought of his horse first. So Johnny and Virgil had killed the breed and the Mexican and taken their horses. He went over the story again and again, phrasing it in different ways. Nobody contradicted him. Joe Grey Shirt nodded his head.

'We got 'em!' said Old Man Prescott. He lifted his reins above the saddle horn and moved his horse forward.

They rode until the canyon turned and then the old man lifted Billy to the ground. 'Stay there, boy,' he said. 'You stay there. Mind what I say?'

Walter James looked at his son, the smallness of the boy there beside the old man's great horse. His face white, and his eyes looking up at Old Man Prescott, looking at nobody but Old Man Prescott, who shifted round in his saddle to say 'You want to stay with the boy, Walt?' Walter shook his head, and the old man shouted, 'Joe Grey Shirt!'

'Sure, Mr Prescott, I stay.'

Then something hummed violently above them, and there was the bang of a Winchester, bouncing down, wall to wall, from the rocks ahead. The Regulators fell from their horses and scrabbled down behind the boulders. Old Man Prescott caught Billy and pulled him down beside him. There was another vicious whirr, the bang of a gun, and Virgil Owens' insane laugh.

'Johnny Owens!' called the old man, 'Johnny Owens! You and Virgil come on down!'

The only answer was another laugh, and Old Man Prescott turned over on his back and pulled his hat-brim down over his eyes.

From where he lay Walter studied the rockfall and the rise of it to the sky. He looked long at the south face and then he looked round at the Regulators where they were hunched behind cover, their faces turned in question to Old Man Prescott and doubt in their eyes. The old man ignored them, and the air was still in sardonic silence. A red-tongued lizard flicked out of its hole a foot from Walter's face, blinked at him nervously, and then was gone in one green-yellow movement.

Walter pulled himself to his knees, held his body as if it were an aimed projectile, and in one quick roll flung himself across to the stone where Joe Grey Shirt squatted contentedly with eyes closed. The Cherokee's expression was non-committal as he answered Walter's questions. He pointed once to the south face and chopped his hand through the air conclusively.

Walter went back to his rock and he called 'Mr Prescott!'

The old man came over in a queer, aged crouch, and Virgil's Winchester spat up the dust behind him. Old Man Prescott swore. 'You figure you're too old and infirm to step over to me?' he asked bitterly.

'I don't want the boy to know.'

'What? Know what?'

'What's your plan, Mr Prescott?'

'Ain't got no plan.' The old man looked reflectively at Walter's tight face. He pushed his hat back, pulled his pipe from his shirt and thrust it between his teeth. 'Them Owens boys can't get out. If we want them though, we got to go up.'

'They'll kill some of us.'

'Maybe. You know any way round that?'

Walter James told him.

'You don't have to do that, Walt.'

'Joe Grey Shirt says it can be done.'

'If I told him to do it and meant it, then he'd say it couldn't be done.'

'I'll do it.'

Old Man Prescott wiped his chin with his hand. 'You doing this because of the boy?'

'I'm doing it because I thought of it.'

'No you ain't,' said the old man, 'We're waiting for sundown and then we're all going up. We'll all be heroes together.'

'I'm sorry, Mr Prescott,' said Walter. He stood up suddenly and ran into the open, down the slope to where the horses had drifted. He felt the nakedness of what he was doing as if the temperature of the air had suddenly changed. He heard Virgil's high yell, and a bullet stabbed the dirt to the left of him and a little ahead. And then others. And one catching his shirt-sleeve and ripping it. He reached the horses, he gripped the saddle-horn of one, swinging himself up as the animal began to move. He heard Old Man Prescott shouting above the gunfire, and then there was nothing but the sound of the pony's hooves, and the swing and the sway of it beneath him.

When Old Man Prescott got back to the boy he saw the expression on Billy's face. 'Now, look here!' he said, and he tried to control the anger within him. 'Do you know why your Paw let them Owens boys whip him around?'

The boy said nothing. He put his face in the crook of his elbow.

'Boy, don't you know your own Paw?'

Billy said 'Why'd you let him run away, Mr Prescott?'

The old man bit savagely on his pipe, and snapped the stem of it between his teeth.

*

Walter pulled in the horse at the mouth of the canyon. His tongue was dry, and appeared to be swollen. It was not only the dust that gave him this sensation, there was that old feeling with which he had been familiar enough five years before. A man less familiar with it might have been ashamed. He lifted his canteen to his lips, washed his mouth and spat out the water. The sun was now two handsbreadths from the horizon and he could feel the sweat beginning to cool beneath his blouse. He passed his hand over his chin, over the rasp of stubble. For a moment the incredible foolishness of what he intended to do paralysed his mind. This, his memory told him, was the moment of decision, when a man might easily become a coward. He tried to erase his mind of all but the immediate problem.

He looked back at the canyon. It went into the rock-face like an arm-thrust, crooked at the elbow. He tried to translate what he remembered of it, and what Joe Grey Shirt had told him of it, into a map's precise contours. The arm, from shoulder to elbow as it might be, ran from south to north, and the forearm from east to west. At the elbow the Regulators lay behind their cover, and somewhere on the steep south wall of the forearm were Johnny and Virgil Owens.

Yet, if Joe Grey Shirt were right, a man of courage might climb the escarpment, look down on the Owens boys and turn their advantage against them. Walter thought of it in half-remembered military terms – scout, flank, attack – but this did not seem to simplify the problem.

Darkening against the sinking sun the high rock ridge ran like the turreted wall of a fortress, and Walter remembered that the Cherokee had given it its old Spanish name *Ciudad Coronado*, the crowned city. He looked up at it and felt his imagination stir. Then he pointed his horse off the trail and rode towards the shattered rise of shale at the foot of the escarpment.

At first it was a gentle slope, and the pony's plunging feet sent the loose stones down in little sibilant falls, but it ended suddenly where the red rock face rose perpendicularly.

Walter dismounted. He unbuttoned the old cavalry blouse, pulled it from his shoulders and hung it on the apple of his saddle-horn. He pushed the hand-gun round to the small of his back, tightening the waistband of his levis. He tugged his hat firmly over his brow and walked up to the rock-face as a man might walk boldly up to an opponent.

The climb was deceptively easy at first, for the shallow strata, pushed out by their prehistoric cooling, formed a rough but adequate stairway, ledges of crumbling stone the width of a man's boot-sole. But as he went higher the strata became deeper, and in some places the next ledge was beyond the reach of his upstretched arms. He unstrapped a spur from his right heel, sweating fingers slipping on steel and leather. With the spur he began to cut a painful hand-hold and foot-hold. Once he grasped a scrag of brush, which some miracle of wind and germination had set to grow there, and as he grasped it he saw it slowly pull free from the thin soil that had given it life. He fell ten feet down the rock-face, spread-eagled, pressing his body against it, feeling the tearing of shirt and flesh on his chest, until his feet jarred on the ledge he had just left and held him.

Then up again, by kicking heels and jabbing spur, feeling the agonizing snap of his nails, seeing the blood oozing darkly below the dust, a furnace breathing in his lungs. He lived a year of his life on the escarpment, now climbing directly upward, now moving to the left or to the right in a ridiculous, slithering slide along the ledges, until suddenly there was nothing left of the wall to climb, and he was lying on his belly with his legs still hanging in space. He listened indifferently to the faint, ringing descent of the spur as it dropped from his fingers and fell back the way he had climbed.

He pulled himself forward until his legs were no longer hanging free, yet still he lay there, unbelieving, until the report of a Winchester jarred his brain. He lifted his head and shoulders. The gunfire came up from his right, up from the dark canyon, and before the echoes had bounced away, he heard Virgil's laugh and Old Man Prescott's answering shout of anger.

He lifted a hand to wipe the sweat from his face, and he saw the blood running down each finger from each torn nail. He was suddenly full of a wild exultation, a pride in having come this far, and he wanted to shout. But the feeling passed quickly into fear. He pulled himself forward on his belly, pretending that the drop of the rock-face was no longer behind him, yet fearing it still, as if it had the power to pull him down.

Away ahead of him stretched the hog-back of the ridge, and he realized that his climb, although it had seemed perpendicular, had in fact carried him along the parallel of the canyon until he was now above the elbow. Below, to his right, the canyon was a black river, yet on his left the sun still rolled redly to the horizon.

A cat, he thought, would have trouble walking along that hog-back. He must crawl, taking the cover of each boulder and looking down always for a sign that would tell him where the Owens brothers lay hidden.

So he crawled. He crawled first to the shelter of an outcrop of hard rock where he braced his feet, forced his buttocks into a niche, and took the hand-gun from his waistband. He broke it and blew the dust from the barrel. He spilled the shells from the cylinder and then spun it. He worked the action once, twice, and then a third time. The gun was heavy and unfamiliar in his hand. There was a crack in the butt that bit the ball of his thumb. The foresight had been filed away, and he wondered if he would be able to sight it by the hammer alone. He weighed it in his hand, and he felt no sympathy between him and it. He hated it.

With his shirt-tail he cleaned the shells. There had been five when Old Man Prescott had given him the gun, but one had been used on Johnny Owens' horse. Now, because his fingers were trembling, he lost another. It bounced from the rock between his feet and went spinning down, a momentary yellow fleck before it was lost. With terrible care he held the remaining three in his mouth until he had wiped each and inserted it in the cylinder. He lowered the hammer to an empty chamber. Again and again he examined the gun to make sure that when he thumbed back the hammer it would fall on to a full chamber. At last he thrust the gun into his waist-band, butt hard against his ribs.

He crawled on, marvelling at the heat of the rock beneath his hands and thighs, his throat closing in dryness that was part thirst and part fear. He crawled, and he halted for long minutes, looking down into the dark of the canyon for a sign.

When the sign came it was sudden and ridiculously unexpected, the flare of a match that lit Virgil's cupped hands, his long nose and deep eye-sockets, the crouch of his body, the stroke of a rifle below his armpit. When the match died there was still a sign, the faint patch of the neckerchief which Virgil had tucked beneath the Rebel cap to keep the sun from his neck.

He was thirty, perhaps forty feet below Walter, and there was no sign of Johnny Owens. He could be below Virgil still, or between Virgil and the rim.

Walter rolled silently over the edge, and with torn hands, that had miraculously found a skill in this, lowered himself rock by rock until he lay on the flat top of a slab fifteen feet above

Virgil. He took the gun from his waist and lay there with his thumb on the hammer.

Now, away from the last glow of the sun, his eyes grew accustomed to the dusk of the canyon. He saw the floor, the stipple of greasewood, the boulders where the Regulators lay, and beyond them their horses, neck-stretched to the sparse earth.

Johnny Owens' voice came out of the rocks below. 'Virgil, get them horses.'

The voice drew Walter's eyes down to where Johnny Owens sat below Virgil, on his heels behind a rock, his hat hanging by its thong between his shoulder-blades, a white grin bisecting his black beard.

Virgil pressed his cheeks against the rifle stock. He fired once and swore, pumped the lever and fired again. Old Man Prescott's yellow horse sat down suddenly on its haunches, rolled over squealing.

'Try another, Virgil,' said Johnny.

In the dusk below, Billy's tiny figure skidded out from cover and began to run towards the horses. Walter saw the muzzle of Virgil's rifle move from one of the horses and follow the crazy path of the boy. The spark of Virgil's cigarette glowed.

Walter stood up and leapt downward. The stones rolled as he hit the slope.

Virgil turned, bringing the rifle down. He opened his mouth. He shouted '*Johnny!*'

He fired the rifle once towards Walter. He worked the lever again and vaulted on to the rock, bringing the stock up to his shoulder. Walter braced his feet, lifted the hand-gun until barrel and arm were a line from his shoulder, and he fired. The bullet took Virgil in the throat, twisting his body as it dropped.

Walter fell behind the rock that Virgil had left, and he listened to the rolling fall of the dead man going down to the floor of the canyon. The noise lasted a long time.

Then there was silence, an unsympathetic silence out of which at last came the thudding of his heart. In the dust beside him Virgil's cigarette burnt acridly where it had fallen. Walter ground it out with fierce satisfaction.

'Owens!' he shouted, 'Johnny Owens! You hear me?'

There was no reply. Then the faint scrape of a spur on stone.

'Owens, this is Walter James! You hear me?'

A single stone rattled in the darkness below.

'Owens, I'm coming down!'

A cough. Then a harsh voice. It said 'Don't talk. Come down!'

Walter looked back up the cliff face. Although the sky was red above the wall of rock, below was black and formless. He had that advantage, the only advantage. He pushed himself to his knees and then to his feet, crouching on his heels, and he moved as silently as he could to the left-hand edge, forcing to his mind the one glimpse he had had of Johnny Owens, hoping the man was still in the same spot, but only half-believing he would be.

He picked up a rock with his left hand and threw it to the right. As it fell, unseating others, he stood up and stepped out.

He saw a shadow rise from the ground, the flash of a gun, firing to the right where the stone had fallen, and then the shadow turned quickly to meet him.

He waited for it. The shadow became a body, a body crouched, the smear of a face and white teeth. He fired at it. He fired again as Johnny Owens shot once more, this time at a target he could see.

*

When he heard the first report of the hand-gun Old Man Prescott said 'The Lord be with him.'

They heard the roll of Virgil's body falling and wondered. 'Lord be with him, too,' said Old Man Prescott.

One of the Regulators called. 'How about that, Mr Prescott? You want we should do something?'

'Ain't nothing to do yet, son.'

He bit his yellow moustache, and then they heard Walter's voice. It echoed from rock to rock. Old Man Prescott put his hand on the boy's shoulder. 'Hear that, Billy? That's your Paw.' He wished that he could see the boy's face in the dusk.

Then there were three more shots, but the second and third so close as to appear almost one. And silence now. One by one the Regulators stood up, staring into the darkness.

'Mr Prescott, sir ... ?' said Billy.

'It's all right, son.' He took off his hat and rubbed his eyes, staring, as they were all staring.

They heard footsteps coming down, coming down in the way a tired man will walk when he knows that there is no hurry. One of the Regulators pumped his rifle and Old Man Prescott swore at him blasphemously, asking the Almighty's pardon in the same voice.

A single spur was striking the stones prettily, and a long-legged shadow came out of the dusk. It paused for a moment and then came on. In its right hand it carried two pairs of boots, and they were the boots of Johnny and Virgil Owens. Old Man Prescott yipped and slapped his thigh with his hat. He threw it on the ground and stamped it delightedly.

Walter James did not look at the grinning Regulators. He dropped the boots in the dust, and he took the gun from his waistband and dropped that too. Then he walked towards his son.

Almighty Voice

I first heard the story of Almighty Voice when I was a boy, before my tenth birthday, when I lived along the South Saskatchewan. There was a *Métis* boy who went to school with me and who had the blue-black hair and high cheekbones of his grandmother's people, the Crees. So perhaps it was from him that I first heard the story, for Almighty Voice was the last great warrior of the Cree Nation, or so it seems to me.

Almighty Voice had made his stand and had died in the Minnechinas Hills eighteen years before I was born, but he was a living man to me as I dug in the slough holes in search of an arrow-head that might have been his. Every fall I saw the vision of him riding in the dust behind the rolling tumbleweed. The Canadian West was still not old when I was young and if you listened, if you sat on a bluff above the river, you might hear, if you were ten years old, the creak of a Red River cart, the thunder of passing buffalo, or a bugle call. You might hear Almighty Voice singing his death song as the field-guns exploded shells above his head and the North West Mounted Police waited for him to die, lying in their scarlet coats among the prairie crocus.

Nor did I have my imagination only to make a reality out of Almighty Voice. Once the Crees came down from their reservation at Duck Lake to take part in the great rodeo in Saskatoon. A cloud of red and yellow and blue, of black and white, riding past the Hudson's Bay Store, the hooves of the ponies hiding the street-car lines. Among the buckskin and the nodding warbonnets there rode John Sounding Sky who was the father of Almighty Voice. Among the women was Spotted Calf who was the mother of Almighty Voice, and both were very old. I liked to think that if some miracle had saved Almighty Voice he, too, would have ridden before me thus. For a dime I could have sat on a hardwood bench above the arena and seen him.

This is his story ...

When he was very young and ran naked about his father's lodge he had so strong and powerful a voice that his grandfather, the war-chief One Arrow, picked him up one day and gravely named him *Mitchi-manito-wayo* – The Voice of the Great Spirit. Even at the hour of death his voice was loud and strong, though he had then been three days without water.

He was born at a time of change for his race. There had been years when the Crees – of the Forests, the Parklands and the Plains – had been masters of all the land between the Peace River and the Qu-Appelle, between Eagle Hills and Hudson Bay. If they were among the last of the Plains Indians to adopt the horse they were among the first to use the gun, and with both of these they drove before them the Blackfeet, Bloods, Piegans, Snakes and Assiniboins. They became as mighty in the Canadian northwest as were the seven tribes of the Lakota in the United States.

They grew rich selling pelts and hides to the Fur Company factors. Their young sons were trained and ready for manhood by the age of ten. They painted their faces black until they had endured the Sun Dance and earned the rights of adulthood. There were many, many of them, and when winter came in the Moon of Popping Trees, and they set up their villages in the deep coulees, the barking of their dogs and the chatter of their women could be heard for miles across the snow.

But such greatness passed, and it was at the time of its passing that Almighty Voice was born. The plough, the telegraph and the railroad had come to the Plains. The government in the east split the Territory into the districts of Alberta, Athabaska, Saskatchewan and Assiniboia, and policed them with six hundred scarlet constables. The land was broken into sections and given to settlers who housed their families in sod huts, and who ploughed up the buffalo wallows, and wheat began to grow where before there had been but short grass.

The great chiefs of the Crees – Poundmaker, Big Bear, Little Pine and One Arrow – put their thumbs to treaties that would shut them into reservations, but this they did only after Poundmaker had fought and whipped Colonel Otter in seven hours of battle at Cut Knife Creek. Some of the Indians who fought then were placed in prison because the government could not trust them to live tranquilly in reservations. One of these was John Sounding Sky.

Thus, when Almighty Voice consummated his manhood in his sixteenth year by taking a girl of fourteen for his wife, his father was in prison, and he had only the stories of old men to remind him of the past. He was bitter against the white men, and on One Arrow's reservation there were mixed feelings about his bitterness, although all admired his god-given voice and his fine skill in running and hunting.

He was tall and of great breadth at the shoulders, but the white men said he was immoral, for he did not keep to this girl of fourteen, but took another for wife. This girl, also, he left for another as young. The Duck Lake Indian Agent, a dour and earnest man called McKenzie, rode over in his black coat and buckboard to talk with One Arrow, and to explain that no young man, red or white, could now behave as Almighty Voice was behaving. A man should take one wife only, said McKenzie, that was the law of God and the Queen.

But, even as McKenzie argued thus, Almighty Voice had taken a fourth wife, the grand-daughter of a tame Indian at Fort la Corne, and to this girl Almighty Voice was faithful.

There was a restlessness in him. In their youth his father and his grandfather had ridden into the great buffalo herds to kill their meat. Now there were steers only, which the Government bought on the rangelands and which were given to the Crees for meat. It was one such steer that set Almighty Voice towards his death in the Minnechinas.

He found it on the edge of the Reservation and he cut its throat, and his wife was already stripping and drying the meat over a green fire when Sergeant Colebrook of the Police arrested Almighty Voice for killing a government steer. He was taken to the police post for trial, and there he said that he believed this steer to have been his father's. He said this arrogantly, with his back straight and his head up, and with an air of great contempt for such laws about cattle.

Agent McKenzie, who was also a Justice of the Peace, sentenced the boy to a month's imprisonment, reflecting that in this time Almighty Voice might also have time to think upon the responsibilities of marriage. That night Almighty Voice lay in the wooden guard-house, wrapped in his blanket, with an iron ball chained to his ankle, and while he lay there a fool called Dickson, a corporal of the Police, came to the window and thought it a joke to tell the Cree that the penalty for killing a government steer was hanging.

The boy believed this, and later that night he lifted the iron ball in his hands, and stepped from his blanket. While the guard slept he stole the keys and freed himself from the ball and the cell. He climbed the palisade of the post and he ran without halt six miles to the Saskatchewan. This he swam and ran another fifteen miles, arriving at his mother's lodge before morning.

He said to Spotted Calf 'They will never hang me. I shall fight and die.'

He took his wife and two ponies, and he took an old muzzle-loader with powder and shot, and he rode northwards to the Barren Grounds. This was in 1895, in October, the Moon of Madness.

Up in the Carrot River country, a week later, Sergeant Colebrook was on patrol with a *Métis* tracker called Dumont. They were looking for Almighty Voice, and they were passing through young spruce bush when they heard the heavy report of a muzzle-loader. The sergeant put his horse to the gallop and broke out of the brush to the prairie. Two hundred yards away Almighty Voice was bending over a fallen prairie-chicken. Behind him his wife held the bridles of their ponies.

Colebrook pulled his horse to a trot and rode forward, holding his right hand upward in its gauntlet to show that he wanted no killing. Dumont rode behind him, muttering about the foolishness of approaching a bad Indian thus.

Almighty Voice straightened his back and began to reload the gun. There was no paint on his face and no feather in his hair, and he wore leggings and a thick, trader's shirt against the October cold. When the policeman was thirty yards away the Cree called out.

'What does he say?' said Colebrook.

'That he will kill you if you go closer.'

'I have my duty to do,' said Colebrook and rode on.

Almighty Voice called out again, and brought up his gun. The sergeant did not halt, and Almighty Voice, who did not wish to be hanged for killing a steer, fired. The shot took Colebrook in the neck and tore him from the saddle. Dumont looked down and knew that the policeman was dead. He sat there, feeling very sick, while Almighty Voice reloaded the gun. Then the *Métis* pulled his horse about and kicked it into a gallop as the Cree fired again.

Dumont came into the Carrot River settlement with a shattered arm and blood on his jacket. He took the settlers back to the brush, and there they found the dead sergeant. There were tracks of unshod ponies going north, but, with Dumont in great pain from his arm, there was no one skilled enough now to follow the trail. So the settlers went back, and within a day or so the wires carried the news across Assiniboia and Saskatchewan that Almighty Voice the Cree was wanted for murder, and that one hundred dollars would be paid for his capture.

Two constables from the Duck Lake Post rode to the One Arrow reservation and questioned Spotted Calf. They spoke to her and she did not answer. No one in the village would tell the Mounted Police what, if anything, they knew of Almighty Voice.

Then, some weeks later, at the old trading post at Fort la Corne, where the north and south arms of the Saskatchewan join hands, a young Cree girl came into the Hudson's Bay store and asked for flour, offering pelts in exchange. The factor recognized her and sent for a constable. But all through the questioning the wife of Almighty Voice sat silent with her hands folded. She was only fifteen, and she was with child.

For nearly two years the white men were given no word of Almighty Voice. He disappeared northward to the Churchill River where the Forest Crees may have hidden him, and perhaps he was happy with them, for these were Indians not yet gathered into reservations.

He was not, of course, forgotten by the North West Mounted Police. His description was pinned to the walls of the posts at Battleford, Yorkton and Prince Albert. At last, in May, 1897, the Moon when Ponies Shed, the police released John Sounding Sky from prison, believing that an opportunity of seeing his father again would bring Almighty Voice back from the northern wilderness.

This was a clever thing to have done, for when Almighty Voice heard the news he came south to his village, and sat for many hours with his father and grandfather. At the end of the council the young man stood up and said 'I shall not run any more. When the policemen come again I shall show myself and fight.'

He went about the village and he told his cousin, Going Up To Sky, and his brother-in-law, Topean, of his decision. They were young men and they swore to join him and to fight with him.

There was a half-breed scout called Napoleon Venne who worked for the police post at Duck Lake, and Inspector James Wilson ordered him to watch the reservation now that Sounding Sky had returned to it. So, day by day, the *Métis* sat his horse in the shadows of the spruce-crowned bluffs, his leg crooked over his saddle and his fingers rolling cigarette after cigarette. His blood a mixture of Cree and French-Canadian, Venne had resolved these confused loyalties by service to the British, and he had no sympathy for Almighty Voice. One day he came back to the post with a question for Wilson. Did not the inspector find it odd that John Sounding Sky should make the same journey, at the same time every day, to the same distant corner of the reservation where poplar and spruce saplings were thick above the coulees?

Thus Wilson knew that Almighty Voice had returned.

The next morning Corporal Bowdridge and Napoleon Venne rode out of Duck Lake to Minnechinas Hills. By afternoon, as they halted, and Venne relaxed to smoke another cigarette, they saw two young figures run into a copse a quarter of a mile away. Bowdridge told Venne to ride to one end of the copse, and he would ride to the other and flush the Indians out.

So Venne took his position below the low hill, and as he sat there, leg crooked, reins on his arms and back bent, Almighty Voice and Going Up To Sky watched from the brush.

Going Up To Sky touched his cousin's arm. 'Let me shoot him.'

'Shoot him, then,' said Almighty Voice, 'but do not miss.'

So Going Up To Sky, who was only fifteen and had never killed a man or counted coup on an enemy, fired and fired badly. The ball hit Napoleon Venne in the chest and he fell off his horse, scattering his cigarette papers and tobacco. He lay on the grass where he swore in French and English and Cree. Bowdridge came round the bluff at a gallop, pulling out his rifle, but Almighty Voice and Going Up To Sky had slipped away. Almighty Voice was angry with his cousin for not killing the *Métis*.

That night the telegraph chattered from Duck Lake to Prince Albert, down through Humboldt to Regina. At Regina, where Colonel Herchmer was preparing to send a contingent of Mounted Police to Queen Victoria's Jubilee in London, orders went out that the whole field force of police in Assiniboia must be ready for action in case this boy Almighty Voice did something to bring the Cree Nation into revolt.

At midnight, on Thursday, 27 May, the bugler of F Division, Prince Albert, sounded Boots and Saddle, and Captain Jack Allan rode southward at the gallop with two non-commissioned officers and nine constables. In the lodges of their fathers Almighty Voice, Going Up To Sky and Topean made ready to die.

Shortly after Friday's dawn Allan's detachment reached the Minnechinas. It was a fine spring day and the grass was still green with the life of melted snow. The constables were saddle-worn, with dust on their scarlet tunics, and before their tired eyes the sea of grass moved oddly. *Métis* scouts were out at point, and soon one of these came riding in to say that he had seen three antelope among the poplars on a bluff a quarter of a mile away. Or they may not have been antelope, he said, they may have been men.

Allan stood up in his saddle and focused his glass on the bluff. Then he slapped the glass shut, raised his arm and brought it forward. The police went on at a trot.

Out of the poplars and the scrub, down to the foot of the bluff, came the three young Crees, with Almighty Voice in the centre. They were stripped to the breech-clout and their bodies shone. Allan waved his arm to right and left, and his constables deployed into wings on either side of him. He rode straight at Almighty Voice.

The Cree brought up his gun with a shout. He fired when Allan was within a few yards of the bluff, and Topean and Going Up To Sky fired too. A shot shattered Allan's upraised arm and knocked him from his horse. Another shot hit and broke the thigh of Sergeant Raven and he fell forward in the saddle, his horse swinging about and trotting away. The Crees slipped back into the bush.

Corporal Hockin, seeing Allan fall and Raven wounded, seeing the fortress thickness of the trees and scrub on the bluff, called off the constables, and they wheeled about and galloped back, with the shrill, derisive shouts of the young Indians following them.

Allan crawled to the edge of the trees and lay there on his stomach. Above him a meadow-lark was calling, and slowly he lifted his head. He looked up into the eyes of Almighty Voice, where the young Cree was half-hidden by silver leaves. 'Throw me your cartridge belt,' said Almighty Voice.

Allan shook his head, and he heard the *click-lack* as Almighty Voice cocked the gun. He shook his head again, and bent it, waiting for the Cree to fire. But when he looked up the Indian had gone. Two constables came in at a gallop, picked up the Inspector and carried him away.

Now buckboards and farm-horses were bringing up settlers from Duck Lake. There was Postmaster Ernest Grundy, and there were Pozer and Davidson, and Bell and Cook, all of whom had come to Assiniboia to farm or work, and who wanted to live without fear of the Crees. At noon Doctor Stewart drove up on his buckboard from Prince Albert, and the wounded men were glad to see him.

Corporal Hockin studied the bluff through Allan's glass. The little hill rose like an island from the prairie and was perhaps 150 yards long and 50 wide. Stunted poplar broke from it in clumps, and the ground was thickly entangled by brush. Three men within that had the power of a regiment, and the thought did not please Hockin. He stationed his constables in a ring about the bluff, although he was wise enough in his knowledge of Indians to realize that these boys had decided to die where they were. But it was Hockin's problem to prevent them from killing as they died.

All afternoon he waited, and the sun was hot and the flies spun about the picketed horses. Now and then from the brush came the singing of the young Crees, and this singing increased when they saw their people coming from the reservation to watch them die. Spotted Calf sat in her blanket and did not take her eyes from the bluff.

As the day cooled into evening Corporal Hockin called for volunteers, and all his constables and as many civilians answered. He chose seven of them, and he formed them up in open order and led them down at the run towards the bluff. They went down with the light of the falling sun dropping aslant the scarlet coats and tartan mackinaws. Hockin was the first to reach the fringe of the brush, and there Almighty Voice killed him with one shot, and touched the body with his gun to count coup. Constable Kerr was killed too when Going Up To Sky, it may have been, shot him in the head and counted coup also with a cry of 'This is mine.'

But none of the volunteers, breaking into the brush, saw any of the Crees. They forced their way through, and somewhere in the middle Almighty Voice, or perhaps one of his friends, shot and killed Postmaster Grundy.

Then the charge reached the other side of the bluff, and behind it the Crees called triumphantly. The policemen and civilians passed back through the brush, and this time none of them was killed, but one claimed that he had shot and hit Almighty Voice in the ankle.

Suddenly the whole prairie was quiet, and in the half-light the crown of the bluff grew black against the sky. Constable O'Kelly looked down to it and he said to his friend Constable Cook 'I believe Hockin is still alive, will you come down with me and bring him out?'

So they lifted their rifles to the trail and ran swiftly towards the corporal's body. At the edge of the brush they were fired upon, and they dropped on their bellies. They were very close to the Crees, for no sooner had they fallen to the ground than Topean, with a great shout, leaped into the air before them.

He was instantly killed by Constable O'Kelly.

But the policemen could not move from where they lay. Almighty Voice's gun broke the twigs above O'Kelly's head with every shot, and Going Up To Sky splintered the log behind which Cook had taken shelter. Now Doctor Stewart, who was much liked by the Crees, came down to the bluff, standing up in his buckboard and showing no fear. He pulled up below the trees and called out to O'Kelly 'I've got the buckboard, can you bring the corporal?'

Neither of the Crees fired at him, although it would have been impossible for them to miss.

Cook and O'Kelly crawled back, and they picked up Hockin's body and placed it on the buckboard. Then they ran, and Almighty Voice, unable to stand on his broken foot, fired one shot that tore the spur from O'Kelly's heel.

It was night, and the smell of the dead brought the coyotes in close to the camp-fires. The waiting Indian women began to keen. More civilians came from Duck Lake, for although they were peaceful men they could not but feel excited by the fact that here, before their eyes, was the sort of thing they thought had gone from the prairies for ever.

Inspector Wilson also came from Duck Lake, bringing more constables. Two hours after sunset Superintendent Gagnan arrived from Prince Albert with still more constables and a seven-pounder field gun. The gun was unlimbered, and in the dark it fired ranging shots that exploded above the poplars, and the roll and thunder of the explosions went across the prairie. When the firing ceased Almighty Voice called strongly from the bluff.

'What does he say?' asked Gagnan.

'That you have done well, but must do better,' answered a *Métis* with grudging pride as he remembered his own Cree blood.

It was very cold that Friday night, and there was no moon. The young Crees sang their songs, and now and then fired shots at the ringing fires. In her blanket, her head uncovered, Spotted Calf went down and stood on a gopher's mound outside the bluff. She called to her son by name and he answered her with hers. She reminded him of the courage of his father and of his grandfather, and of the greatness of his people. She told him that he must not weaken, that he must die fighting.

He answered that she could have faith in him and in Going Up To Sky. Topean had died bravely, he said, and without foolishness. Now, with the repeating rifles they had taken from the dead policemen, he and his cousin would also die well. But, he said, their throats were dry from the want of water, and their stomachs called out against their emptiness.

Gagnan listened to the conversation uneasily, without understanding it, and he sent a policeman to bring in the woman. The constable took Spotted Calf's arm in the darkness, saying, 'Come away, old lady. If you stay here you'll be hurt.'

She was offered food. 'I am weak,' she said, 'but while my son starves and thirsts I shall not eat or drink.'

Towards dawn Almighty Voice called again. Gagnan turned to the *Métis* for translation. The half-breed said 'He says they have had a good fight. But they are hungry. He says if you send them food and water tomorrow they will finish the fight.'

The birds in the bush flew up to meet dawn on Saturday. Black smoke from the encircling cooking-fires rose steadily in the still air. A constable came in with news that had been received by wire. Early that Saturday morning a field force had left Police Headquarters in Regina, taking the cars northwards. It was commanded by the Assistant Commissioner, Colonel McIlree, a fine, handsome man with sweeping whiskers and a high-bridged nose. With him he had Inspector Archie McDonell, 24 other ranks, 13 horses, and a nine-pounder field gun. They expected to arrive at the bluff that evening.

So, throughout Saturday, there was a lull. Now and then the seven-pounder fired a shell, and the waiting police and waiting civilians watched the fragments snap the leaves and branches of the poplars. As the noise of each shot died away Almighty Voice's ululating yell answered in derision.

At noon a crow sailed in from the prairie and hung above the trees, and there was a strange silence as all eyes were turned upon it, and all knew what it meant to the two Cree boys. The bird hung black and motionless for a minute it seemed, until Almighty Voice fired, and it fell into the trees. There the Indians tore it apart and sucked its blood and ate its meagre meat.

The Regina Force reached Duck Lake at five o'clock that afternoon. By ten in the evening they arrived at the bluff, and McIlree immediately ordered both guns to open fire. The shells burst in orange and scarlet against the dark sky and then there was silence.

There was silence for an hour until the voice of Spotted Calf was heard calling to her son from the hummock where she stood. Once more she called upon his courage, and he answered that it had not left him, but that he and Going Up To Sky were suffering greatly from hunger and thirst. They had, said Almighty Voice, torn bark from the trees to eat. They had dug down in the dry earth to their arm-pits in search of water, and found none. Going Up To Sky was weary, and he, Almighty Voice felt the pain of his wounded ankle, but their spirits were strong.

Then the air was quiet again, until Spotted Calf began to sing her son's death-song, and he joined her in it, and the *Hi-he-yeh!* throbbed in the night, and no one among the white men had the strength to order the woman away.

In the dark hours before dawn on Sunday Almighty Voice and Going Up To Sky fired often at the campfires. One constable, it is said, claimed that a shot once came from *behind* him, from the prairie and not from the bluff. It has been further said that on Sunday, after it was all over, a bloody moccasin was found in the grass outside the besieging ring, as if Almighty Voice had laughed at the police by crawling past their posts in the darkness, firing this shot at them and then crawling back to die with his cousin, Going Up To Sky.

At seven o'clock on the morning of Sunday 30 May both guns opened fire. For an hour the shells burst over the trees and the shrapnel whipped the leaves and branches like a great wind. Now and then the gunfire was answered by a rifle shot, by the death-song of Almighty Voice.

The guns were stilled for an hour, so that they might cool, and then they began again, and fired until noon when James McKay and William Drain, who led the civilian volunteers from Duck Lake, went to McIlree for permission to charge the bluff. There were, they said, now over a hundred men besieging the two young Crees, and it was time to end the humiliating business.

But McIlree, who knew how tenuous was the hold his police held on the Territory, and how much their prestige was at stake in this affair, saw no wisdom in allowing the two Crees to kill more white men. So he refused permission, and he ordered the guns to fire again. He sent to Duck Lake for spades, so that his men might advance on the bluff by entrenchments.

At one o'clock McKay came again to him, and pointed out that there had been no return fire from the Indians for some time. They must be dead. So McIlree ordered a detachment of his constables to join the advance.

The white men went forward in open order, in the sunlight, firing, some of them, as they ran, stumbling in their heavy boots. The dark green mackinaws, the scarlet coats and yellow striped breeches went forward across the grass, watched by the old men and boys, the women and children of One Arrow's village.

The charge went through the brush, and there was no one to stop it.

The white men found Topean lying where O'Kelly had killed him. They found a shallow rifle-pit that had been dug in the centre of the bluff. Leaning against its wall was Going Up To Sky who was only fifteen, and it is said that he was still breathing, and someone put a rifle to his head and killed him.

At the bottom of the pit lay Almighty Voice with seven wounds on him. These had not killed him. He had died from a shell splinter that had parted his skull from crown to chin.

All about the pit the bark had been stripped from the trees, where the young men had reached up to peel it and eat it. And in the ground, just as Almighty Voice had told his mother, there were two deep holes, as deep as a man's arm is long. There the Crees had dug for water. The earth to the bottom of them was dust and without moisture.

All the police and the civilians now came crowding into the trees, jostling one another about the pit and looking down. The women of One Arrow's village keened at the edge of the bluff, waiting for the moment when they would be allowed to take away the bodies of the young men. The legend of Almighty

Voice began to grow from that moment, and part of this legend says that near the spot where there had been fighting on Friday evening some characters were found carved on the bark at the foot of a poplar tree. A *Métis* squatted down to study them and, when asked, he said that they were by way of being an honourable epitaph. He called out their meaning in English: '*Here died three warriors!*'

'Meaning Almighty Voice and the other two?'

'No,' said the *Métis*, 'Almighty Voice carved it for Corporal Hockin, and Kerr, and Grundy.'

Spanish Stirrup

The Old Man sat on his sorrel beneath a cottonwood. Its big, varnished leaves kept the sun from his face, but even so the strong light hurt his eyes, and he pulled his hard-crowned Mexican hat low on his forehead, tightening the thong. It occurred to him then, as it had occurred to him many times, that total blindness would have been better than this damnable mockery of being able to distinguish between light and dark and no more.

A breeze tugged at the skirts of the yellow linen duster that covered him from shoulder to knee. The wind also brought him a confusion of noise from the bottom of the hill where his brand was being put on the last of nine hundred head of cattle – the six-inch mark of a Spanish stirrup on a steer's left thigh, a steeple-fork crop from each ear. On some invisible tablet in his mind The Old Man recorded a decision to have the weaker calves shot before the herd was driven north, and the meat given to the Tonkawa village. It would be one way, the only way, of repaying the Indians for keeping raiding parties of Comanche from the range during the War.

There was a shift of feet in the earth to his right.

'Riders coming down the draw, Mister Ferguson.'

The Old Man did not take his folded hands from the saddle-horn, and he fought an impulse to turn his useless eyes towards the voice. 'That you, Jubilo?'

'It's Ole Jube, Mister Ferguson.'

'How many, Jubilo, and how far?'

''Bout two miles, Mister Ferguson, and three of 'em.'

The Old Man pulled back the right skirt of the duster and tucked it beneath his thigh so that his heavy hand-gun was free. The negro horse-herder watched the action sadly, and wondered what a blind man could do with a pistol.

'I want Adam Carthage up here, Jubilo. Fast!'

'Yes, *sir*, Mister Ferguson.'

The Old Man heard no footsteps leaving. He listened for a few seconds and then said sharply 'You gone, Jubilo? Damn you, why don't you say when you go?' There was no reply. The sorrel lifted a foreleg and hit the earth with it once. The Old Man passed the palm of his right hand down the animal's neck, from cheek to saddle-skirt. The hair was smooth, and he remembered how beautiful the sorrel could be in the sun.

He heard no approaching hooves from the west, but knew that these must be hidden by the noise from the branding fire. He thought he could smell the acrid sting of hair and hide beneath the iron. but he knew that he was too far away for this and that it was only a memory, come like others to plague his blindness. He lifted his eyes and deliberately faced the painful glare of the sun. Although he could no longer see it yet it was there, all about him, this beautiful ranging Texas land of the upper Brazos, green with oak and mesquite, bright with mustard and bluebonnets, red-slashed by river banks. Cattle land wide under the sky, and lush with grass and water. A man could ride seventy miles from the Pease River to the Brazos and still be on John A. Ferguson's Estribo Range. This was what he had built and this would have been his son's, had Johnny ever come home from the War.

Mexican spurs jingled below him, a stone slithered away, a hat was slapped once against a thigh. The dust from it touched The Old Man's nostrils.

'Carthage? Who are they?' He was not answered. 'Damn you, Carthage. . . !'

'I heard you, sir, but the sun is behind them,' Adam's voice was gentle, and its kindness hurt The Old Man. He jerked at the sorrel angrily, standing in the stirrups. 'You'd tell me *nothing*!' he said, and thus Carthage knew, and hated knowing, that The Old Man had been thinking of Johnny again.

'I can see them now. Three of Colonel Wheeler's riders. You want me to stay?'

'No. Not now. You get back.' The Old Man listened to the ring of departing spurs, remembering the day he had given a pair to Johnny, a pair to Adam, and the sound of each pretty, dying note was like a pain.

When the Wheeler riders came they halted on his right. There was a tight creak of leather as a man put his weight on the stirrups and eased his buttocks against the cantle. There was another man's sigh, a horse's shuddering sneeze. From such sounds The Old Man created a picture of what he could not see.

'Who are you? Say who you are!'

'It's Lake, sir. Colonel Wheeler's hand.'

'I remember you, boy. I remember beating the breeches off you when you were a kid. Now what do you want with me?'

A young man laughed easily. 'That's right, you did, Mister Ferguson, sir. The Colonel says he's taking his cattle north a month from now, and do you want him to take yours along too.'

'You tell the Colonel I'll have my herd in Kansas before he leaves Texas.'

Someone whistled softly. Then Lake said '*You're* taking them, Mister Ferguson, sir? To *Kansas*?'

The Old Man turned his body to face the voice. 'You got some opinion on that, boy?'

'Hell, Mister Ferguson, sir! It's more'n maybe a thousand miles to Kansas through the Indian Nations, and no trail to follow. Ain't nobody taken cattle that way yet, leave alone a bl ...' Lake stopped.

The Old Man said heavily '*Mister* Lake, sir, last year, we got these longhorns out of the brush, over eight hundred head from yearlings to four-year-olds. They are *my* cattle on *my* range, *Mister* Lake, sir. I'm rich in cattle like the rest of us down here, but they aren't worth fifty cents apiece in the South. Up in Kansas, I'm told, they'll fetch forty dollars in Yankee gold.'

'Hell, I know that, Mister Ferguson, sir.'

'Then you know it's drive them north or starve. You tell the Colonel that Estribo will cut a trail for him.'

Lake laughed again. He looked at the other two riders and then back at The Old Man. 'Adam Carthage going as your trail boss, Mister Ferguson, sir?'

'You got some opinion on that, too, boy?'

There was a pause. 'No, sir, I ain't. I hope you get through, Mister Ferguson.'

'The Lord will protect us, boy. He has said *For all the beasts of the forest are mine, and so are the cattle on a thousand hills.*'

'If He said that, Mister Ferguson, it wasn't Texas He had in mind.'

'You get out of here, boy. Blasphemy don't sit kindly in my ears. Tell Dutchy to give you some coffee.'

They went, the noise of hooves turning, sliding, dying, and The Old Man was alone again. There had been much in Lake's laugh and easy impudence to remind him of Johnny. He stroked the sorrel's neck and called out in bitterness *'I will lift up mine eyes unto the hills, from whence cometh my help!'*

The Wheeler riders stopped at the bottom of the hill, in a shallow draw by Dutchy's fire. The German cook gave them coffee, and they washed the dust from their mouths, spat, and then drank. The Estribo herd, yellow, paint and black, flooded away to the banks of the Brazos, and the riders looked at it critically. Sughrue, his old face a map of incredible lines beneath his Confederate cap, was pushing a pony at a steady pace behind a loping steer. The longhorn rocked awkwardly, but man and horse moved with a beautiful rhythm. When he was five yards from the steer Sughrue's right arm, which had been swinging a big standing loop, jerked forward. The rope slipped easily over rump and hind legs of the steer, travelled forward over the horns, fell, and tightened about the forelegs as Sughrue flung back his arm to close the noose.

'Dale vuelta!' yelled Lake approvingly, although he knew that Sughrue had made the difficult, unnecessary throw only to impress the Wheeler riders. Sughrue took three dallies of the rope about his saddle-horn, and his pony squatted with legs braced. The rope thrummed and the steer went down on its right cheek with a grunt. *'Link!'* shouted Sughrue.

The boy called Lincoln rode up, yellow hair bare, hat hanging down his back by the strings, and he swung a rope that held the hind legs of the winded steer. Stretched out on its right side, all legs held, the longhorn lay still, red of eye. Adam Carthage rose up from the fire with a stamp iron, swung it, and rested it momentarily on the steer's left thigh. 'Crop him and turn him loose,' he said, and he walked over to Lake.

The young men looked at each other. Lake saw Adam's thin, angled face above the yellow bandana. It was an older face than he remembered from the War, but in it was the same quiet, waiting expression of the eyes, the same warm smile. Lake bent forward from the saddle and put out his hand.

Adam took it. 'Ben. You come about the drive? What did The Old Man say?'

'That he'd damn well drive his own cattle north and the Lord was on his side. You think he can do it, *compadre?*'

'We'll do it.'

Lake's grin became crooked. 'So you *are* bossing the drive?'

'That worry you, Ben?'

'No, *compadre,* but I hear he blames you for the grass waving over Johnny. Someone ought to tell him.'

The smile left Adam's lips slowly. 'You, maybe, Ben?'

Lake laughed. 'Not me, but somebody.'

'Not while I'm on Estribo. You spread that around, Ben.'

Lake tossed the cup to Dutchy and gathered his reins. 'Johnny ain't worth killing for, Adam. Somebody'll tell The Old Man one day.' He raised his hand and turned his horse. '*Vaya con Dios!* Thanks for the coffee.' The Wheeler riders went up the side of the draw in a cloud of red dust.

Adam felt the sweat at the small of his back, pain as muscles relaxed and anger ebbed. Sughrue came to his side, bringing the smell of leather, horse and tobacco, that was as much a part of him as his bald head and lined face. 'The man's right, boy. You'll kill somebody some day, on account of Johnny.'

'Anyone,' agreed Adam, 'who tries to tell The Old Man.'

'Tell him what?' asked Sughrue innocently.

'Don't laugh at me, Sughrue.'

Sughrue pulled off his hat and hit the young man on the shoulder with it. 'I'll laugh at you, boy, ain't I the right? Eternal damnation, I have! I was there that day The Old Man found you under a wagon tree after a Comanche raid. Ugly little crittur. The Old Man picked you up from under a sack . . .'

'I know.'

'You know, boy, you know! The Old Man held you up and he said "What do we call this dogy, Sughrue?" and I picked up that sack and it had on it *Adam, Corn and Seed Merchant, Carthage, Illinois,* so I said to call you Adam Carthage. I'll laugh at you, boy, on account of you owing me your name.' But Sughrue did not laugh, he spat between his feet.

Adam pulled off his gloves, thrust them through his belt, and wiped the sweat from his hands to the faded cavalry breeches he still wore. He looked up to the cottonwood and saw The Old Man there still, a long, straight-legged figure in a yellow duster and black hat, his full moustache white against his brown face. The leaves above him were shining like red metal.

'Sun's setting,' said Sughrue, and then 'This is a darn-fool thing we're doing, Adam. Where'n hell's Kansas?' Adam said nothing, his thoughts still with The Old Man. Sughrue went on. 'You know what one of them Wheeler riders told me? He said Pedlar Norton took his wagon and daughter up into the Indian Nations with the first thaw this Spring.'

This is a bad day for memories, Adam told himself. First Johnny, and now Johnny's girl, Solace Norton. He said 'The Pedlar trades with friendlies every Spring.'

'He got ambitious this year. Decided to do business with the hostiles. The Kwahadi Comanch'.'

'Sughrue, there are no Comanche north of the Red.'

'There's a heap this year. Just waiting for us. Antelope-eaters, Buffalo-eaters, Honey-eaters and Wanderers, the whole pack of them gone north for peace talks they say with Yankee cavalry along the Cimarron.'

The relief that Adam felt surprised him by its strength. 'If they're talking peace then Solace will be safe enough.'

'I surely hope and pray,' said Sughrue without conviction.

The Old Man was coming down the hill, his body erect and leaning backwards against the incline, his feet outstretched and tooled leather flaps swinging below each stirrup. The sorrel halted at the lip of the draw. The Old Man's sightless eyes ranged from left to right. '*Sughrue?*'

'I'm here, John.'

'How about it, is it finished?'

Sughrue spat silently. 'Ask Adam, he's here too.'

'I know he's here. I could hear those damn fancy spurs a mile away, but I'm asking you.'

Sughrue burst out angrily 'Eternal damnation, John! When you going to stop prodding the boy? Do you think he could help Johnny never coming home?'

The shadow of the Old Man and the sorrel, red-black in the falling sun, dropped across the two men, and it seemed to grow in the long pause before Ferguson spoke again. He said 'Is it finished, Adam?' But the use of the given name put no warmth into the question.

Adam looked at the herd and the branding fire. 'By nightfall,' he said.

'Put Daly and Bridges on night-guard. We'll point the herd north tomorrow. Sughrue!'

'I'm still here.'

'Mount up and see me home.'

Adam watched as they rode up from the river to Estribo's gateway. They were black against the far stretch of plain. This was The Old Man's wide country, and he rode across it like a king, yet Adam felt a great and terrible pity for him.

*

The air in the adobe house was thick and sweet with the smell of sweat and leather, a horse smell and a cattle smell. The one window was shuttered and kept out the night air. The lamp smoked on its broken chimney, and in its light the boy Lincoln lay with his mouth open as if he were calling silently in his dream. The pale flame of the lamp glowed again on the bar of a belt-buckle, on the spur of an empty boot.

A tangle of emotions kept Adam awake – excitement, impatience, and a fear to which he could put no name but which seemed somehow related to Solace Norton. He kicked back his blanket at last, pulled on his boots, opened the door and sat on its sill. A big-bellied moon hung over the Brazos, reflected on the river like a spilled handful of silver dollars.

A coal-oil lamp was burning in the ranch-house, in The Old Man's room. The adobe and timber walls were black where the shadows fell, but a creamy white where the moon struck. High above the door, where The Old Man had nailed it in his youth, was the big wooden *estribo*, a Spanish stirrup ten times its normal size. When it had been put there The Old Man had been a young man, and Texas had been a sovereign and independent republic, and the Estribo range promised to be the greatest between the Red and the Rio Grande.

Adam and Johnny had shared that dream in their youth, listening to The Old Man as he told the story of how he had built his herd, beginning with black, high-flanked *cimarrones* that had been running wild in the mesquite since the days of the Spaniards. He had gone south to hunt cattle in the Brasada. He had played poker with yearlings as stakes, and won a hundred head in one night, playing cards in the light of a tallow candle, in a border *cantina*. Some of the Estribo herd had been wet cattle, taken in night raids on Mexican ranches across the Rio Grande. Some had been taken from Comanches who had themselves stolen the steers. The Old Man had killed two white men and many Indians to hold his land and to increase it. All might have been what the dream promised but for the War between the States, which took away first Johnny and Adam, and then the other hands, even Sughrue in the end. Estribo's stock had drifted back to the brush.

But last year, thought Adam, that *was* a year, the year of the greatest cow-hunt Texas had ever known. Its men home from the War, Estribo had rounded up nearly 800 wild cattle, corraling them in thorn traps by water-holes, stalking them like antelopes. It had been hard, it had been dangerous, and the hunt had ended on the day when an old *zorrila*, an ugly lean longhorn with a line-back and a speckled belly, went on the prod, ripping the guts out of The Old Man's horse and throwing him on his face in scrub.

When The Old Man had been turned over on his back his eyes had been no more than a smear of red dust and red blood.

The picture was strong in Adam's mind this night as he rolled a cigarette and put it unlit in his mouth. He heard Curly Bridges far off, riding night-herd and singing sadly, with his leg crooked, no doubt, about the saddle-horn, and his pony finding its own way.

> 'Once in the saddle I used to go dancing,
> Once in the saddle I used to go gay...'

The light was still burning in The Old Man's room. Few men, thought Adam, lose two fathers in one lifetime. He remembered the day he had come home from the war. There, waiting at Estribo's gateway, had been The Old Man, in black hat and duster, and all he had said was 'Where's Johnny? Where's my son?'

The answer had not been easy, for it was scarcely the answer at all. 'He was lost in The Wilderness.'

'*You* came home?' said The Old Man in fierce hate, and thus easily had all love died between them.

Now Adam wondered if Solace knew. She must know, and that was why she had not returned to Estribo where everything could only remind her of Johnny. It was five years since Adam had seen her. She had been seventeen when Johnny and he rode away. For most of her life she had lived at Estribo with them, a boy as much as they until, in one night almost, she became a girl suddenly, a girl sweet and wild by turns like a mountain cat, with black eyes and a heart-shaped face, with lips held immobile by some inner humour. A girl who, as Adam remembered, kept her brightest smile and softest word for Johnny Ferguson. Everyone had accepted the fact that Johnny was cutting a rusty for her.

If it had been Adam who taught her to ride, if it had been Adam to whom she brought a finger for bandaging or a stirrup leather for repair, it was Johnny whom she kissed. That was on the day they left for the War.

The night before there had been a dance, and some folk had ridden thirty miles or more to attend it. Solace had sashayed about in a fine blue skirt, and her shoulders almost bare above it. A girl with a woman's face and a woman's manner suddenly, as if she had taken these out of the settle with the blue skirt. Her eyes had shone as Johnny whirled her about the floor, while the fiddle sawed and men and women hit the boards with their heels.

At last Adam had been alone with her, outside in the dark. He had wanted to touch her hand but could not. She had moved so close to him that her head was almost resting against his shoulder, and she had sung softly. Then, suddenly, she whirled away, struck the earth with her foot and cried 'Adam Carthage, you ... *mule*!'

At dawn next day he and Johnny stood by their horses, reluctant now to go. The Old Man took Adam's arm. 'Bring Johnny home, Adam. *Bring him home!*'

The grey light had warmed itself on Solace's cheeks, and her eyes had seemed larger than ever. She drew Carthage away. 'Adam, will you do something . . . ?'

'I know!' He had said it almost angrily. 'Bring Johnny home!'

At first he thought she would laugh, for her throat bubbled, her cheeks swelled, and she caught at her lips with her fingers. Then she burst out 'You're still a *mule*, Adam Carthage! But you do that, won't you? You just bring Johnny home!'

Then Johnny had come up, and caught her about the waist, and she had kissed him full on the mouth, her eyes looking across to Adam. When they left Johnny bent down, picked her up with one arm, drew her to the saddle, and rode for half a mile with her thus, she with her foot in his stirrup, and her hair blowing out. Then Johnny dropped her on a clump of buffalo grass. She laughed as she rolled over, a small girl again, her low-calfed boots kicking at the blue skirt. When she stood up she began to cry and, still crying, turned from them and ran back.

That was five years ago, that was what Adam remembered of Solace Norton. Now her fool of a father, more pious than prudent, had taken her up into the Nations.

Adam snapped a match between thumb and forefinger and lit the cigarette. Curly had made a full circle of the herd and was nearer now.

> 'Once in the saddle I used to go gay,
> Got shot in the breast and I'm dying today.'

Adam stood up. Behind him one of the blankets unrolled itself and Jubilo said throatily 'Mister Adam, you need me?'

'No.' Adam stood with his feet astride, and he could see the horse-herd in the corral, the grey smudge of Jubilo's bell-mare. 'How's the *remuda*, Jube? You think it'll make the drive?'

The negro's teeth flashed in the moonlight. 'Further than your steers, Mister Adam. I got you a good night-horse, that little paint.'

'That's Sughrue's, Jube.'

'I done do a trade for you, Mister Adam.'

Another blanket stirred, and Shelby's voice said brutally 'You going to talk all night, black boy?' The flash of Jubilo's teeth was abruptly extinguished.

On a quick impulse Adam walked up to the house, wondering, almost immediately, why he had not the sense to leave things as they were. He lifted the latch and stepped into the room.

'Sughrue? That you, Sughrue?'

I should always wear those damn spurs, thought Adam, that way he would always know.

The Old Man sat in a yellow pool dropped by the shade of the lamp, a red and black Tonkawa blanket over his shoulders. The light shone through his hair and sharpened the jut of cheekbones and jaw. His eyes were unnaturally blue. There was a cowhide folder open between his hands, and Adam knew that it contained two fading tin-types, facing each other across the folder and across the empty years of The Old Man's life. That on the left was of Mrs Ferguson whom Adam had never known, a girl whom The Old Man had brought from the east and who had wasted away and died in Texas as she gave life to Johnny. It was her son's picture that faced hers.

'No, it's Adam.'

The folder closed with a snap between The Old Man's hands and he pushed it into his shirt. He pulled himself to his feet by the arms of the chair and the blanket slipped from the great breadth of his shoulders. In the silence they both heard the pretty ticking of the brass carriage clock which had been all that Martha Ferguson had brought west. 'My hands don't come into this room. What do you want?'

'It's Adam.'

'I heard you. You heard me. What do you want?'

Adam scratched his mind for a reason. How was it possible to comfort a man who shut his heart against comfort? He said 'The drive tomorrow ... Where do we point them?'

'North,' said The Old Man, and added with disgust, 'Is there any other way?'

'There's more than one northward way. The Kansas line or Missouri.'

'North,' said The Old Man again, 'We'll follow the tongue. Get Dutchy to point his wagon tongue at the North Star each night, and come morning we'll follow it.'

'To Kansas,' said Adam.

The Old Man's moustache was lifted. 'You got a preference, mister?'

Now Adam was angry. 'I'll point your herd where you wish and get them there. I just wanted to know.'

'You're forgetting, mister. It's Kansas or nowhere. Two hundred and fifty thousand head were driven from Texas to Missouri last year, and most of the drovers were robbed on the border by blue-bellied Yankees. You point Estribo to the Kansas line, mister, or get your gear and leave.'

Adam was suddenly tired. 'If that's what you want,' he said, 'I'll leave.' The Old Man's shoulders slipped, and when he did not reply Adam went on. 'One thing more. Where will you ride?'

'Where're you putting Sughrue.'

'I was putting him on right swing, that paint of his being a good worker, but Jubilo's traded the pony for me.'

'I'll ride with him, you keep him there. You think a horse is all there is to trail-driving, or maybe that Sughrue's going to ride the same horse from sun-up to sundown? Sughrue's a better man than any of you.'

Adam said 'Make him your trail-boss then. I'll ride where he says.'

The Old Man's expression changed. His eyes opened wider, as if he were desperately trying to see Adam's face. There was no harshness now in his voice. 'Adam I can't ask you this again. How did Johnny die?'

There was still no answer to the question. 'I didn't see him die, Mr Ferguson.'

Slowly The Old Man turned his back.

*

They reached the Red at Chouteau Creek within seven days, an average drive of fifteen miles a day, but on the first day out from the Brazos the pace had been hard. The herd had bunched into a spread across a front of half a mile, and the swing men rode wide to gather. When the cattle bedded down that night they had travelled more than twenty miles and were tired. The Old Man swore as he stood erect by Dutchy's fire, the flames playing shadows on his face. 'You'll run the tallow off them! We're not taking bones and hide to Kansas!'

He did not ask for Adam, who was out with the first night-guard. He said 'You'll keep it down, all of you. You tell Carthage that, Sughrue. I want them driven off the trail to graze at noon, and I want them grazing with their noses still pointed north. You gentle them at point. Shelby, or you'll quit this drive!'

When The Old Man had gone Shelby rasped a hand over his chin. 'I know something to run the tallow off *him*.'

Sughrue looked over the rim of his cup. 'Dally your tongue, big man. We all got to learn.'

On the morning of the second day Adam put Jubilo and the forty horses of the *remuda* ahead of the herd to give it direction. For two more days the trail ran uncertainly across wide park-lands, over clear streams that were sleeved with spring-green timber, and by the end of the third day the cattle found their own leader. An old, yellow mossy horn, with scars on its ribs and flanks, and a horn-spread of five feet, nosed its way forward to the head of the drive. The herd swung behind it, three, four, sometimes five, but rarely more than six abreast, and a mile long almost, with the weaker-footed, the cows and the unkilled calves, coming up in the thick dust of the drag. There, behind them and with a bandana across his mouth, rode Daly, who was only 17. With a leader of the herd chosen Jubilo fell back to the flank, and the lazy swing of his voice could be heard above the lowing, the rattle of hock and horn. *'Hep, hep, come away there!'*

Every day, from dawn to dusk, Adam worked through six changes of horse from the *remuda*. When the herd lurched to its feet in the morning he mounted and rode on, five or six miles ahead of point, scouting the land, looking for water, marking a concealed cut-bank. Then he rode back to high ground to await the herd, watching it as it came up, a black snake crawling with horn-tips glinting, and a tall feather of dust rising. He called it on, this way or that, with a swing of his hat.

At night the herd was bedded down on a hill slope among the stunted post-oak, the flank men working it into a compact space. The lead steers were already down, chewing, by the time

Daly brought up the drag, beating the dust from his shirt but still smiling. Adam slept little, he snatched at sleep when the herd nooned, or in the saddle as he waited for it to come up to water. For six nights he rode with the night-guard from dusk to dawn. The feel of saddle and horse was between his thighs even when he dismounted.

He watched each man carefully. With the exception of himself, Sughrue, and the sullen Shelby, there was not one rider over 22. Daly, Carlisle and Bridges and Lincoln were like young animals, brawling, laughing, singing, snapping. Adam made his judgements and stayed by them. After that first day he never put Shelby on point with Carlisle. Bridges and Lincoln were too close in friendship and horseplay to work well together. He put them on opposite flanks and faced down their objections.

It was Shelby who worried him, a man black-faced, black spirited, but a good man at point when his impatience was curbed. But Shelby had been in the Texan Brigade and knew about Johnny. When he looked at Adam, or at The Old Man, it was with a sly, mean twist to his lips.

On the day's drive Dutchy collected wood and cow chips for his fire, pushed his oxen ahead of the herd to reach the site Adam had chosen for nooning or night camp. A dry, taciturn man, Dutchy was an oddity. He hammered coffee beans with a gun butt instead of boiling them whole. He had a withered right leg which was still strong enough to operate the brake of his wagon, and which, he said, had taken a lance thrust in one of the Emperor of Austria's wars. Nobody believed him. There was not, said Sughrue, an Emperor of Austria, nor an Austria for that matter.

The Old Man rode with the drive like its conscience. When the trail was rough, in the broken lands south of the Red, his sorrel was roped to Sughrue's pony. From far off, on scout, Adam would see that flapping yellow duster, and he thought of it as a guidon.

They grew filthy, all of them. Their faces were rough with scrubby beards. They stank, and did not notice the stench as they crouched at dusk over Dutchy's salt bacon, beans and black coffee. They rode hard through the daylight hours, and at night they were too tired to think of the miles yet to ride, to wonder whether there would be cattlebuyers across the Kansas line, to wonder at all what they were doing. On Sunday, in the middle of those first seven days, before the drive went forward as on any other day, The Old Man spoke over the dawn fire's smoke:

'The Lord is my light and my salvation; whom then shall I fear? The Lord is the strength of my life; of whom then shall I be afraid?'

The hands said 'Amen!', wiped greasy fingers on their thighs, tightened girths and mounted. Thus it was to be every Sunday, and if anyone forgot the names of the days The Old Man did not, marking them down in his mind.

From the Brazos to the Red the trail was good. To the east rose up the rough, hilly Cross Timbers that banded Texas to the Indian Territory across four hundred miles. It was a country smudged with green dwarf-oak and burnt black in mile-long patches by fire. It was a country that ran with clear water as if it were weeping, and it was a country that rolled gently like a troubled blanket.

The Red was reached two hours after dawn on the seventh day. Shelby pointed the drive across the saline flats and wire grass to a narrow ford that Adam had found. The water was yellow and swift, but the herd took it well, crossing the current obliquely and crawling out on the far bank like an idling cottonmouth. The hands swam the Red naked, holding clothes and gunbelts above their heads. Their bodies pink and white beneath brown faces, Bridges and Lincoln raced each other up and down the north bank, yelling and laughing until The Old Man rode sightless into the noise they were making and swore them back on the trail.

North of the Red and into Indian Territory the land was good too – low, flat sandhills with sweet green valleys. There were narrower draws choked with oak and hickory brush, and these Adam scouted each day, looking, hoping for some sign of Pedlar Norton's wagon. Instead he found a hunter called Matthewson at camp, a greasy man decorated with buckskin thongs. He was unsurprised by the news that Texas drovers were coming north, but sardonically doubted whether they would find Kansas worth the trouble. He had heard of no railhead there. But his knowledge, or lack of it, was a year old. He had wintered, he said, in an Osage lodge, and he wanted to talk about Indian women. Of more value was his advice to scout to the north-east where, he said, Adam would find a trail cut by the trader Jesse Chisholm. To Matthewson's mind it went as far north as the Cimarron, and maybe further.

When Adam found this trail he was awed by the ruts, cut more than a foot into the red earth by Chisholm's wagons. He turned the herd on to the trail, and the hooves broke down the walls of the ruts and obliterated them.

The further north the herd had been pushed the colder the nights had become, as if men and cattle were hanging on to the tail-shirts of winter. The Wichitas lay to the north-west, bare eroded granite heads above the open plain. On the afternoon of the second day across the Red, twenty-five miles into the Nations, the weather changed. The sky above the Wichitas turned a blue-black, and the grass an electric green. The eastern sky was inflamed. Misting rain, turning to sleet, blew up ahead, and the cattle lowered their heads before it. The mossy horn lost its lead and turned on its own trail, with Shelby lashing at it. The whole herd turning away from the weather, moving at an unhappy lope south-eastwards towards the protection of timbered hills. They bobbed awkwardly past Adam's stirrups, like drift going down a river, and nothing could hold them. He caught one glimpse of The Old Man's duster, far out on the flank, and then he rode on in the direction the herd was taking, shouting to Bridges and Lincoln to point it into a wide draw. There it halted at last.

By nightfall the wind had dropped and the sleet ceased. The air was still above the herd, but thunder drummed along the top of the Wichitas, and lightning, livid and long-legged, danced madly out on to the plain. Adam put all men on to night-guard, and he wished that he had The Old Man's faculty for prayer.

At midnight the storm moved down from the mountains towards them. Lightning sparked across four or five miles of the plain before it died. The air was thick with a sulphurous smell. Sughrue rode up to where Adam sat on the rise. He was wearing a blanket over his shoulders, his head through a hole in its centre. He spat dexterously between the ears of his pony and he said to Adam 'You need some tobacco juice, boy, to rub in your eyes. Keeps you awake.'

Adam looked down into the darkness of the draw. 'How is it down there, Sughrue?'

'Bad. There's an old curly horn with a mean disposition that's going to give trouble if that lightning don't stop. The rest are pretty spooked too.'

'Will they run?'

'They'll run lest you know a good prayer, boy. You'd better get them young fools Daly and Lincoln out of the draw. And cache your spurs and pistol or that lightning'll burn you down to Dutchy's bacon.'

A three-legged flash strode up to the mouth of the draw. It lit the wide plain and the black, uneasy mass of the herd. It shone blue on Sughrue's face. He said *'Here we go!'* He pulled out his gun and pushed it into his shirt, and he was leaning from the saddle, fumbling with spur leathers when, in another flash, Adam saw the steer with the corkscrew horns rear up and begin to run.

The air was now full of shuddering light. In one second the whole herd was on its feet and moving. It turned in a great coil like a striking snake and threw itself forward. In its path were Daly and Lincoln. Adam, from the rise, saw Daly's horse swing round and plunge up the slope towards him, clear of the stampede, but in some madness Lincoln set his pony to race the herd. He had gone no more than fifty yards when the black horse he rode put a foreleg into a prairie dog-hole and went down, rump and tail going up into the air. For a moment Lincoln seemed suspended between earth and night-sky, and then he fell. The herd passed over him.

'Sughrue!' shouted Adam. There was sudden darkness. *'Where's The Old Man?'* Lightning again. Adam saw Sughrue riding down towards the head of the run, spurless heels kicking, his hand jabbing towards the top of the rise. Looking there Adam saw the yellow duster motionless and safe, and then he was away himself.

He rode towards the noise of the run, finding the herd in moments of unreal light, a racing, rolling, inexorable mass in which, now and then, a horn gleamed white, an eye red. He thought he saw the crazily swinging white top of Dutchy's wagon pulling away. He thought he saw the *remuda*, manes and tails fanned out, speeding across the front of the stampede with Jubilo yelling behind it. For a mile, two miles, the herd ran in a bunch, as erratically as a ball rolling in a saucer. Then it seemed to gather itself into a column, twenty or thirty abreast, but still unpredictable, still making maddened swerves to the left or the right.

When Adam reached the head of the run, the paint pony carrying him beautifully, he saw Bridges riding there, and Shelby, and Sughrue who was the closest of the three to the herd, rope swinging, feet kicking, throat screaming a Rebel yell as he rode for the leader. He appeared, disappeared and re-appeared with each flash of lightning.

Adam shouted *'Get 'em milling!'* as he passed Shelby and Bridges, yet knowing that this was what they were trying to do. Sughrue's left boot was now kicking at the mossy horn's flank, his rope lashing its neck, while the steer's great horns cut the air a foot before his pony's forelegs.

'You damn fool Sughrue!'

Sughrue turned his head and grinned at Adam like a boy. The strap of his cap was below his chin, its visor on his nose, and his eyes shone out of the mask of dust that covered his face above the bandana.

Then, suddenly, and for no reason except one perhaps understood by the steer itself, the mossy horn swerved in a great curve to the left away from Sughrue's boot and rope. He drove closer to it, turning it back on itself and on the track of the stampede. *'We done it!'* he yelled, and he stood in the stirrups.

Slowly, wonderfully, its pace slackening, the herd began to coil itself up like a spring as the leader, running in narrowing circles, gathered the rest after it, turning, turning, until it was penned in the centre of the mill and the run was over.

Carlisle, Daly and Shelby rode about the horn-swept mass of dust and cattle, whistling to it, calling and cooing soothingly like pigeons.

How long the run had lasted Adam did not know, but as he pulled his horse up to the rim of a bluff, and felt the pain growing in thighs, buttocks and arms, he saw the red smear of sunrise over the Cross Timbers, and he knew that the storm was over. He released his body slowly, allowing it to slip from the saddle, guiding it down with both hands on the horn, until he lay on his back and felt the taste of the pony's sweat as it fell to his face. He heard the grunts of Sughrue and Bridges as they dropped beside him. There was no sound of hooves from below now, only Carlisle's sweet singing, and the frustrated lowing of the steers. The dust rose in a bowl and glinted in the morning sun.

Sughrue sat up, wiped his face and spat. He swore lovingly and slowly. 'Ten miles they run, I'd say. Took a one-way ticket to hell and couldn't wait for the stage. But we turned 'em. Adam, there's good waddies in Estribo.'

Bridges pushed himself up on an elbow, and grinned out of a young face grey-bearded by dust. 'Ten miles back the way we come ain't good, you old grissel-heel!'

Sughrue hit the boy on the shoulder, and then the two of them rolled in the grass, laughing and punching in joy. Adam let them wrestle the emotion from their bodies and then he said stiffly 'Curly, take Daly and a spade from Dutchy's wagon, wherever that is. Bury Lincoln. You'll find him back where the herd broke.'

Bridges sat up quickly. 'Link ... ?'

'I'm sorry, Curly.'

Bridges walked to his horse. He looked at it long before he pulled himself into the saddle. Sughrue watched him ride away. He said 'Won't be enough of Link ... I'll go too, Adam.'

They found Lincoln at noon, and they dug the earth away from beneath what was left of him, and they let it slide into the shallow hole. They piled stones over the grave, and at its foot they laid out smaller stones, little niggerheads in the shape of the Estribo brand.

All that day and night the herd rested where it had ended its run. At dusk The Old Man came through the firelight's rim. The muscles of his cheeks were tight, his voice harsh.

'Eight killed, and a week's fat run off the rest. We'll drive slow for three days. Lincoln's folk will get his pay as if he made the drive. That's fifteen a month, mark that, Carthage. And they'll get forty cents a head bonus on every steer we sell in Kansas.' He paused. He turned away and then turned back. 'You ought to know this, you did well.'

When he had gone Shelby stood up. He swore. His face was marked with dust and the rims of his eyes were red. '*Forty cents?* Thirty's what he promised us, and Lincoln ain't got no folks but a drunken old man.'

Adam looked up. 'So be it,' he said.

'You shut your mouth, Carthage! If you're too scared to cut that old fool down I know how to make him crawl!'

Adam stood up and faced Shelby. 'You know what?'

'You forgetting I was in the War with Johnny too?'

'Shelby you're a snake.'

'*Adam!*' warned Sughrue softly.

'Shelby, you'd cut your own mother's throat.'

Shelby's desperate, tired face was puzzled. He rubbed a hand over it, as if to clear his thoughts. 'You prodding me to a fight?' he asked.

Adam stepped forward and hit the big man heavily on the mouth. Shelby lurched forward, but he did not lower his hands below his belt. With childlike surprise, his red lips quivering, he said 'You're trying to kill me.' He looked at the others. '*He wants to kill me.*'

'I'll kill you, Shelby, if you try to put into words what's in your mind.'

'We got visitors,' said Sughrue laconically.

The tension passed. Shelby laughed and turned his back on Adam.

'I say we got visitors,' said Sughrue again, and jerked his thumb beyond the fire.

Into the light, leading a mud-coloured pony on a grass hackamore, came an Indian. At the stink of him even Sughrue spat. The Indian was an old blanket buck, with toothless mouth open in a foolish grin, greasy hair swinging in one plait over his right shoulder, and a tall beaver hat on his head. Behind him came a young squaw, her eyes demurely lowered.

He squatted by the fire and stretched out his hands. His knee-joints cracked like kindling wood. He looked about him, nodded, and said '*Wohaw!*'

'He wants beef,' said Sughrue. 'Shall I kick him out?'

Adam shook his head. 'Tell him to help himself from a steer killed in the run.'

'He's done that,' said Sughrue. The woman had pulled a red steak from the parfleche on the pony's neck. She cut a string from it and gave it to the buck. He chewed it noisily between his gums, leant over and shook Sughrue's hand. 'You stinking, filthy siwash,' said Sughrue amiably. The Indian grinned and nodded.

Adam turned away to his blanket, knowing that although it had not come this night the time *would* come when he would have to kill Shelby. Because of Johnny. No, not because of Johnny, because of the Old Man. He did not like Shelby, but he did not hate him. Shelby was a good cowhand. There wasn't a better on point or flank. Yet the thing would be. Shelby would ask to be killed.

He put his head on his saddle and he put his hat over his eyes. He awoke, almost immediately it seemed, to the hard pressure of Sughrue's hand on his shoulder, but he realized that he must have been asleep for some time. The rest of the hands were rolled in their blankets, and the Indians were gone.

Sughrue said 'Keep your back covered with your belly, son, no call to move.' He sat back on his heels and looked at Adam carefully. 'Once I got upwind of that old buck I talked with him. He says he saw the Pedlar and Johnny's girl along the Washita two days back.'

For the moment Adam could think only of the fact that Sughrue still called Solace 'Johnny's girl'. Then he saw the expression in the old man's eyes. 'Go on, Sughrue.'

'He says 'bout three hours later an Indian raiding party cut the Pedlar's trail and followed it.'

Adam sat up. 'Kwahadi Comanche?'

'He thinks so. A big party, son. Twenty warriors, maybe, and three thieving Kiowas. And there's more, boy . . .'

'Go on,' said Adam again, feeling suddenly cold.

'The old buck said he followed the party. Said he was going

to see what they were up to so's to tell the Army, but I reckon he went along to pick up their leavings.'

'Get to the point, Sughrue.'

'Well, he followed the Comanch' until they hit the Pedlar's camp. He saw Norton by the wagon, holding out his hands to show he'd got no gun. Solace was there too, Adam. The buck described her pretty good. The Comanch' rode down on 'em both, whooping and yelling. The old buck lit out fast then, deciding it wasn't healthy to stay.'

Adam reached for his boots and gunbelt. Sughrue held his arm and said gently, 'Boy, this was two days ago. It's too late.'

*

Adam rode far ahead of the herd and wide, seeking some sign of Solace and her father. He found nothing, not even a wheel-rut. He shut his thoughts behind the angled hardness of his face, and he scarcely spoke.

At dusk, on the nineteenth day of the drive, the herd reached Washita. Jesse Chisholm's trading trail led down through rich prairie to an oxbow bend of the river. Although there had been lush grazing for two days there had been no water, and when the lead steers smelt the river they loped into a bouncing trot that stretched out the herd over two and a half miles. The yearlings and the cows, taking shorter steps, lost their sense of direction, and the riders on swing had to push them hard. Bridges and Carlisle worked through eight changes of horse between sun-up and sundown.

The cattle were strung out to drink along the red clay banks of the Washita, the lead steers downstream so that they would not foul the water for the rest. Dutchy unyoked his oxen in a willow grove. He was a man of some compassion despite his taciturnity, and when the hands rode in after the herd was bedded he rewarded their sweat and their saddle galls with a big turkey gobbler that he had shot on the trail. That evening the sky rode high, pricked with bright stars. The Washita murmured over the shallow, rock-bottomed ford, and Daly brought out his Jew's-harp. To its thrumming Bridges sang.

'Calico girls are fine and dandy,
But the marrying kind wear gingham!'

Adam had found buffalo signs on the plain that day, deep, dry wallows and wide roads where the hooves had scoured the earth. He found another sign, too, and this he brought back and dropped at Sughrue's feet. 'Comanche?' he asked shortly.

It was a small buckskin bag, worked with red, yellow and white quills, its neck closed by a thong. Sughrue picked it up silently, loosened the throat, and tipped out the contents. There was a spiral of fence wire fashioned into crude tweezers, a triangular fragment of looking-glass, a twig pounded into short fibres at one end, two ear-rings of Spanish gold, an army button, a shell with a razor-edge, and a lump of dry fat.

'Where'd you find this, son?'

'In the Cross Timbers yonder. There were a lot of tracks, too, Sughrue. Unshod ponies going north.'

Sughrue touched each article reflectively. 'You found a Comanche's toilet-bag, Adam boy. This here's wire he plucks his beard with. With this here he cleans his teeth. How many ponies?'

'Hard to tell. Twenty, maybe.'

Sughrue silently returned each article to the bag, with the exception of the ear-rings, each of which he bit and then placed in his vest. Then he dropped the bag on the fire and watched it burn.

'Well?' said Adam.

'Tell you something more, boy. This morning young Daly found a cow that couldn't keep up with the drag even. Bellowing fit to bust. Udders been cut. Some young Comanch' got into the herd last night and drank himself some milk and blood. Makes 'em feel good.' Sughrue looked up. 'What do you figure?'

Adam answered with a question of his own. 'Is this the party that found Solace and the Pedlar?'

'Maybe.'

'Maybe isn't good enough!' said Adam in sudden anger.

'Maybe it ain't, boy, but maybe's all I know.'

Adam turned away, and went to where The Old Man sat by the tail of Dutchy's wagon. His hands were on his knees, his back was erect, but the lines on his face seemed to have been cut more deeply than nineteen days before. When his ears caught the sound of feet he said 'Who's that?'

'Adam. I'm scouting to the south-east tomorrow.'

'North's our trail,' said The Old Man.

'I'll join the herd before sundown. I found Comanche sign today. And three nights ago that old buck told us he saw a war-party raiding Pedlar Norton's camp.'

The Old Man frowned impatiently. 'Norton knows this country. He knows its risks.'

'He also knows, or knew, what would happen to Solace if the Comanche took her. So do you.'

'Johnny's girl?'

'Yes,' said Adam coldly, 'She was with him.'

'Johnny's girl,' said The Old Man. He turned up his face and Adam was surprised by the passion there. 'You find her, Carthage, *you find her!*'

'I aim to.'

He left the herd two hours before dawn, riding to the south-east where the country became rough and hilly, belts of brush and stunted trees slashed with rich prairie and broken by narrow canyons. He rode a roman-nosed grey that had proved itself in endurance, a horse that weighed less than six hundred pounds but which was iron in stamina. Dawn was already moving in uneasy light when Adam heard hooves behind him. He halted, dismounted, put one hand gently on the grey's nose and pulled his rifle from the scabbard with the other. He listened. The following rider was coming at a steady, relaxed pace. Adam heard the ring of a stone struck by a shoe, and he knew that whoever was riding it, this was a white man's horse. When the rider came over a rise Adam saw the cold light shining on the flat of Sughrue's cap. He pushed the scabbard gun home and called out.

The old man slipped down, grinned and spat. 'Good-morning, boy. You rode hard.'

'Who's with the herd?'

'Shelby'll take care of 'em. Listen!' He cocked an ear, and they heard the faint, distant music of the cattle as they forded the Washita. 'You need me with you.'

'The herd needs you. I'll do this alone.'

'Something you ought to know, son. The Old Man sent me to look after you.' Telling Adam this seemed to amuse Sughrue.

Adam paused. Then he put his foot in the stirrup. 'Mount up, you old fool.' Sughrue grinned.

By mid-morning they cut the Comanche trail at the point where Adam had found the buckskin bag. Sughrue dismounted, prodded the hoof-marks with his finger. 'Three days old, but a baby could follow this. Now what, boy?'

'Hunting party? Raiding party? Any women with them, Sughrue?'

'You ask a lot from some pretty hoof-marks, boy. How do I know? No, no women I'd say, but that don't prove nothing.'

Adam kicked the grey into a long lope, pointing it up the Comanche trail, and thus silently he rode for more than two hours until they nooned in a wide gully. There the trail was lost on stony ground. Sughrue walked his horse up the slope, backward and forward, leaning from the saddle, studying the earth for half an hour before he returned. He loosened his saddle-girth, poured water into his cap from a canteen and let his horse drink. Then he sat in the pony's shadow and chewed thoughtfully on a piece of jerked beef. Adam lit a cigarette. 'How do you see it now, Sughrue?'

The old man squinted at him in disgust. 'Who'd you ask all these questions of if'n I'd gone back? You want me to make guesses?'

'I want to know, Sughrue.'

'Then I guess that the old buck was lyin' and the Comanch' didn't raid Pedlar Norton. Then again I guess he was telling the truth and they did and the Pedlar's dead. Then again, I don't guess anything on account of being old and wise.' He pulled the peak of his cap down over his eyes, folded his arms and went to sleep.

That afternoon they scouted a dozen of the narrow, waterless gullies, looking for a sign, and when they found one, a mill of hoof-marks about a water-hole, Sughrue grunted and slipped to the ground. He broke the horse-droppings with the toe of his boot and touched them with his finger. 'Warm,' he said, 'This here's a new trail, hour, maybe two hours old. Son, you feel nothing breathing down your neck?'

'Why should they hang around here for two, three days, Sughrue?'

'Why should a Comanch' do anything, boy, most of all breathe?'

Adam looked up to the serrated rim of high ground where a harsh stone outcrop held back a wash of green scrub. He turned the grey towards it, halting below the rim, dismounting and climbing the rest of the way. At the top he lay on his belly and there Sughrue joined him. To the north and the east the thinly timbered hills dropped away into a basin corrugated by shallow arroyos in which red clay soil looked like blood running. The air was dry and crystal sharp. With the brim of his hat pulled low over his eyes, with sweat pricking the back of his neck, Adam slowly studied the broad, broad land.

'Sughrue, do you see that? To the right of that ox-bow strip of brush?'

The surface of the basin moved tremulously in the heat.

A thin skein of dust lay over a shallow depression two miles to the north-east.

'The dust? I see it boy. Could be anything, buffler perhaps?'

'Look below it, see that?'

Beneath the dust there was an occasional glint of sharp light. Sughrue put both hands above his eyes, stared, and said 'Eternal damnation!'

Suddenly they heard a single, heavy, booming explosion, then a series of perhaps eight, or nine, shorter and sharper sounds, a ragged volley of shots, and the splintering glitter of light increased.

'Buffler gun,' said Sughrue, 'and if it weren't crazy I'd say the others were horse-pistols.'

A thin tremble of crying voices came to them across the long, yellow land. Away from the arroyo there burst a score of minute riders, each trailing a feather of dust and each moving rapidly. In pursuit of them followed a darker, larger body and a thicker cloud of dust. This body did not break, but kept its formation for half a mile and then halted, turned and moved back. Flashes of light came from it as the sun struck on metal.

'Cavalry,' said Adam softly.

'Bluebellies?' Sughrue began to laugh.

Adam gathered the reins and pulled himself into the saddle, setting the grey down the slope towards the arroyo. The distant, scattering riders had now disappeared into the broken land, and the dust of their passing grew thin in the air. Adam rode towards the cavalry, and he heard Sughrue following. As he came up with the soldiers he saw that they had now dismounted. A dozen horses were held by the handlers, and a group of troopers were beating the dust from their clothes or looking down into the arroyo. A Pawnee scout, with a single feather upright in a black hat, was still mounted and staring to the north-east. A sergeant, yellow stripes so faded as to appear almost white, his chest swelling against scrubbed suspenders, walked towards Adam and Sughrue. He frowned, lifted his hat and wiped his forehead with his arm.

In the bottom of the arroyo Adam saw Pedlar Norton's wagon, lying broken-wheeled on its side, its oxen dead, arrows thick as quills in their bodies. Beyond them four soldiers were digging a grave.

The sergeant held Adam's bridle. 'Who are you?' He looked over his shoulder and called 'Lieutenant, sir!'

A young man turned away from the wagon and took a white hat from his head. His hair was thick and fair and there was an expression of sickened gravity on his boy's face. He came up slowly and stared at the two cowhands.

'Adam Carthage. From the Brazos.' It was nearly two years since Adam had seen a Yankee uniform, yet the old uneasiness stirred within him instinctively, as if this man were still his enemy. 'Driving cattle to Kansas.'

'Texans?' The lieutenant closed his eyes suddenly and put his hands over them.

The sergeant moved forward quickly. 'Sir . . . ?'

'It's all right.' The officer straightened his back and put out his hand to Adam. 'I'm Vaughan. Lieutenant, C. Troop, Fifth Cavalry.' Adam took the hand uncertainly.

'What you bluebellies doing down here?' inquired Sughrue with amiable insolence.

The sergeant moved his shoulders. 'Buckle your tongue, Reb!'

Sughrue leant on his saddle-horn and spat. 'Never saw a

Yankee horse-soldier this close afore. You wouldn't stay to get acquainted during the War!'

'All right, Sughrue, rope in your tongue.' Adam dismounted. 'Lieutenant, who was with that wagon?'

The officer's tanned face seemed suddenly green. 'An old man ...'

'Nobody else?'

'Just an old man ... or what was left of him.' The boy pulled his shoulders back. 'The Indians had tied him upside down to a wheel ...' He stopped with throat working.

'An' lit a fire under his head?' asked Sughrue in a hard voice, 'That's a 'Pache trick, but the Comanch' aint slow to learn.'

'My men are burying him,' said Vaughan. 'They had shot arrows into him, too. After he was dead.'

Adam walked to the edge of the arroyo and looked down. A blue spiral of smoke was still twisting from the fire by the wheel. He smelt it, and he smelt a sharper uglier smell. The tightness of the muscles in his cheeks hurt him. He turned back. 'There wasn't a girl ... ?'

'*Adam, boy!*' said Sughrue.

'Damn it, lieutenant!' shouted Adam. 'That man had his daughter with him.'

The soldier looked at him curiously. 'We came on them suddenly. We saw their fire-smoke. But they burst out of here.'

'There was a girl with him!'

'We didn't see her, sir,' said Vaughan stiffly.

The Pawnee scout called from the rise, his hand pointing westwards. The lieutenant moved quickly. '*Sergeant!*'

But Adam was already in the saddle, kicking with his heels. Five hundred yards from the arroyo, where the land dipped down again into a bottom tangled with grape-vine and green briar, he saw a flash of colour, a red skirt and a white blouse. He pulled up above it, and forced his way through the brush on foot. It was Solace. She lay on her back, her body stiff and straight, her right arm bent across her eyes. As Adam knelt and touched her she screamed. She brought her arm away from her face and struck him with her fist. Her eyes were so wide that the whites were clean about each iris. Her face was ugly with horror. Her scream tore open her mouth in agony, her tongue doubled back. She struck at Adam again and again, her back arched. Then she fainted. He picked her up and carried her back. Her dark hair, unbraided, fell over his arm and brushed against his hips, and he felt as if he were carrying all the pain there was in the world.

The troopers watched him curiously. Some, who thought that Solace was dead, pulled off their hats. Adam laid her on the ground, and took her hands between his and rubbed them. He pushed back the hair from her white face. It was five years since he had seen her, and although the image of her had always been vivid in his mind he had not remembered how beautiful she really was.

'Leave her, boy,' said Sughrue gently. He crouched beside her and splashed water on her face. 'Leave her. Your hands are trembling fit to break.'

The girl's eyes quickly opened. They looked beyond Sughrue's shoulder to Adam's face, but there was no recognition in them. She sucked in her breath in a silent scream that quivered down the length of her body, and then her eyes closed again. 'All right, boy,' said Sughrue. *'All right!'*

Adam stood up. 'Where's your post, lieutenant?'

'Fort Gibson, sir, on the Cimarron.'

'You'll take her there, of course?'

Vaughan pulled at his gauntlets uncomfortably. 'I'm sorry. It's not possible.' He saw the sudden fury in Adam's face. 'Mr Carthage, I'm on an extended patrol with orders to scout the Washita as far as the big bend, and south of there to the Wichitas and the Red. That's a long scout, Mr Carthage. I can't take a woman on it.'

'Bluebellies!' said Sughrue with disgust.

The sergeant moved angrily. 'With the lieutenant's permission...'

'At ease, sergeant!' Vaughan looked at Adam unhappily. 'Mr Carthage, surely you can take her with you?'

'A cattle-drive's no place for a woman either, lieutenant. We've got four, maybe five hundred miles before we reach any place in Kansas where she can be cared for. There'll be women at your post, can't you take her back there?'

Vaughan looked down at Adam's breeches. 'I'm right, Mr

Carthage, am I not? You were in the War? You understand what orders mean?'

'If we hadn't come up you'd have left her here?'

The officer's face reddened. 'Your coming was providential, sir.'

Sughrue spat firmly into the dust. 'Yankee horse-soldiers!' he said, and he looked at the lieutenant. 'You got any idea what you're looking for, sonny?'

'Comanche and Kiowa hostiles,' said Vaughan coldly. 'I'm to bring them in for the peace talks.'

Sughrue looked across to the wagon. 'Looks like they ain't interested in peace talks. Sonny, you were lucky today. Next time they'll see you first. Now be a good boy and go back and tell your Colonel, and take Miss Norton.'

'I am under General Sherman's orders, sir.'

'Tell *him* then, sonny. He's got a mite of sense.'

'Damn your eye, Reb!' said the sergeant.

'Ask your scout,' said Sughrue easily. 'Those Kwahadi bucks've got reputations to make, and they'd as lief make them on you. They'll cut you up in the mountains and then come raiding us. Now you want us to take the girl along?'

The lieutenant ignored Sughrue, but his back was straighter as he spoke to Adam. 'Sir, we can give you escort to the Washita if you've a mind to it.'

'*Escort?*' shouted Sughrue. 'We don't need no help from Yankee horse-infantry!'

'We're obliged to you,' said Adam wearily. 'We'll ride along with you to the ford.'

'Ain't no yellow-legs going ...' began Sughrue, and Vaughan turned to him swiftly.

'I am an officer of the United States Cavalry, sir. I believe even the Army of the Confederacy, while it was in being, understood the meaning of orders.'

'Sonny,' said Sughrue slily. 'Maybe you never met that Army, *while it was in being?*'

'No, sir,' said Vaughan simply. 'I never had that honour.'

The sergeant stepped in front of Sughrue. 'I met it, and I never saw a Johnny Reb that was as big a fighter as he was a talker.'

'All right, sergeant!' said Vaughan harshly, but his voice softened as he turned to Adam. 'If the young lady ...'

'We'll see to it,' Adam knelt on one knee beside her and said 'Solace ...'

Her dark eyes looked at him incredulously, and her head lay in the pool of her black hair. *'Adam?'* she said.

Then, when he touched her hand, she screamed again. Scream followed scream. The troopers' horses backed away, rose up against the grip of their handlers. Adam took Solace in his arms impulsively, pressed her shuddering body against his, calling her name until the screaming stopped. Then great, racking sobs came from her throat. She clung to him, clenching and unclenching her fingers and calling 'Adam ... Adam ... !'

He stroked her hair, and he looked up from her to the unhappy lieutenant. In that moment he realized the great conflict of the boy's emotions.

'It's all right, lieutenant. We'll take her.'

'I'm obliged to you, sir.' Vaughan walked to his horse. The grave-diggers had finished, and Pedlar Norton was now beneath the earth, a wheel-spoke for his marker. The sun was sweetening the air with the smell of the dead oxen as the patrol lined up and Vaughan, with hat tilted forward at an angle of boyish gallantry, with gauntlets folded neatly through his belt and sabre held tightly by his left side, walked the line.

Adam watched, old memories stirring. There, as he had seen it many times, were the troopers standing to the left of their mounts, each face impassive, chests in line with the horses' mouths, right hands holding the reins six inches from the bit, nails down. The whole a splash of dusty blue and yellow. And the whole of it pathetically unnecessary out here, thought Adam.

'Prepare to mount ... *Mount!*' The creak of leather and the ring of metal, legs swinging, boots going home in the stirrups.

'Help me, Sughrue.'

Adam stood up, lifting Solace in his arms, knowing that she was still staring at him in wild bewilderment. While Sughrue held the bridle of the grey, he placed Solace on the saddle, mounted the rump behind her and gathered the reins. He nodded to the lieutenant.

The boy raised his hand, brought it down pointing west, and

they moved off. Beyond them the sun lay bloodily on the black timber. Sughrue rode to Adam's stirrup. He looked at Solace's closed eyes and he whispered hoarsely.

'They wouldn't touch her, Adam ...'

'What the hell are you talking about?' said Adam in anger.

'What you're thinking about, boy. They wouldn't touch her till they'd finished with the Pedlar. But why didn't it happen three days ago when that old buck saw them?'

*

They camped that night by the Washita where the herd had crossed, the marks of hooves still deep in the mud on the south bank, and more again in the red clay on the north. During the ride Solace had said nothing, and Adam had been grateful for this. He did not know what words could have comforted her. When he looked down at her face, where her head lay against his shoulder, he saw her eyes still staring at remembered horrors.

That night she lay in Adam's blanket by the fire, looking at the flames until her eyelids at last fell from exhaustion and she slept. He pulled the blanket about her shoulders and touched her forehead once.

He sat on his saddle, making himself a cigarette. The horses moved gently at the picket line, and against the pale edge of the river he could see the slanted shadow of a carbine on a sentry's shoulder. The lieutenant squatted beside him. He looked towards Solace and he said 'She is a very beautiful girl, Mr Carthage. She seemed to know you.'

'We were children together. Long ago, before the War.'

The lieutenant eased a finger through the knot of his neckerchief. 'The War,' he said, 'It's not easy, Mr Carthage, to come into an army *after* a War.' He seemed embarrassed by what he had said.

'I understand what you mean, lieutenant,' said Adam. 'I've no bad feelings about you. The War's over.'

The officer's face was split by a boy's smile. 'Thank you, Mr Carthage. My father commanded a brigade in the Army of the Potomac. He always spoke well of your soldiers.'

'The War's over,' said Adam again.

'Yes,' said Vaughan. 'We'll leave you in the morning. The Pawnee tells me that hostiles crossed the river two miles upstream and appear to be following it. I am sorry I can accompany you no further. You'll be all right?'

Adam smiled. 'We'll find the herd by noon, I reckon.' Then he hesitated. 'Will you take some advice?'

'I'd consider it a favour, sir.'

'What Sughrue said about the Comanches ... he was right. They'll try to cut you up. I should keep your scouts well out and forward.'

'We'll be all right, Mr Carthage. They've run from us once.'

'Yes,' said Adam, 'and they'll remember that. Good night, lieutenant.' He turned to his blanket roll.

He awoke before dawn, and he went down through the cold mist to the river, and threw water on his face. Then he returned and saddled the grey, rode it through the ford, up the north bank and for two miles beyond. He climbed a bluff and started to the north as dawn came. Ahead of him the Cross Timbers swept to the west and he saw only its scrub-green hills. He thought he saw, far away, a thread of dust on the horizon, but the herd was nowhere in sight nor did he expect it to be. He had ridden out thus to calm the thoughts that were in his mind. These were all concerned with Solace, and when he rode back they were still unresolved.

He crossed the river and found the lieutenant squatting on his heels by the water, shaving. The boy smiled a bright greeting. The smoke of the breakfast fire was blowing to the south in blue curls. Upwind of it sat Solace, erect on a McClellan saddle, her head bent, and her black hair flowing forward. She was combing it with her fingers. The fine line of her exposed neck was white and strong. There was a little cloud of soldiers passing backwards and forwards before her on spurious errands.

Adam's spurs rang as he dismounted behind her, and at their music Solace turned her head sharply, one quick, graceful movement that lifted her chin and flung her hair behind her. She smiled. 'Adam ... Those spurs, I never forgot them.'

The smile puzzled him, he had not expected such resilience of spirit after yesterday. He looked at her without speaking.

For a moment her eyes clouded, and then she smiled. He saw

now the brittleness of it, and he knew that it would crack at the slightest pressure. To his surprise she suddenly leapt up from the fire and ran to him, locking his arms to his side with hers. 'Adam ... It's been so long!'

Then, as abruptly, she released him and stepped back, her eyes bright and her face flushed. 'Sughrue says that Estribo is taking the herd to Kansas. You'll let me come?'

'There's no other choice. I wanted the lieutenant to take you to Fort Gibson.'

'Why?'

'You should be with women.'

'You're thinking of yesterday.' Her voice trembled and she was back against him again, holding him to her fiercely, her nails digging into his back.

'I'm sorry,' he said foolishly.

'Paw said they would treat us fairly. And they did, Adam. They came twice and went away after just staring. But then they came again and tied Paw to the wheel ...'

'Don't talk about it.'

'The soldiers came, and I ran. *Oh, Adam ... !*'

He thought she would cry again, and this he might have understood. But she released him and stood back with her head lifted. Her chin was firm and her full lips closed. She said quite clearly 'Was he dead, Adam?'

'The soldiers buried him, Solace. I don't believe he suffered.' And he hoped that the lie was convincing.

'I promise you, Adam ... I promise you I shan't cry again.'

'I should understand.'

She shook her head. 'I want to look at you. You've changed. It isn't just that it's been so long. Your face is sad. Was it the war?'

He rubbed his hand over his chin and tried to jest. 'Maybe if I shaved, like the lieutenant.'

'Is it because of Johnny, Adam?'

'What have you heard about Johnny?' he asked, and she frowned at the hard tone of his voice.

'That he was killed,' she said slowly.

'The Brigade lost four hundred men in the Wilderness.'

'Poor Johnny,' she said softly.

The patrol was mounted, the fire still hissing from the coffee poured upon it, and the lieutenant came across with his hat crushed in a gauntleted hand. He bowed shortly, put on the hat and saluted. 'Good-bye, Miss Norton. I'm sorry . . .'

Her eyes were unnaturally bright again as she turned to face the boy, red skirt swirling and held by her hand. Her voice trembled. 'Thank you, lieutenant. You did all you could.'

'Yes, ma'am,' he said, and saluted again. He looked once to Adam, gravely and apologetically before he returned to his patrol. He mounted, and his young voice called high against the song of the Washita. The troopers swung easily into twos and rode to the northwest along the red bank. Adam and Solace saw the lieutenant pull out from the head of the column and stand in the stirrups for a minute looking back at them. He raised his hat, held it high, and then rode on.

Sughrue came to their side. 'More courage than hindsight, that one,' he said. 'Do we move out now?'

It was late that afternoon before they came up with the Estribo herd. The mark of hooves lay beaten in the grass and brush for them to follow, a long, snaking, northward-pulling, trail. Twice they passed the bodies of newly-born calves, half-eaten by coyotes. They had been shot. Sughrue looked at them. 'Shelby ain't allowing nothing to hold up the drive.'

'He did right,' said Adam.

It rained at noon, a heavy shower that lasted half an hour, falling from a single dark cloud above them while all about it the sun shone on the rest of the plain. Adam wrapped his blanket about Solace and gripped his pony's flanks with his knees to hold his seat. The rain gathered in tiny jewels on the girl's dark hair where it broke free from the blanket. After a while the grasp of her arms about his waist relaxed, and he knew that she slept. The raincloud moved away to weep over the table-land, and the coats of the horses steamed in the sun.

The herd came into view as they topped a low rise at dusk, black and shining, and just bedding down among the oak, cotton wood and thickets of wild plum that lined the South Fork of the Canadian. There was no dust, for the rain had turned the trail to mud. The canvas top of Dutchy's wagon glowed lividly in the half-light as they rode towards it. Daly, bedding down the last of the drag, saw the riders first, and he raised a high, yipping yell, pulling out his gun and firing three shots to the sky.

'Blamed fool!' said Sughrue. 'Does he want to start another run?' But he, too, was excited, and he kicked his horse to a canter.

Solace stirred against Adam's chest. She lifted her head and her face was close to his, her eyes wide. 'Are we there, Adam?' He nodded. She pulled herself away from him, looking down to the camp as she spoke. 'He's blind, isn't he, Adam? Mr Ferguson, I mean?'

'He's blind,' said Adam.

'There's something between you both, Paw said. That's why he wouldn't take me back to Estribo. He wouldn't say, but it's because of Johnny, isn't it? What happened to Johnny, Adam?'

For a reply he kicked at the pony, urging it towards the camp. He saw Dutchy's dirty white apron, saw Bridges and Carlisle running, stumbling awkwardly in boots never made for walking men. They waved their hats above their heads and yelled. Adam wondered irritably why one of them, at least, was not already riding night-herd. Then he saw The Old Man, immobile by the unsaddled sorrel, his yellow linen duster torn in one place on the skirt. Ferguson's face was bitterly weary.

Adam ignored the voices about him as he lifted Solace from the grey, and then slipped to the ground himself. He took her arm and led her to The Old Man.

'I found her,' he said harshly.

The Old Man put out his arms. 'Solace?'

For a second she hesitated, and then she ran to him. His arms folded about her, and his head bent over hers. She murmured to him quickly, turning first one cheek against the duster and then the other, and her shoulders shook. Now she cries, Adam thought. The Old Man raised a hand to the girl's head, and all heard his voice as it called.

'Yea, like as a father pitieth his own children, even so is the Lord merciful unto them that fear him.'

He turned and led Solace to the wagon.

Adam uncinched his saddle and pulled it from the grey. The horse nuzzled his shoulder and he tore a handful of grass from the earth and began to wipe its sweating coat. His arm was touched cautiously, and there was Dutchy, leaning over his withered leg, a smile of unusual warmth on his frosted face, a cup of coffee in his hand. 'For you, Adam. Not find the Pedlar, eh?'

Adam took the coffee. 'He's dead. Look after her, Dutchy. She must ride with you on the wagon, so look after her good.' He drank the coffee quickly. It was hot, and it scalded his tongue and throat, but the pain seemed to give him pleasure.

Shelby rode in two hours later, his horse caked with mud to the belly, and blood was mixed with the mud. Adam looked at the raking wounds with anger. He hated a cowhand to ill-use a horse.

The black beard was thicker on Shelby's face, and his two days as trail-boss had given him a swagger. He left the horse with Jubilo and brought his saddle into the firelight, dropping it to the ground. He looked at Adam and he looked at Sughrue, and he held his head to one side and slowly wiped his hands down the back of his thighs. He said nothing at first, but as he began to unbuckle his leggings he looked up and said 'You got back. You brought a girl, too, Jubilo says.'

Sughrue cackled. 'You hoped maybe to leave us behind?'

Shelby dropped the leggings over his saddle and stood facing Adam. He seemed changed, there was an aggressive confidence in his carriage that acted on Adam as a warning.

'We got Comanche trouble, I hear,' said Shelby. 'Jubilo says a war-party killed the Pedlar, and maybe's following us.'

'There's a Yankee cavalry patrol after them,' said Adam. 'Following them up the Washita.'

Shelby laughed. The laugh was his opinion of soldiers.

Adam stared at his face, trying to read the thoughts behind it. The firelight glinted ruddily on the sweat that clung to the big man's beard. Adam recognized it, he had seen it often enough during the War. It was the sweat of a man who had tightened his courage and was keeping a grasp on it.

'You hearing me, Carthage?' said Shelby loudly.

'I hear you. Speak your mind.'

Shelby took a pace to the right, and a little to the rear. Adam was coldly aware that while this movement put Shelby deeper into the shadows it also sharpened his own silhouette against the fire's light. He wished that he were not so tired.

'I want you to listen to me, Carthage.'

Adam's eyes were fixed on the big belt buckle at Shelby's waist, gleaming in the thin light. 'I'm listening, Shelby.' The big man wiped his hands on his pants again, and let them hang by his side. 'You listen good, then, Carthage, on account of I want you to get my meaning. I didn't sign on to fight Comanches for the Army, or take cattle where no buyers are waiting.'

'You signed to ride for Estribo, not boss it.'

There was a tension in Shelby's voice that lifted it to a nervous note. 'This here's the South Canadian. I say we follow it east downstream apiece to the Shawnee Trail and take that to Missouri.'

'We're going to Kansas, Shelby.'

For a moment there was a desperate appeal in what Shelby said, 'There ain't no sense in that, Carthage, you know it! Not another five hundred miles, maybe, and not knowing who's to buy the cattle when we get them there. And having to fight Comanches maybe.'

Adam said 'It's not your problem, Shelby. You can pack your gear and ride off tomorrow. I'll get The Old Man's note for your time.'

Shelby's feet shifted until they were astride, and his body rested on them evenly. 'I don't want no paper, Carthage. I put sweat and guts into this drive, more than any of you. I want what it pays, and it'll pay if we take this herd to Missouri, not Kansas.'

'The Old Man says Kansas.'

Shelby swore. 'That blind old fool! Only thing that keeps him upright is his pride,and I know how to take the salt out of that!'

'Shelby ...' said Adam.

'I don't want to fight you, Carthage, but you been prodding me all along. Now I call your play. I'm telling The Old Man about Johnny and maybe then he'll see sense. You want to stop me, then you got to kill me.'

'I'll kill you, Shelby. I promised you that.'

Adam heard a rustle behind him as the others drew away

from the fire. A shadow came to his side and he knew by the tobacco smell that it was Sughrue. 'Adam boy!'

'Keep out of this, Sughrue.'

'Boy ...'

'Keep out of this!'

The shadow went. Adam thought, this is hatred. Hatred of what the Comanche had done to the Pedlar, of the fact that Solace had seen it done. A hatred of The Old Man's hate, of the long drive to Kansas, of greasy saddle-leather and horse-sweat, of galls and lice, of beef, dust, and the fogging sleep in his mind. Yet there was no hatred of Shelby.

'Shelby ...' he said again.

Sweat was now on his own face, stinging his eyes, but his body seemed cold. Shelby was a shadow only, faceless and handless. Only the belt buckle still gleamed in the light, and Adam knew that when Shelby moved a hand towards a gun a shadow would pass across that buckle and extinguish its gleam momentarily.

'You want to try, Carthage?' shouted Shelby shrilly.

Adam said nothing, and the shadow passed over the belt buckle.

Shelby fired his gun once, but wildly, and his thumb was on the hammer for a second shot when Adam killed him. The heavy bullet struck Shelby above the buckle and, big though the man was, lifted him from his feet and threw him on his back.

The sound of the two shots rolled back with dimming resonance. Adam stood there, looking at Shelby's body, the upturned boots, the worn hole on one sole. Slowly he pushed his gun back into its scabbard. His face hard, he turned to the fire. Sughrue did not look at him, but spat once into the flames. Daly's open face was staring at Shelby with frank astonishment. Jubilo came forward, his big hands spread out. 'Mister Adam ...'

'Bury him,' said Adam harshly.

'You hit, Mister Adam?'

'No. *Bury him!*'

He heard The Old Man's voice. 'Who fired those shots? Sughrue! Damn you, Sughrue, what's going on here?'

Adam turned. The Old Man was standing with Solace, hat and

duster off, his vest black against his white shirt, and his striped pants bagging over his boots. But Adam did not look at him for long. He looked at Solace. Her blouse and skirt were splashes of harsh colour against the blue darkness. She was staring at him with horror.

*

Even at the beginning of the drive Estribo's hands had been scarcely enough to handle the herd, and now with two men gone, Lincoln in the stampede and Shelby before Adam's gun, the work was hard on the remaining riders. Adam kept Daly on drag, put Carlisle and Jubilo on swing, and Sughrue and Bridges at point. He thought *Seven men to drive eight hundred head, it's impossible.*

He did not like leaving Jubilo's horse-herd unhandled, but the old caponera, the grey bell-mare, led it well and it did not stray from the note of her bell. In her turn she kept close within sound of the negro's singing voice on right flank. Adam watched and he thought *We shall do it if The Old Man prays hard enough.*

But the work was hard, unceasing, saddle-galling, and by the end of a day though the steers may not have travelled more than fifteen miles, the swing men had ridden sixty on frequent changes of horse. Adam spent less time ahead on scout, but worked with the riders, even on drag with Daly. If he found it hard that the boy no longer smiled at him as once had been, Adam did not show this in his cold, emotionless face.

For Shelby's ghost was riding with the herd, and the manner of his death was in every man's memory. The big cowhand was not mourned, he had never been liked, but it was not easy to understand why Adam had killed him. Shelby had been buried by the trail, his grave covered with stones. The Old Man had spoken over the grave, with a morning wind whipping dust about his feet.

'*I will wash my hands in innocency, O Lord, and so will I go to thine altar*. Sughrue, did Shelby draw his gun first?'

'He did, John.'

The Old Man thought of this, and then said 'Mount up!'

The herd crossed the South Fork of the Canadian that day,

the twenty-first of the drive. The grazing was rich, the land unbroken, and Estribo made good time across the ten miles of prairie to the north fork. No one spoke to Adam unless he made talk necessary. Each man turned his eyes away from Adam's face, yet it was as if Adam could feel the touch of them between his shoulder-blades once he rode on. At night, about the fire, there was a silent uneasiness when he was present. Once he rode in from scout to hear Bridges improvising a melancholy song.

'He was a tall man, a killing man,
Who shot our partner down . . .'

At the sound of Adam's spurs Bridges stopped, and looked up at Adam with a face suddenly tense. *He thinks I might kill him for that,* thought Adam, and on the heels of the thought came an angry bitterness. As if in revenge, the next day he rode each man relentlessly, with such brutal tongue-lashings that Sughrue broke away from point and took his arm. 'What are you trying to do, boy, prove you had to kill Shelby?'

'You want to prove I hadn't, Sughrue?'

'Cut your own trail, son,' said Sughrue sadly, and turned back to point.

Solace rode on Dutchy's wagon, sitting erect behind the yoke of four oxen, her red skirt torn at the hems, her blouse covered by a cowhide vest that Bridges had given her. Her dark hair was knotted below her right ear with a strand of rawhide. Hour after hour the jolting, swinging, springless wagon tried her body. Her face grew tight with the strain. The dust gathered on her high cheekbones like purple shadows. In the hot nooning, when Adam rode up and dismounted by the cook-wagon, he searched his mind for words that might break through her cold reserve, and he could find none.

It was as if each time she saw his face, or his thin dark-shirted figure riding, the vision of Shelby's fallen body came between them.

Adam knew that he was accompanied by four hands, a *remudero*, a cook, a blind old man and a girl, yet he knew that he was also alone. He withdrew into himself, and his arrival, with spurs ringing, at camp-fire or nooning, was enough to produce a tense and cautious silence. Sughrue watched it all unhappily, wondering if this was how a professional gun-man was made, not by his own choice but by the pressure of other men's emotions.

Then something happened that destroyed the tension, or at least eased it.

Halfway between the North Fork of the Canadian and the Cimarron, on an upland plain noisy with the whirring of prairie chicken, Estribo realized that the Comanche raiding-party was once more following them. The night-guard was, inevitably, inadequate, and for three nights in succession a Comanche slipped in among the herd, cut a cow's udders and drank its milk and blood. Adam rode wide, to the east and west of the trail, looking for signs and finding none.

On the fourth morning, shortly after dawn, he found an arrow thrust into the earth on Jesse Chisholm's trail. It was long, with two straight black grooves on one side and two spiral grooves on the other, running from its turkey feathers to its iron barb. It was roughly daubed with red clay, and tied to the shaft were three cavalry buttons. Adam took it to Sughrue who ran his fingers along the black and red grooves. 'Comanche war arrow,' he said.

It was Daly, wide-eyed, who asked 'How can you tell?'

Sughrue spat his disgust. 'On account of a hunting arrow ain't barbed like this.' He touched the head. 'And this here fancy bit of metal is set at angles to the notch. Know why? Cause your ribs run across your body. A hunting-head's set the other way cause a buffler's ribs run down.'

'What about the clay and the buttons, Sughrue?' said Adam impatiently.

Sughrue broke the arrow between his hands. 'Who knows, boy? Maybe a Comanch' invitation to any horse-soldiers spoiling for a fight.'

On the twenty-seventh day of the drive the first Indian was seen. Adam was three miles ahead of the drive and looking for water. He found it, a narrow creek running out of the sandstone plateau. He was squatting by this, with his pony drinking beside him, when he saw the Comanche on a rise, less than a mile away. The Indian was motionless, shield hanging over the left flank of his horse, a short lance up-pointed. He seemed to be wearing some sort of cap, but he was too far away for any detail to be clear. Adam stood up, drew his rifle from its scabbard between stirrup leather and fender, and he waited. The Indian remained on the rise for perhaps two minutes, and then he went. One second he was there, and then he was gone.

Adam rode back to meet the herd. It was noon. A mile from the lead steers Adam stood in his stirrups and held his hat high above his head, remaining thus until Sughrue and Bridges, at point, saw him and turned the herd off the trail. He watched Dutchy's wagon make a wide half-circle before it halted. He saw the red and white movement of Solace as she got down, and then cattle, men and horses were all stationary in the wide basin, and the dust began to fade.

He rode in. Sughrue was talking to The Old Man, and Adam called him away with a beckoning hand.

Sughrue said 'Ain't you found water, boy?'

'There's water up ahead, not much, but water. And something else, Sughrue, Comanche. One at any rate. About four miles up.'

'What now, boy?'

Adam was vaguely irritated that Sughrue had no suggestion of his own to make. He dismounted and loosened his saddle-girth, speaking to it rather than to Sughrue. 'As I see it, maybe they're not interested in us, maybe they're looking for soldiers to fight. But we're so easy for them. I figure they may hit us at the Cimarron when we're crossing, or maybe just before.' He looked up at Sughrue.

'How about the water you found,' said Sughrue. 'These steers are dry.'

'It's not much, not enough, they'll have to last to the Cimarron.'

'A dry herd and the Comanch'. We got trouble sure enough.'

'Sughrue, I want the others told. Carlisle and Bridges won't carry saddle guns. I know it makes riding swing harder, but you tell them to get guns out of Dutchy's wagon. Young Daly's handgun is never cleaned. You get the boy to work on it.'

'And then... ?'

'And then I don't know. Do you Sughrue?'

Adam found The Old Man by Dutchy's wagon, clumsily pushing cold beans on to his knife with his fingers and passing them to his mouth.

'It's Adam. In a day, two days, maybe more, or maybe never, I think the Comanche are going to raid us.'

The Old Man put his knife on his plate slowly. He wiped his moustache with two quick sweeps of his hand. 'You afraid?'

The brutality of the question was bluntly deliberate, and Adam tightened his lips before he replied, just as brutally. 'A blind man is no good in a fight. I'm afraid, maybe, but I want to know what you want done with you. I'm bossing this drive.'

'All right,' said The Old Man with surprising tranquillity. 'I hurt you, Carthage, and now you've hurt me.'

'I'd like an answer.'

The Old Man put his hands on his knees and turned his face upward. His pale eyes stared unblinkingly at the high sun. His hands trembled slightly on his knees as he said '*The Lord is my light and my salvation, whom then shall I fear?*'

'All right,' said Adam softly, as if he had been given an intelligible answer.

That night he spoke to Solace. He went to her where she sat with her back against a wheel of the wagon, a blanket across her knees, and her hands resting on it. Her head was held back and her eyes were closed. There were real shadows beneath them now, not dust, and Adam wondered at the inner strength that made it possible for her to endure the drive, to suffer the fierce heat, the dirt, the sweat, the relentless push northwards. Her hair was unknotted and it fell over one shoulder in a dark, shining curve.

She heard the sweet music of his spurs and opened her eyes. She saw his tall, thin body, a body that seemed composed of balanced angles, resting geometrically on the strategic points of hips and shoulders, a horseman's body that seemed somehow incomplete on foot. She saw his young-old face, the hair thick at the nape of the neck, the eyes that were harsh. He stood before her, looking down, pushing his gloves through his gunbelt, and his eyes searching her face as if looking for an opening through which he might find an entry to her thoughts. 'Solace, are you all right?'

'Thank you, Adam.' There was no invitation in her voice.

He crouched on his heels and now his face was closer to hers, and in the firelight she saw even more clearly the loneliness of his eyes. She wanted to take his hand.

'Solace, there's something you must know. That Comanche war-party is dogging us.' Her mouth opened quickly, the lips drawn back slightly over the teeth, and he went on quickly, almost whispering. 'I think they'll hit us some time soon, how I don't know. If it comes when we are on the trail get in the back of the wagon, lie there on the boards and don't get up until you hear my voice. I can't . . .'

She interrupted him quickly, raising a hand as if she wished to press the fingers on his lips. 'Adam, I want to ask you a question.'

He paused in surprise. 'What question?'

'Why did you kill Shelby?'

Her hand fell on his own, where they were clasped between his knees, and he felt the urgent pressure of it.

'You threatened to kill him before. Curly told me.'

'What else have you been told?'

'That you'd changed when you came home from the War. Sughrue said that. He said that all men were changed by the War, but I know it's more than that with you. Carlisle said you're a hard man to work for now. He said you wanted to kill Shelby. They all say that, except Sughrue.'

'They're wrong.'

'They say Shelby wasn't the only man you wanted to kill. Sughrue said you tried to fight Ben Lake.'

'They talk a lot about me,' he said coldly. 'And what does The Old Man say?'

'Adam,' she said desperately. 'I can see something is wrong. I didn't expect you to be the same, not after a war. But it isn't that, because I think I've changed too.'

'Like you say,' he said gently. 'You've become a woman. That Yankee lieutenant said you were beautiful.'

She seemed puzzled by the tone of his voice, and then she shook her head. 'Mr Ferguson . . .'

'What does The Old Man say about me?' he interrupted.

She was angry suddenly. 'You think I've been asking about

you? I didn't ask, they all told me, they thought I could help.'

'What does The Old Man say?'

'Why is it so important to you what The Old Man says? He doesn't talk about you. Adam, tell me about Shelby. It was because of Johnny, wasn't it? And it's because of Johnny that you worry about Mr Ferguson.'

He stood up, pulling his hand away from hers, and she leant forward quickly. 'Adam, can't I help?'

'There's nothing to help,' he said. 'Do as I tell you, Solace. Stay in the wagon, lie on the boards.' He turned and as he was about to leave her he heard the rustle of her skirt. She gripped his arm fiercely, pulling him round to face her. 'Adam, I want to know! Why did you kill Shelby?'

'I killed him,' he said heavily. 'Why should it matter?'

The firelight shone on the anger in her eyes. She spat the words from her mouth in distaste. 'They are right, then. You've become a killing man!'

He caught her wrists, and saw her wince at the pain of his grip. 'Like you say,' he said again. 'Ask Bridges to teach you his song. The tall, killing man who shot our partner down.'

She began to cry, and at that moment Jubilo's voice called from the horse-herd, there was a single booming report of a pistol, roll of hooves receding into the darkness, a triumphant skirling cry. Sughrue appeared suddenly by Adam's side, chest and arms scrawny in his red flannel undershirt, his bald head shining. He held his boots in one hand and his gun in the other. He said *'Comanch'!'*

'Jubilo!' Adam began to run towards the darkness, pulling a gun from his belt. He saw the restless movement of the horses, heads and manes tossing, and he heard the nervous ringing of the bell about the grey mare's neck. The herd parted and Jubilo came through. He too had a gun in his hand.

'Too late, Mr Adam. They got away from me, with that old claybank and a chestnut. Three of 'em, Mister Adam, they snuck up on me in the dark.'

Now they heard Daly whistling shrilly from the night-guard, and Adam slipped on to the bare back of the little paint and rode down to the dark mass of the herd, calling the boy's name.

The whistling guided him down the draw, through a patch of blackjack where, in the moonlight, Daly sat in his saddle looking down at the bodies of two steers. Blood was still bubbling from their slashed throats, spreading black on the lemon-coloured grass. The rest of the herd moved unhappily against the scent of blood.

From the distant darkness there came the throaty gobble of a turkey-cock. It was answered to the north. Adam could see nothing out there, just the moon shining on the frosty mica that encrusted the stone outcrop. When Sughrue came up Adam nodded towards the ridge. 'You get what it means, Sughrue?'

'Two gobblers staying up late for an augurin' match, maybe, but since that ain't like gobblers it's most likely Comanch' congratulating themselves.'

Half to himself Adam said 'We'll need all the men we have now.'

Sughrue scratched his left arm-pit reflectively. 'Could have used Shelby,' he said to the darkness.

'We could have used Lincoln, too,' said Adam in a hard voice. 'Maybe I'm blamed for his death as well?'

'Ain't said you're blamed for anything,' Sughrue said, and went back to camp.

Adam rode with the night-guard until dawn, feeling the ache of his body, the sharp grit in his eyes, the itch of a sweat-caked shirt. He was afraid and he knew that the others were also afraid. It was no use for him to try to imagine what the Comanche would do, for he had no answer in his mind. There had been twenty in the party that killed the Pedlar. Maybe there were less now, maybe more. There was no way of knowing. Indian war-parties had a way of dwindling away after one success, or even increasing, it all depended on the character of the leader. Nor was there any way of knowing how they would attack the herd, if they would attack the herd, whether they would come at night, or ride down suddenly one noon. However they came, if they came, it did not seem possible that they could be stopped, not by five riders, a cook, a blind old man and a girl.

At midnight the disc of the moon lay on the horizon. The herd rose to its feet with a long, rustling sigh, stretched itself and settled down again, just as it did every night. It would not move again until dawn. There was another problem. The cattle were thirsty. The creek where Adam had seen the Comanche had been drunk dry by the first fifty steers, and the bed ploughed into mud by the rest.

*

Estribo put the herd on the trail at first light. Adam judged that the Cimarron lay seven miles ahead, and he hoped that it was not dry. He watched the black snake coil into movement, horns swinging, the dust coming up slowly. Before he rode on to scout he stopped at Dutchy's wagon. The old German, leaning wearily on his withered leg, was priming a muzzle-loader. He had a pistol stuck into his waistband. He looked up from it to Adam, and seemed to be considering the value of a smile before he let it drift across his lips. Solace sat on the wagon-seat above him. She had heard Adam's approach, but she did not turn her head towards him.

'Dutchy, stay on the flank of the herd. No call today to go ahead to make noon camp. And Dutchy, look after Miss Norton, will you?'

'Sure thing, Adam, I do that. But what you think?'

'I don't know. But keep the wagon close in to the herd. Bridges is swing man on this flank, and he's a good gun.' Adam looked up to Solace, as if he were about to speak to her, but then, with reins held high above his saddle horn by the left hand, he turned his horse towards the head of the drive. As he loped past Sughrue and Jubilo at point he saw that The Old Man was riding there too, the skirt of his duster tucked beneath his right thigh, his right hand resting on his gun. Adam thought, *Maybe he knows something from the Psalms to fit this situation too.*

He raised a hand briefly to Sughrue and pushed on ahead at a canter.

He was three miles from the Cimarron an hour later, and could see its silver gleam, when the Comanche burst out of a coulee half a mile to the north. They emerged in a great, flowering shock of colour that shortened Adam's breath.

He halted and counted them as they came out. There were

seventeen. He remembered that the old blanket buck had said that there were twenty Comanche in the war-party and three Kiowas. He wondered where the rest were, whether they were still hidden in the coulee, whether they had deserted the war-party, whether they were back on the flank of the herd, or even at the rear, waiting.

In line, the Indians watched him. He could see the wind moving the ponies' tails, fluttering along the feathers. He saw the sun shimmering on greased skins. He turned his horse and moved away at a slow walk, until the land dropped down and he was out of sight, then he whipped his horse to a gallop. A mile from the lead steers he raised his hat above his head and kept it there. He saw a flurry of dust at point where Sughrue and Jubilo fought to turn the herd off the trail. He heard the calling, the thin, piping, whistling. He saw the sorrel, with The Old Man in the saddle, move slowly to the west, to the left near Dutchy's wagon, and he heard Jubilo crying sweetly to the *remuda*.

He rode down. Sughrue came up at a gallop, pulling in his horse so hard that it went back on its haunches with a beat of hooves. The old man was angry. 'Eternal damnation, Adam! It's an hour or more to noon yet. We can't hold 'em much longer, they smell water.'

'Comanche, a mile or more ahead.'

'How many, boy?'

'Seventeen.' Adam moved on to the herd. 'Sughrue, get Bridges and Carlisle up closer to point, and tell Daly to stay in close with the drag. I hope that damned gun of his is clean!'

The Old Man was dismounted, standing by the sorrel's head, with a hand on its bridle. 'Carthage, are you there? What is it?'

'Comanche. Dutchy, hitch Mr Ferguson's sorrel to the tail of your wagon.' Then he saw Solace. She was sitting on the seat, feeding shells into a repeating rifle. She had tied a bandana about her hair and knotted it below her throat.

'*Solace . . .!*'

She did not look at him. She levered a shell into the breech and laid the rifle on her knees.

'Dutchy, give the hands what they can have sharp and cold!'

Adam did not eat himself, but stayed in the saddle at the head of the herd, waiting and watching. One by one the Estribo hands joined him. He did not look back to them, he heard the occasional creak of leather, a hoof beating the earth, the slow, wheezing exhalation of Sughrue's breath. He spoke once. 'Daly are you all right, boy?'

'He ain't here,' said Sughrue. 'He's back with the drag where you said. Take it easy, son.'

'Sughrue!' The old man came up to Adam's side. 'What do you figure?'

'You tell me, boy, is it wise to wait?'

'We walk the herd up to meet them and we have no chance. Sooner or later they'll come to see what's holding us up.'

'I hope and pray,' said Sughrue.

They waited for three-quarters of an hour, and even the cattle seemed infected by the suspense and were oddly still. Great heat pricked the back of Adam's neck, and his pony dropped its head wearily towards the earth. Then the Comanche topped the rise ahead, one by one and slowly, until they were strung out along it in a line, a thousand yards away and looking down on the herd. They made no movement until, at last, one rider in the centre raised his hand, palm towards the herd.

'Sughrue?'

'They want to talk.'

'That all?'

'For the moment, anyhow.'

Adam tightened the neck-thong of his hat. 'Sughrue, take Bridges and Carlisle and get back of the herd. Do it slow and gentle. Bunch it up close if you can, without moving it off. I'm going up there to talk. If they do anything worse than talk, get the herd moving towards them fast.'

'You talk Comanche maybe?' inquired Sughrue amiably.

'Meaning what?'

'Meaning I'm coming with you, boy.' Sughrue called over his shoulder. 'Curly, you heard Adam. Bunch up this herd, and, if you have to, get it on the run fast. They won't take much prodding, they smell water.'

'Carthage!' It was The Old Man.

'I hear you, Mr Ferguson.'

The Old Man opened his mouth, and then closed it. He gathered the duster about his shoulders and at last said '*His faithfulness and truth shall be thy shield and buckler.*'

'Yes, sir,' said Adam. 'Jubilo, get Mr Ferguson over to the wagon and hitch his sorrel to it.' He looked once towards Solace. She was sitting with her back straight, the gun on her knees, her face uplifted and her eyes staring towards the Comanches.

The Indians did not move as the two white men approached. At first Adam had the startling impression that these were not Comanches at all but negroes, for their faces were painted black.

The cowhands halted fifteen feet from the Indian line, before the warrior whose hand was still raised. He was a young man, with two bands of yellow paint breaking the black of his face and running across the bridge of his nose from cheek to cheek. He was tall for a Comanche, but he had his people's light skin, and it shone with grease. Apart from a breech-clout his body was naked, and his legs hung on either side of his pony. He wore a badger-skin cap that was decorated with a rosette of scarlet feathers above his right eye. His chest, arms and thighs were striped with vermilion and yellow, and his moccasins were thickly beaded, and each had a pendant of feathers on the heel.

He wore his hair in one plait, and it was studded with silver discs, graduated in size until that at the bottom of the queue was no larger than a button. The hair was interwoven with coloured rags. There was a lance across his back, a war-shield on his pony's flank, and in his left hand, across his wooden saddle, he carried a cavalry carbine.

Adam looked at the gun. He looked too at the army saddle-cloth beneath the Comanche's saddle. In the corner of it was the insignia '5'.

The warrior next to the leader was riding the claybank from Estribo's *remuda*. He wore a cavalry blouse with a lieutenant's bars on the shoulder, and hung about his neck was the fine silver watch which Adam and Sughrue had last seen in the hands of Lieutenant Vaughan, C Troop, Fifth Cavalry.

'God rest the boy's soul,' said Sughrue softly.

If the leader was tall for his race, the other Comanches were conventionally short and stocky, their chests broad, their legs bowed. Some carried bows, but almost all had cavalry carbines, and some of them pistols, holstered and slung across their shoulders by the belts. One had a bloody gash across his face, and the arm of another hung loosely and at an ugly angle by his side. Now Adam knew what had happened to the other six members of the party.

'Them yellow-legs put up a fight at any rate,' said Sughrue and calmly spat in front of the war-chief's pony. There was no change of expression on the Comanche's face.

Away to the right of the line were three Kiowas, their foreheads wrapped in scarlet and yellow cloths, and they were tall men with narrow shoulders. They wore no paint except a single band of yellow, an inch deep, across their faces below their eyes, the lids of which were daubed with scarlet. One of them carried a lance with three bloody scalps near the head. The highest, Adam saw, was red, red like the cavalry sergeant's hair. The Kiowas grinned happily.

At last the war-chief lowered his hand, and at the movement tiny bells, hanging from the lobes of his ears, rang gently. He studied Adam's horse, its bridle and saddle, and his eyes lingered over the Mexican spurs.

'Ask them what they want, Sughrue.'

Sughrue pushed back his hat, wiped his mouth, and chopped the air with his hand. He grunted a few halting words. The warrior in the lieutenant's jacket laughed, holding his hand over his mouth like a woman. The war-chief did not smile. He placed his hand over his breast and spoke with great passion in a language so sonorously beautiful that Adam found it hard to believe that this was the same tongue that Sughrue had just used.

'What did he say?'

'I didn't get all of it, son. But the meaning's plain. They're Kwahadis, all right, down from the Staked Plains. He says this is the land of the *Nemena*. That's what the Comanch' call themselves. The People, as if there wasn't another blamed soul in the world. He says this is their land and what the hell are we doing on it. He says his name is Tasajillo. He's got some other name that sounds like Carrying His Lance Forward, but Tasajillo's what the Mexicans call him, after that damned rat-tailed cactus with the thorns.'

'What do they want from us?'

'I'm getting to it, boy. Course, he wrapped it up some, but he says if we give him a hundred head to take back to his people he'll let us through.'

'Would he?'

Sughrue spat. 'Why should he? Any Comanch' can steal a steer. These ones figure to take our hair back as well.'

'Who are they, Sughrue?'

'I told you, boy. Antelope-eaters. Some of Quanah's young men, though I don't suppose that old buzzard knows what they're doing. The Kiowas are from Satanta's band, I reckon, and here with his blessing.'

The war-chief brought his hand across his body and said four angry words. 'He says we're wasting his time.'

'Ask them why they aren't up on the Cimarron talking peace with the cavalry?'

Sughrue sighed and put the question. Tasajillo smiled momentarily before he answered. The fun-loving warrior on his right hit a thigh and mimicked great amusement. One of the Kiowas lifted his gun and gave a long, ululating call, turning his pony in rapid circles.

'In as many words, son, he says don't we wish they were.'

'Tell him the cavalry will punish him.'

'Adam, boy ...'

'Tell him, damn you! We need time for Bridges to bunch the herd.'

This time Tasajillo did not smile. He leant across to the warrior in the cavalry jacket, tore the officer's bars from its shoulder and threw them at Adam's feet. This time all three Kiowas called and circled their horses excitedly. The Comanches sat with proud, still faces.

'You got any more light conversation, boy?'

'Yes. Tell him I'm angry to see one of our horses ridden by his young men. But tell him I forgive him this, and can let him have a steer and some tobacco. But tell him this herd is going through, and it would be a pity for such young men to die.'

'Meaning us, of course?'

'Tell him!'

Sughrue shrugged his shoulders. When he heard the message Tasajillo smiled again. He looked down at the herd and spoke.

'Adam boy, he says he'll take Solace along with the hundred head, and he's quite willing to fight you for her.'

'Tell him we'll discuss it with our chief.'

Tasajillo sneered and nodded. The Indian line had closed in on the centre, but it made no movement forward. The wind rippled along the feathers and the horse-hair. The sky behind the slash of red, black, yellow and white seemed a deeper blue. It seemed to Adam that he was facing not a line of horsemen but an arrow drawn back on a string to the head. He turned his horse and began to walk it slowly down towards the herd. Beside him Sughrue said hoarsely, 'My back is a mile broad.'

They had gone two hundred yards when a high yell rose behind him. Adam looked over his shoulder and saw that wave of colour suddenly break down the slope. Tasajillo held the carbine to his shoulder with his right hand, his cheek along its stock. Adam saw the puff of blue smoke, then heard the report. There were other shots, wild ones from the Kiowas, and an arrow sighed swiftly between him and Sughrue who gave a shrill Rebel yell and cried *'Ride, boy!'*

Adam put the paint pony to a gallop. The herd was less than seven hundred yards away. He saw the ox-wagon jerk forward, and behind it the sorrel threw up its head and followed. There was a volley of shots, a high crying as Bridges, Carlisle, Daly and Jubilo drove the steers into a run. The black pool of beef lurched clumsily at first, with the lead steers swinging in alarm, and then suddenly, miraculously and wonderfully, the whole moved forward in a great roar of hooves.

The first steers were already plunging past Adam as he swung his horse in a wide curve and turned it back to face the Indians. The Comanches were coming down in a close charge, a rare manoeuvre for them, but one which showed their confidence. They rode knee to knee, but fifty yards from the herd their line broke, fanning out on the flanks. For two of them the break came too late, and the old mossy horn and a big black steer caught their ponies. The Indians went over, hit the ground, and were lost in the dust and the hooves.

With wild elation Adam knew that he had been right, that in the herd he had the momentary advantage of a brigade of cavalry. The noise was now so great that he could hear no shooting, but in the dust he saw flashes from the Indians' carbines. He saw Sughrue riding straight-backed towards an approaching Kiowa, his jaws moving rhythmically over his tobacco, and his hand-gun held out straight from the shoulder. The Kiowa suddenly crumpled, slid round the neck of his pony and fell. Sughrue yelled.

Now there were no Indians before the run, but racing in the dust along its flanks, hanging over the far side of their ponies, one hand knotted in the mane, the other firing beneath the animal's neck. The steers, smelling water, ran hard up the slope and down the other side in flood. Adam stood in the stirrups and peered into the dusk. *Fourteen left,* he thought, as if solving some casual problem of arithmetic, *but where are they?*

And where was the wagon? He could not see it ahead of him, and he turned quickly. Back through the dust-cloud, on either side of that heaving mass of head and horn, he saw flashes of light, saw here and there a naked body. A steer passed him with five arrows in its body, yet able to plunge another fifteen yards before it fell, bringing down two others.

Adam halted, with his rifle out of its scabbard and held across his chest. Out of the dust suddenly, mouth open in a yell, rode a Comanche. Adam saw a lance leave the Indian's hand just as he brought up the rifle and fired. The Comanche fell or slipped to the far side of his horse, but something grazed along the side of Adam's head, and the sun-glinting dust exploded into darkness. He dropped forward, grasping the saddle-horn. He shook his head and straightened his body. The rifle had slipped from his hands and he brushed his forearm across his eyes, swung his horse round to the run and pulled his pistol from its holster.

Ahead of him now there rolled the crazily-swinging white top of the ox-wagon, its two wheels bouncing, the sorrel keeping pace with it, and The Old Man riding erect and calm, a pistol in his hand. Two Indians, a Comanche and a Kiowa, were riding at the wagon from the left, across Adam's path. The Kiowa raised a carbine and pointed it at The Old Man. Adam kicked the paint, felt its barrel-body heave and rise, and then, in a second it seemed, he struck the Kiowa's pony. The rider disappeared.

As Adam passed, the Old Man's mouth was wide in a desperate cry, '*God in mercy, let me see!*'

The other Indian, the Comanche, was Tasajillo, and when he saw the Kiowa go down before Adam's horse he swerved away and moved up to the front of the wagon, his arm outstretched. Dutchy was lashing at the oxen, but yet they moved so slowly that the Comanche pulled in his horse to a lope. Adam saw Solace fire the rifle once, and then Tasajillo had plucked it from her by the barrel and flung it away. His white teeth shone against the black of his face. He had lost the badgerskin cap, and the single queue of his hair danced across his shoulder-blades, the silver discs shining.

He was yelling when Adam drove along beside him, grasped that plait of hair, slipped his feet free from the stirrups, and pulled.

They fell to the ground together, and the force of the impact knocked the breath from Adam's body and plunged him momentarily into singing darkness. He felt the Comanche's greased body slipping and writhing beneath him, and he clawed at it desperately. Then, out of the darkness, Tasajillo's face appeared below him, lips drawn back over the teeth, the black paint masked grey with dust.

He struck at it once with the barrel of his gun, and the black paint and the dust were suddenly red. He felt a hand groping urgently across his back. It was lifted and it struck, and yet there was no pain beyond the shock of the blow. He struck again with the gun, and again, yelling as he struck, seeing the face disappear, eyes, nose and sneering mouth disappear redly until the struggling body beneath him arched in one great convulsive movement and was still.

Blackness came over Adam in a compassionate silence.

He awoke to that darkness still, but to a movement over his face, a coolness touching his mouth. Then there was no darkness above him, like a shadow passing. There was a throbbing in his head, and he felt as though a great pleat had been taken in the flesh of his back.

'Adam?'

There was the sound of water moving gently over smooth ground, and there was the face of Solace above him. Sughrue wheezed at his shoulder. 'Sughrue, the Comanche ...'

'Gone, boy, gone fast.'

'And the herd?'

'Strung out for five miles along the Cimarron, bellies fit to bust. We whipped 'em boy!'

Adam closed his eyes, and he felt the coolness of Solace's fingers on his cheek.

*

Three days passed before Estribo gathered all the cattle scattered by the Comanche raid and the run. Fifteen steers and four cows had been killed, trampled or brought down by bullet and arrow. Two horses from the *remuda* and another five steers had died in the quicksands along the south bank of the Cimarron. It had taken five hours to rope and drag another six free from the sands. Cattle had drifted upstream, or lost themselves in the blanket folds of the treeless plain. Apart from Adam, only the boy Daly had been wounded, a bullet graze across his buttocks that hurt his pride more than his flesh. He found it hard to sit a horse, but harder still to endure Sughrue's grave references to his stirrup-standing riding as 'cantle-polishing'.

During those three days Adam lay on his side by Dutchy's wagon, his right arm and shoulder numbed by the stroke of Tasajillo's knife, and his head still aching from the lance-blow. Albeit illogically, the Estribo hands now accepted him as they had done before the shooting of Shelby. Bridges brought in Tasajillo's badgerskin cap, its rosette of red feathers dusty and broken, and he impulsively offered it to Adam. They brought in the Comanche's scalp, too, and this, with the cap, was nailed to the side of the ox-wagon.

But Adam was restless. It was thirty-two days since Estribo had left the Brazos. The Salt Fork of the Arkansas and the Kansas line were, he estimated, fifty miles to the north, three to four days' drive away. Beyond that, how far would the herd have to travel before finding a railroad and stockyards, a hundred miles, two hundred, or were they really there at all? And if they were, had Estribo now the strength to reach them?

He watched the men as they came in to camp at dusk, the dirt and beards on their faces, shirts torn, leggings and boots scuffed, broken finger-nails scratching at lice. Their eyes were deep-sunk, and there was a listlessness in their movements as if they slept as they walked. Daly now looked a man. Bridges and Carlisle had become old men. Jubilo's black skin was ashen with fatigue. Adam wondered what it was that kept them together, and he decided that perhaps they did not know the answer to this themselves.

The Old Man came to Adam once, standing above him with the wind moving the yellow duster. 'Is it bad?'

'No,' said Adam. 'It's nothing.'

'I've prayed for you, boy,' said The Old Man uncomfortably. '*Thou shalt not be afraid of the sickness that destroyeth in the noon-day*.'

'I'm obliged to you, sir.'

The Old Man's face was cold again. 'It's my Christian duty,' he said.

Solace tended Adam. She changed and washed the bandages which she had made from her underskirt. Yet her manner was distant, and she spoke no more to him than was needed. He watched her, finding fresh reason to marvel at the great strength in her fragile body. He watched the line of her neck, the short straight nose and the firm chin. He watched her in the morning when she parted and braided her hair with a comb that Daly had made for her from a turkey's wing-bone. He saw, in her walk, the grace of a woman combined with the litheness of a horseman. He ached for the sound of her voice.

Her face was burnt and cracked by the plains sun. Her hands were rough and never clean. She never complained, but on the evening of the second day that Estribo waited by the Cimarron Adam thought he heard her crying in the darkness.

He arose from his blanket at dusk on the third day and said that he would be sick no longer. He rode as night-hawk that evening, and came back to camp with his face hard from the pain in his shoulder.

At dawn on the fourth day Estribo crossed the Cimarron

and moved north once more. And the days passed. The sun was high and the broad prairie rolled. Each mile was like the last, and there were times when it was possible to believe that the herd was stationary. The hands rode with backs arched and tongues dry. Curly no longer sang at the evening fire, and there was a nettle-sting in Dutchy's voice. Tasajillo's cap and scalp fell from the nail on the wagon, and it was a day before their absence was noticed. Yet, for an hour, Bridges and Carlisle argued who should go back to find them, as if they had been a talisman that should not be lost. When Adam stopped the argument harshly, they stared at him with a re-awakening of old hostility.

Then there was The Old Man's sudden decision to speak the Word over the camp before he turned to his blanket at night. In a high, trembling voice he exhorted the sweat-soaked riders to repent their sins before they reached Kansas. They listened to him patiently, and Jubilo called out 'Amen!' Once, at nooning, when men, horses and cattle were motionless and gilded by the sun, The Old Man stood up and declared triumphantly, '*Many oxen are come about me. Fat bulls close me in on every side!*'

There was something hysterical in Carlisle's quickly-stifled laughter.

Gently Solace took The Old Man by the arm and led him away. Adam saw that the hands were looking from Ferguson to him, and he knew then that although, in the beginning, Estribo had accepted the blind man's leadership without doubt, now they saw Adam as their leader. He was the hub and the rim of the wheel of which they were but spokes. The knowledge gave him no comfort, for he felt himself bound to The Old Man by stronger ties than expediency.

Perhaps it was the mirror of this knowledge in his face that made Solace speak to him again of Johnny. She said 'Adam, don't you know? What's happening to Mr Ferguson is because of you. He lost Johnny, and now he thinks he has lost you. Won't you tell him, Adam?'

'There's nothing to tell him.'

'Is there nothing you want to tell me?'

'There's nothing.'

But he told her. Not then, but later, on the morning after the day Estribo met the four riders from Kansas.

Forty miles or more north of the Cimarron, within smell of the Salt Fork, the riders appeared suddenly on the trail, a mile ahead of the lead steers and they halted there. For a moment they remained immobile, and then they stood in their stirrups, waving their hats and calling. The sound of their voices came thinly. Adam, riding at point with Sughrue, held up his hand. 'Turn 'em off,' he said, 'it's noon, but watch me.'

'Who do you reckon they are, boy?'

'I aim to find out.' Adam touched his pony and cantered towards the riders. When they saw him coming they galloped down to meet him. Adam pulled a rifle from its scabbard and waited. They arrived in a cloud of dust through which they still yelled. Three of them were dressed like cowhands, northerners with wide-winged chaps and tall-crowned hats, but the fourth was a big, red-faced man in a long black Prince Albert and a hard hat. 'You from Texas?' he shouted.

The strong Yankee accent pricked Adam's suspicions, but he said, 'Estribo, from the Brazos. Who are you?'

The big man hit his thigh and leant back. He looked at the herd approvingly. 'You don't say? From the Brazos? How much beef you got down there?' He saw the slant of Adam's rifle and he hit his thigh again and laughed. 'You afraid of us, son? Put your pop-gun away. We're just what you're looking for.' He pushed out a hand. 'Sugg's the name. Joe McCoy's personal representative to the State of Texas.'

Adam took the hand. The grip cracked his fingers, and he did not like the thought that this was his right hand, his gun hand, and locked. 'McCoy?'

'Joseph Geiting McCoy of Springfield, Illinois, which state is also my own, sir. You going to ask us down, Mr. . . . ?'

'Adam Carthage.' But he did not turn his horse and he did not sheath the rifle.

'Mr Carthage, you don't know how glad I am to see you! By now I guess Joe McCoy's got his stockyards waiting for that beef of yours, and a rail laid right to the door. Mr Carthage, give me your hand again!' He took it, and pumped it up and down.

'Stockyards?' Now the truth was coming to Adam, and he grinned.

'Yes, sir, stockyards! You didn't know? You never saw Joe McCoy's handbills? Mr Carthage, Texas must be bigger'n Texans say if you didn't, for last winter I flooded the damn place with those handbills.'

'Not much comes up the Brazos to Estribo,' said Adam still grinning. 'But we like it that way.'

'Well, sir, I'll tell you. You drive that herd of yours due north by the star over the Kansas line to the Arkansas. There you'll find a plough furrow that'll lead you straight to Joe McCoy, and the best price you ever heard of for cattle. Ain't worth much in Texas are they?'

'Not worth the hide,' agreed Adam.

'Mr Carthage, then shake my hand again, because you'll never meet a happier man to see than me.'

Adam laughed. 'You've a hard grip, Mr Sugg. Come on down for coffee.'

They rode down at a gallop, with Adam yelling like a boy now, and waving his hat in wide sweeps across his head. He saw Solace come out from behind Dutchy's wagon, head lifted, a hand pushing at her hair. He saw the movement of The Old Man's duster. He saw Sughrue running with a gun in his hand. He rode up to them all, and pulled back his pony, his throat bubbling with a high yell of joy. An answering smile caught the lips of Solace.

'Carthage . . . !' The Old Man called. 'What is it?'

'Riders from Kansas. There's a railroad, buyers and stockyard waiting for our beef!'

'Praise the Lord!' said Ferguson.

Sugg pushed his way forward, his sharp eyes and agile mind quickly appreciating The Old Man's blindness. He picked up the right hand where it hung beside the linen duster, and he shook it. 'Sugg's the name, sir, stockman from Illinois. I'm happy to meet you.'

The Old Man's face softened. 'I am John A. Ferguson of Estribo on the Brazos. I am very much obliged to you for your news, sir.'

Sugg shook the hand again. 'Mr McCoy sent me down into

this territory. Joseph Geiting McCoy of Springfield, Illinois. Sent me down to find Texas drovers and point 'em north to him. Sir, we're obliged to *you*!'

That night something of Estribo's old gaiety came back to the fire, with Curly singing again, and Carlisle thrumming his Jew's harp. Solace smiled across the firelight as she clapped her hands in rhythm and sang with Curly.

'Mr Carthage,' said Sugg. 'Is there anything I can do for you?'

'Your three friends look like drovers,' said Adam, 'and we're short-handed. We lost a man in a stampede and another . . .' He hesitated. 'If two of your friends could ride with us to Kansas maybe?'

'What do you pay, Mr Carthage?'

'Fifteen a month, and thirty cents a head.'

'Confederate scrip or Yankee dollars, Mr Carthage.' The question was asked without malice, and Adam grinned.

'Depends what Mr McCoy is paying in, for that's where the money'll come from.'

'You hear that, Sweet Jim?' Sugg turned to the men beside him. 'You want to make a fortune? How about you, Driskill?' Sugg winked at Adam. 'Course, they ain't Texans, sir.'

The first man grinned. He was a short, bow-legged hand with sandy-hair and freckles on the back of his hands. 'I'll ride with you, Mr Carthage.' The other man, thin and cold-eyed, just nodded.

'Obliged to you both,' said Adam. 'Mr Sugg, is there any trouble along the Kansas line?'

Sugg's eyes shifted quickly from Adam's face. 'Well, Mr Carthage, there is and there isn't, in a manner of speaking.' He looked back. 'You ought to know, and I'd like to get this beef to Joe McCoy. There are some people up there who say Texas longhorns will bring the Spanish tick to their stock. You know there's some kind of Kansas law against Texas steers coming north?'

'That I've heard,' said Adam. 'How does Mr McCoy feel?'

'Well, I'll tell you, Mr Carthage. He figures that Texans make their own laws where cattle is concerned.'

Adam smiled. 'But somebody figures otherwise?'

'Well, sir, there's a lot of settlers ain't going to like it, but right now they ain't your trouble. There's something else, you see.'

'Jayhawkers?'

Sugg moved his shoulders, as if the word offended him. 'That's a Southern name, Mr Carthage. You see, up there they call themselves Union patriots, like the War was still on. Some have moved over from the Missouri-Kansas line, Mr Carthage, aiming to stop the Texas drives, or so they say. For my money they're road-agents and deserters from both armies. Maybe they'll just take a dollar a head from you, or maybe they'll try to take your whole herd. Or maybe you won't even see them at all. Does this change your mind, Mr Carthage?'

Adam smiled again. 'No, sir, we'll take Estribo on.'

'I guess you will,' said Sugg.

At dawn next day he rode southward. He passed the whole length of the drive with his hard hat raised like an inspecting general, and then he replaced it, waving his hand once to Daly before he rode on. Adam put the new hands, Sweet Jim and Driskill, on swing and watched them for an hour until he was satisfied that they knew their job. Then he rode forward to scout the Salt Fork for a ford.

The river was running high in flood, and rising further with each minute, but Adam found one spot where he thought the herd might cross if it came up in time. He was waiting there when he saw Solace riding towards him. She had split the red skirt and sewn it into wide leggings, and she was sitting on Shelby's saddle astride a blood bay from the *remuda*. A brown and white cowhide vest covered her blouse, and a dark hat was tight-thonged below her chin. Adam recognized the hat as Daly's, and he wondered, with vague irritation, what the boy was wearing.

Solace rode with beautiful ease, and as Adam watched her coming up through the sun and short grass he felt a great movement in his heart. She halted thirty yards from him, her head to one side, and then slowly she rode up. He dismounted and helped her from the saddle.

She pushed the hat to the back of her neck, and her dark hair tumbled out of it. Days of sun had cut tiny lines at the corners of her eyes, and bleached the lashes. He felt dirty, unkempt with the scrub of beard on his cheeks, and the sweat holding his shirt to his back and chest. She stared at him, and then looked away quickly to the river. 'It's fast, isn't it. Can it be crossed, Adam?'

'Probably. But it won't be easy.'

'Has nothing been easy for you, Adam? Since the War, I mean?' He did not reply. He felt in his shirt pocket for his tobacco poke and began to make himself a cigarette. Her fingers touched his arm as she moved closer. 'I rode out to talk with you. But I think I know it all. Johnny's not dead, is he?'

'Sughrue told you?'

'Nobody told me. It's true, isn't it Adam?'

He wanted to tell her now. 'It's true. He's not dead. Or at least he wasn't killed in The Wilderness. But I never said that. I never said he was dead.'

'What happened, Adam?'

'What happens in any fighting, Solace. Nothing you want to remember.'

'But you remember, Adam. Tell me.'

His voice, as it began, was gentle, but then it hardened. 'There had been bad days, with the Yankees pushing us down towards Richmond. We were tired, maybe that was how it was with Johnny. Maybe you should see it that way, Solace.'

'I want to see it as you see it. What did he do?'

'He went over the hill. He deserted to the Yankees. The Brigade was no more than regimental strength. It was lying on the ground, I remember. I remember that because I can still see the flowers in the grass, up close against my face. We were lying on the ground below a rail-fence. Does any more matter, Solace?'

'I want to know.'

'It was hot and quiet. Like it is sometimes in the middle of a fight. We could hear the Yankees talking, way over. One started playing a Jew's harp. It was like we were all on a picnic, except for the smell in the air, and if you lifted your head just that high enough you could see the bodies up ahead. Johnny was lying beside me and he suddenly said, *"I've had enough of this, Adam!"* That's all he said, that he had had enough of it.'

'And then?' she asked gently.

'And then he stood up and put his hands in the air, and he went through the rail-fence, and he walked across to the Yankees. They called out to him. They shouted *"Come on Johnny!"* They meant "Johnny Reb", but it was like they were calling his real name. He shouted for them not to shoot him. They didn't. Nor did we. We didn't believe it was happening.' He looked for surprise in her face, but saw none there.

'Shelby knew? That's why you killed him?'

'No,' he said, 'not for knowing. Other men know, Ben Lake, and I think Sughrue guesses. A lot of men know. I had to kill Shelby because he was going to tell The Old Man.'

'Somebody must tell him.'

'No!'

'You've no right to say that, Adam.'

'I've got this right,' he said bitterly, 'All I am and what I am, even my name, belongs to The Old Man, and I can't hurt him. This right too, from the time we were boys I never let The Old Man see what Johnny really was, that he was no good. Maybe it was wrong, but once begun I had to go on.'

'Adam . . . he knew, he knew what Johnny was.'

'Did you?' he asked, 'You were Johnny's girl.'

'I was . . .?' Her mouth opened, and to his surprise she began to laugh. 'Oh, Adam, you mule! Even Johnny didn't think that.'

'The Old Man does.'

She caught his arm. 'Because he thought I would be good for Johnny, the way you were, Adam. *Adam . . .!'*

He dropped his cigarette and reached out with his hands, catching the girl by the shoulders and shaking her angrily until her hair broke free and blew about her face.

'Adam!' She hit him with her fist, and he kissed her.

Dutchy's wagon topped the rise behind them, and they heard the sharp crack of his bull-whip. He saw their faces as he drove up, and he grinned. Adam took off his hat and waved it above his head with a high, skirling yell. The German halted the wagon beside them and nodded, his head rising and falling, his shoulders shaking.

'Dutchy, get your wagon over, the river's rising bad. Where's the herd?'

'Bout half a mile back. I should wait, Adam?'

'Get over, Dutchy!' The whip snapped, the oxen heaved against the yoke and the wagon tipped drunkenly to the water. The river broke yellow above the wheel-hubs in a froth, and washed over the raised, distended nostrils of the oxen.

'It's going to be bad,' said Adam.

'Adam, answer me! Am I spoken for?'

He took her hand. 'You're spoken for,' he said. 'Get across the river.'

She shook her head and laughed. 'I can't, not now.'

They waited, stirrup to stirrup, and his hand held hers across the space between them. The Salt Fork was growing in volume, yellow with mud and dirty foam, and now it was swinging down young trees and smaller drift. Adam looked at it. The herd would have to swim, and he knew that this crossing was going to be very, very bad.

The lead steers came down to rise with Sughrue and Bridges at point. The cattle had their heads down, horns swinging heavily, close to the ground, and Adam could see that they were tired. He said, 'Solace, wait. Don't cross alone.' And then he rode towards the herd. He called to Sughrue to look after The Old Man and then, with the first steers going by him, he rode over to Jubilo. 'They won't take it, Jube, and we can't turn 'em now. Can you point your *remuda* across first?'

The negro grinned and began to peel his shirt from his back. 'We'll do it, Mister Adam.'

The old yellow mossy horn put its forelegs into the water and then swung away, fighting to get back up the bank, but the pressure behind it was strong. The herd broke its formation and spread along the bank upstream, great horns stabbing. The earth began to crumble and three steers were suddenly plunged into the water. Adam saw the lash of longhorns and then they were gone below the river. Thick dust spread along the bank, hazing all outlines. Out of this suddenly came The Old Man, his sorrel roped to Sughrue's saddle-horn. He was coughing, and he pulled his neckerchief over his mouth as he shouted. 'Is Adam here? Carthage!'

'I'm here!' Adam put his hand on The Old Man's arm. Between his knees he felt the uneasy trembling of his horse as the frightened steers thudded against it. He turned it rapidly and evenly in circles, clearing a space as he shouted, 'Sughrue, get The Old Man out of this!'

More and more of the herd was coming up. Two more steers were thrust from the bank by the crush, and one at least came up from the fall and began to swim to the far bank. Adam saw Bridges suddenly in the dust. 'Curly, take the new hands back and hold up the drag!'

'Carthage!' The Old Man shouted. 'Put the *remuda* over!'

'Sughrue,' yelled Adam. 'Get him out of this, damn you!'

Jubilo was bringing the horses up on the right flank, sitting naked on the back of the grey mare. His black body shone as he called, '*Hep, hep, come away there!*' The horse-herd went over the high bank behind him, black, grey, paint and chestnut, horse after horse with manes and tails blown, flanks braced for the leap into the water.

Naked and shrieking, trunk and shoulders only above the water, Jubilo pushed the grey across the front of the maddened steers where they milled at the water's edge. The mossy horn had now been forced into the river up to its belly, and stood there like a rock, red-eyed. Jubilo swung his rope and caught the steer by the horns. Tightening it, he let the current take the grey like a piece of drift. The rope snapped free from the water and thrummed. Plucked from its feet the mossy horn was dragged into the race. It went under, rose up and began to swim. Up-stream Carlisle had roped another longhorn and pulled it in. One by one at first, then half a dozen at a time, then in great numbers, the herd followed, until the yellow surface of the river seemed thorned by their horns.

Adam turned back, looking for Solace. He found her on a rise, her lips parted, her eyes bright with excitement.

'Scared?' She smiled a denial at him. 'Come on then!' He took her reins and led her horse upstream. He gave her no time for fear but rode with her into the river. He felt the sudden wrench of the current as it jerked the paint from its feet. The pony's head went under and water washed over his own face, then he felt that round, hard-ribbed body rise up. The paint's nose broke the water in a great sneeze, and it began to swim.

Solace's blood bay, to his left, had taken the river badly. It was breathing badly, and Adam realized that Solace had not loosened the saddle-girth. The bay fought for a minute, sighed, and slid over on its right side, the weight of saddle and rider pulling it down. Adam slipped from his own saddle, feeling the drag of leggings, gunbelt and boots, and cursing himself for not having removed them. He dropped back on the length of the reins until his right hand caught, held, and knotted itself in the paint's tail. He let his body float up then, free from the pony's kicking hooves, and with his left arm he caught Solace as she was washed from her drowning horse.

A spar of drift struck Adam on the chest, drove the air from his lungs and forced him below the water. He felt Solace's fingers tighten on his shoulders. Then his head was above the river again. He could see little, the lash of water in his eyes, the reflected brilliance of the sun in every bead. He pulled Solace close to him, and there was a terrible ache in the wound on his back.

Then, suddenly, there was the river-bed beneath his feet, the slip and pull of mud. The pony had found it too, and its body made a great lurch forward. They were in the shallows.

Adam released the tail and, still holding Solace, he crawled and dragged himself up the bank. There he lay on his face, hearing the sighing beat of his breath and the great, lowing clamour of the herd. He turned to Solace. Her white blouse and red skirt clung to her body where she lay on her back, her breast rising and falling. There was mud across her face, plastering her hair to her cheeks, but her eyes were brilliant.

She began to laugh, and he laughed with her.

'Adam, the way you go sparking ...!' And she caught his shoulders and kissed him.

On the high bank across the river, naked except for scarlet drawers, his gunbelt and clothes held above his shoulders, Bridges saw them and raised his voice in a tremendous yell of delight. Still yelling, he put his horse to the river.

Wet and shining, heels kicking, horns swinging, the herd spread out on the great grass plain.

*

Estribo crossed the Kansas line on the thirty-seventh day of the drive, heading for the North Fork of the Arkansas where, if

Sugg had been right, would be found the plough-furrow leading to Joe McCoy's stockyards.

For the first two days of the sixty-mile pull to the North Fork, Estribo saw no one. The rolling, rich grass was marked by groves of orange bowdark trees, and but for these the land spread unbroken to the earth's rim. On the third day was met a party of Osage Indians, men and women, who were amiable enough, demanding only tobacco and a steer, grinning as they threatened to raid the herd if they did not get the gifts. They went away with no tobacco, for the hands had none now, but with two steers.

On the fourth day, soon after dawn, an emigrant train of five Conestogas, led by a greasy scout on a buckskin horse, halted to let the herd pass. There were men in farmers' hats and serge pants, women in poke-bonnets standing in the wagon shade, and children who sucked their thumbs in wonder at the sight of Texas cattle and Texas drovers. *Californy!* was white-washed on some of the water barrels.

And on the fifth day there came trouble.

At dusk Adam was scouting the Arkansas, and had found a ford in a flat basin where the river widened to two hundred yards and fell in depth to less than a foot. He was watering his horse there when three riders came to the north bank and halted, watching him. He mounted and pulled his rifle from its scabbard.

The riders then splashed across the river heading for a clump of trees on his side, and there they stopped and watched again for two minutes. He turned his horse and began to walk it back towards the sound of the approaching herd. He was two hundred yards from the river when the riders broke from the trees and came up on his right. He turned his horse to face them, pumped the lever of his rifle and called, 'Far enough!'

They stopped, and one of them laughed, a big, belly-choking laugh. 'Put your gun up, cowboy! We're friends.'

'You'll have to prove that,' said Adam, and the man laughed again.

'We want to talk, cowboy, and we'd rather do it without shouting.'

'Come on up,' said Adam, 'but keep your hands above the

apple.' They moved in to within fifteen feet. 'Far enough. What do you want?'

The darkness was thickening, and he could scarcely see them. The one who had spoken was a length ahead of the others. He was a big man of impossible breadth between the shoulders. He was wearing a fringed hunting-shirt, a stove-pipe hat and Union Army breeches. There was a scabbard-gun beneath his left leg, and a pistol thrust through his belt. His face was almost hidden by a red beard. The two men behind him were younger and slighter. One wore a hunting-shirt too, and the other an Army shell-jacket. A slouch hat, low on his forehead, threw this third man's face into darkness.

'You with that herd coming up?' said the big man.

'That's right.'

'I'm Docherty. Mean anything to you?'

'Means nothing,' said Adam. He moved the gun so that it was pointing at the big man's chest.

Docherty saw the movement and laughed, a red hole in the red beard. 'It will, cowboy. Soon mean something to all you Texas drovers. Where you from?'

'Estribo on the Brazos.'

'Well, I never heard of you neither, cowboy,' and he laughed again. The rider in the shell-jacket suddenly backed his horse.

'It's like this, cowboy,' said Docherty, 'We're Kansans, and we got to say that Kansans don't like you bringing stock up here and giving our cows Spanish fever.'

'Our steers are clean,' said Adam.

Docherty leant forward. 'Now I'm mighty glad to hear that, I most surely am!' He rubbed his chin. 'You figure you could put that gun down now?'

'It stays where it is,' said Adam. 'Speak your mind if you please, Mr Docherty.'

'You're a mighty uneasy man, cowboy, and that's the truth. However, it's like this. There's a toll on all Texas cattle coming up through the Nations to Kansas.'

'Who's fixing it?'

'Who? Why, me, Docherty!' The big man hit his chest.

'And who do you collect it for, Mr Docherty?'

'Who for, cowboy? Why for Docherty.' He rolled in his saddle.

'Keep your hands above the apple, Mr Docherty.'

Docherty straightened his body quickly. 'For a man so polite, cowboy, you're a mite too suspicious of strangers.' Adam said nothing. 'Look here, cowboy, me and my friends want two dollars a head on every steer you got back there. Pay that and you can take 'em through to wherever you've a mind to go. What's more, for that price I'll see no one else bothers you.'

Adam pointed the rifle at the big man's chest again, inwardly cursing the increasing darkness. 'We'll go through all right, Mr Docherty, and we're paying no toll to Yankee border-thieves.'

Docherty rasped a hand across his chin again. 'That so?' he asked, without offence. 'Now how many men you got back there?'

'Enough, Mr Docherty.'

'I'll tell you, cowboy. I hope you have. 'Cause over the river we got twenty good rebel-hating Yankees who'd like to change your mind for you.'

Adam brought the gun to his shoulder. 'Mr Docherty, the War's over, don't try to start it again here. Get back across the river and take your riders with you.'

The man in the shell-packet pushed his horse forward ahead of Docherty. He said, 'Put down your gun, Adam.' He tipped his hat back with the straight fingers of his right hand and his face was now visible.

'*Johnny!*'

'You know this Texas cow-herder?' said Docherty.

'I know him. You let me talk.' Johnny grinned at Adam. 'Paw with you?'

'He's with us.'

'And still eating fire? You got all of Estribo's spread back there, Adam?'

Adam said nothing.

'I asked you a question, Adam.'

'Try one I'll answer.'

'All right. How's Paw?'

'Do you care, Johnny? He's blind if that means anything to

you, blinded getting cows out of the brush last year. Johnny, whyn't you come home?'

'To what? To fingers pointing at me? To eating dirt for fifteen a month like one of The Old Man's hands. What did you tell him about me, Adam?'

'He thinks you're dead. What are you doing with these jayhawkers, Johnny?'

'Lookee here, cowboy,' said Docherty.

Johnny laughed. 'Put it this way. I decided to be on the winning side. I got tired of losing.'

'I don't like this,' said the big man.

'Nobody asked if you did, Docherty,' Johnny crooked a leg about his saddle-horn and began to roll a cigarette.

'Solace is with us back there,' said Adam, and instantly regretted saying it. It was now quite dark and he could scarcely see Docherty and the other man, but the white splashes of their hands were still above their saddle-horns.

Johnny put the cigarette in his mouth. A match flamed in his hand and Adam saw the young-old face, the soft mouth and the hard eyes. The light went suddenly as Johnny threw away the match. The scent of the tobacco was strong.

'Damn you, Adam! You think I'd go back and crawl to Paw and all you brave Southern veterans.'

'You figure stealing from Estribo is better?'

'I shan't take anything that isn't my own.'

'I told you, Solace is back there.'

'Who?' And Adam realized that the name really meant nothing to Johnny any more.

'It doesn't matter. You there, Docherty, take your men and ride. Don't try to stop us coming through.'

'Adam ...'

'Get out of here, Johnny. I've a mind to kill you.'

Johnny unhooked his leg from the horn and fitted the foot into the stirrup. He gathered his reins. 'Docherty's a man of his word, Adam.'

'You know that about me, too, Johnny. You tell your Yankee friends.'

Johnny laughed. 'Adam, you've got maybe eight, ten hands back there. Maybe less. And tired too, I reckon. Docherty's right, we've got twenty or so across the river. Pay the toll and we'll let you through.'

'If it means anything, we've got less than ten dollars between us. Our money's on the hoof.'

Docherty laughed. 'Then we'll take it on the hoof, cowboy. Every steer you've got.'

Adam raised the gun again, and levelled it at Johnny this time. 'I should have killed you, Johnny, that day you walked over to the blue-coats. I'll kill you now if you push me. So ride, damn you!'

Johnny turned his horse slowly, looking back over his shoulder. The light of his cigarette, as he drew in his breath, sharpened the grin on his lips. 'Talk it over with Paw,' he said. 'We'll see you tomorrow.' And then they were gone.

Adam waited, listening to the sound of hooves dying to the splashing as the three riders crossed the river, and then there was silence.

*

By moonrise the herd was bedded down below the sand-hills that separated the river from the grassland. The grazing was rich, and Adam was glad that the cattle no longer strayed at nightfall as they had done early in the drive. When they were watered it was now easy to close-herd them, and they settled down within the half hour. The moon was full and white. It rose two handsbreadths above the horizon and drew long, dark shadows from the sleeping steers. Adam put three men on the first night-guard – Carlisle, Daly and Bridges – and when they saw the tightness of his mouth they did not ask him why two of them, or even one, would not be enough. But he saw the question in their eyes and he said, 'There's trouble coming. If it comes tonight it'll be from across the river.'

Bridges jerked at a cinch-strap, slapped his horse on the flank and put a foot in the stirrup. He looked over his shoulder. 'You care to say what trouble, Adam?'

'I'll answer that. Jayhawkers.' Adam went back to where the horses were rope-coralled by the water. He called for Jubilo, and the negro came out of the darkness. 'Cut me out a good night-horse, Jube.'

'I get you the black with the white blaze, Mister Adam. Walks like a high-toned lady. You sleep up there and he'll bring in the strays on his own.'

'Make your choice, Jube, I'll rely on it.' He went back to the fire, and silently took his coffee and sow bosom from Dutchy. He sat on his saddle, watching the flames. He knew that Sweet Jim and Driskill were looking at him curiously, and that, from somewhere in the shadows behind, Solace was also watching. He drank the last of the coffee and put the cup on the ground. He stood up and began to strap on his leggings. When he had done this he looked at the two cowhands across the fire.

'You've a right to know this, and do what you please about it. You're not Texans, you're not Estribo riders, and I can't ask more than your job. There's border-thieves across the river and we've trouble coming from them.'

The sandy-haired man, Sweet Jim, grinned and said, 'We saw them on the way down with Willie Sugg. Told us to hurry on and bring you drovers up. A big man called Docherty?'

'The same,' said Adam. 'You can ride off now if you wish, both of you.'

Sweet Jim grinned again, and Driskill turned his sour, dark face upwards, twisting his lips as if the suggestion had somehow poisoned him.

Adam said, 'You're welcome to think on it. But if you decide to ride out, ride south, and ride before dawn.' He picked up his saddle and turned away towards the *remuda*. By the wagon Solace caught his arm and spoke his name softly. She said nothing more, but her eyes searched his face, and he looked away from them to Sughrue who stood behind her, chewing methodically. 'You heard what I said, Sughrue?'

'You seen these men, boy?'

'I saw three of them here before the herd came up. A big man, a Yankee by name of Docherty, is their leader. He said he had twenty men across the river, and for two dollars a head they'd let the herd through. Or they'd take the herd. The choice is ours, and we've got till tomorrow to make it.'

'Twenty?'

'So he said. But I don't know. I'm riding out now to make sure.'

'Not alone you ain't, boy. I'll come too.'

'Saddle up, then,' said Adam briefly. Now he turned to face Solace. On a sudden impulse he dropped the saddle and held her by the shoulders, a gentle grip at first that tightened as he felt her body trembling beneath his hands. 'There's more than what I've told you, Solace. Johnny's with them over the river.'

'Johnny?' she said. 'Why ...?'

'Why?' he repeated. 'Could you ever ask why about him? But he's there. He's older and he's harder, but he's still Johnny. Do you still think I should have told The Old Man?'

She came close to him, locking her arms about his waist. 'Now he'll find out this way.'

He said, 'No, he'll not see Johnny. I want Johnny dead and I'm glad The Old Man is blind. I could have killed Johnny tonight. Tomorrow, maybe I shall kill him.'

She raised her hand quickly and put it over his mouth.

Sughrue came back, a saddle dragging from his right hand, a rifle in his left. 'Ready, boy?'

'Johnny's with Docherty over the river.'

Sughrue said nothing. He looked sideways to the earth and spat.

'All right, you old fool,' said Adam. 'So you knew he wasn't dead.' He turned aside from Solace and then halted abruptly. Standing erect and hatless, with the firelight jerking shadows across his face, there was The Old Man. One hand reached out before him.

'*Adam ...!*' whispered Solace.

'Carthage!' The word dragged itself in pain from The Old Man's throat.

'I'm here, sir.'

Ferguson took a step forward. He stumbled, regained his balance and cried, 'Let me be!' although no one had moved to help him. He said, 'Where is he? Where's Johnny?'

'He's not here, Mr Ferguson.'

'But he's alive, isn't he. I heard you wish him dead, Carthage, but he's alive isn't he? This time you'll answer!' He pushed aside the skirt of the duster, a trembling hand pulling at his gun. The hammer caught in the linen, tearing the cloth noisily.

'John!' said Sughrue. 'Put up the gun.'

'Stay away from this, Sughrue. I want this answered, Carthage. You answer me or I swear by the Book I'll kill you!' He raised the gun before him on a straightened arm. It pointed away to the night-darkness.

'Put up your gun, sir,' said Adam with great gentleness. 'There's no call for it.'

'Answer me!'

'Put your gun up,' said Adam again. 'Put it up and I'll tell you. You can use it then if you wish.'

Ferguson's right arm dropped to his side. 'I must know!' he said.

Adam stepped forward quickly. He took the gun and he stood there, surprised by the anger that suddenly rose within him, thickening his voice. 'I'll tell you. Because you've heard half of it you've a right to the rest. I killed a man to keep the grief from you, and now I tell you. You've got to understand what that means!' He wanted to take The Old Man's shoulders in his hands, and the strength he needed to resist the impulse put a great harshness in his voice. 'Johnny wasn't killed in the War. He deserted to the Yankees before Spottsylvania. He went over to the Yankees with his hands in the air.'

It was said, and he watched The Old Man's face. He watched the muscles relax at the corners of the mouth, the cheeks falling, the whole sad, tired face melting. *'Johnny!'* cried Ferguson in great agony.

Yet there was more to say, and Adam heard his own voice as if it were coming from another man's throat. 'I've lived with this for more than three years, and I kept it from you because of what I owe you. I've taken from you what no man would take, because of what I owe you. I killed Shelby, because of what I owe you. But now you've got to hear it all. Johnny was no good, before the War, during the War. He was never any good.'

'He is my son!'

'He's your son. He's your son and he's across the river with border-thieves. He's your son and he'll rob you. And he knows you're blind. Now here's your gun, you can use it if you wish.'

Adam held out the gun and saw that it was shaking in his hand. Sughrue stepped forward and took it, thrusting it into his waist-belt. 'Boy,' he said unhappily, 'did you have to do it that way?'

'I didn't choose it,' said Adam.

A great sob burst from The Old Man. He lifted his head and he stared sightlessly at the sky. He cried out, '*For this my son was dead and is alive again! He was lost and is found!*' Without lowering his head he lifted his hands and covered his face with them.

Solace went to him. 'Mr Ferguson,' she said, 'Poppa Ferguson, *please*!' She took him away.

Adam picked up his saddle. 'Let's ride,' he said harshly.

They rode across the shallow river to the north bank. In the moonlight Sughrue found it easy to follow the trail. The three border-thieves had turned to the north-west, across high grass country that was corrugated by shallow draws. Along the bottoms of these the stalks of last summer's sunflowers were like palisades, tall and white and broken. Adam and Sughrue rode for two miles, and when they lost the trail they kept riding to the northwest, and they did not speak.

Then Sughrue's horse whinnied. He swore and put a hand over its nostrils. There was an answering whinny from over the ridge. 'They're there, boy.'

'Maybe,' said Adam. 'Maybe settlers, maybe a Cheyenne hunting party. Maybe anybody.' He dismounted, unstrapped his spurs and hung them over his saddle-horn. He pulled out his rifle and began to walk up the rise. Three yards from the top he dropped to the ground and crawled the rest of the way. The grass had been scorched by a recent prairie fire and its scent was strong below his face. When Sughrue joined him they lay there and looked down. At first they could see nothing. After the moon's silvered night the draw was dark, but slowly the glow of a fire blossomed below, and in its light other details took shape. There were horses there, unsaddled and loosely corralled. Adam counted them, and counted them again. 'Twenty?' he asked softly.

There was a pause and Sughrue grunted. 'Eighteen, twenty. Hard to say.' There was a ring of shoe on stone. 'Not Indian ponies,' he said. 'Not settlers neither, too many horses and no wagons.'

'Soldiers?'

'See no sentries, boy, and that horse-line's too bad even for Yankee cavalry.'

'Then we've found them,' said Adam.

Wood cracked and fell in the fire below, and a spiral of sparks spun upward. Three men were sitting beside it. Away to their left, beneath a stunted tree, lay a semi-circle of blanket rolls. Adam counted again. 'Twenty,' he said.

Sughrue took off his cap and wiped the sweat-band with the palm of his hand. 'Blamed sure of themselves!'

One of the men by the fire lifted his head and tilted a bottle above it, holding it there for a few seconds before he threw it across the stream. It broke on a stone and the man laughed. It was an unmistakable laugh. 'Docherty,' said Adam, and Sughrue spat.

Adam studied the draw carefully, as if he were drawing a map of it in his mind. It was shaped like a long, steep-sided spoon, and at the far end it flattened to meet the plain. There the stream widened and ran on into darkness. Adam closed his eyes and built the scene in his mind, then he opened them to see where he had been at fault. This he did several times until, with eyes closed or open, he could see it all plainly – the fire, the horses, the sleeping men, the dark stream and the stunted tree, the patch of scrub to the right, the smooth grass walls of the draw rising up.

Docherty stood up. He yawned. He scratched his thighs and arm-pits, and lurched towards the sleeping men. There he seemed to sink down into the darkness. Adam touched Sughrue's shoulder. They slid back and walked down to the horses.

Adam said 'What do you think?'

Sughrue rubbed his hands down his hips. 'Twenty, and ten of us. Take out Dutchy and The Old Man leaves eight. Seven since you got to leave a man on the herd. Then there's Sugg's riders, so maybe we're only five.'

'Maybe,' said Adam, and he mounted and turned the black towards the river. As they splashed across it forty minutes later the rim of the moon was already breaking the edge of the plain. From the trees on the south bank the lever of a rifle clacked and Daly's thin voice called 'You stay put, I'm a right nervous man!'

They halted and the water rippled below them. Adam smiled but Sughrue shouted angrily 'Daly, you darn fool!'

The boy broke from the cover of the trees, his horse's hooves hitting great fans from the water. 'I swear I didn't know it was you, Adam.'

'Get back,' said Adam, 'We're safe for the night. Send Curly and Carlisle in.'

When Adam rode up to the fire Sweet Jim and Driskill were rolled in their blankets beside it, but they heard the sound of his spurs as he alighted, and they sat up. Sweet Jim grinned. Adam walked across to them. 'You've made a choice?'

'We'll ride with you,' said Driskill, and it occurred to Adam that these were the first words he had heard the man speak.

'I'm obliged to you,' he said, and he turned away to find Solace. She was crouched by the tongue of Dutchy's wagon, a blanket over her shoulders, her arms gripped tightly below her breasts. She was not asleep, and she stood up quickly when he approached. He could still marvel at the grace there was in her movements. 'The Old Man?' he said.

For an answer she pointed. Ferguson was sitting on a saddle beyond the fire, his hands on his knees, his eyes staring beyond to the darkness. 'He's said nothing since you left, Adam. He's sat there, all the time.'

'I could have told him some other way, but there wasn't time. He gave me no time.'

She took his hand. 'He knew what Johnny was, it made no difference. You hurt him by not telling him when you came home.'

'I couldn't know.'

'Are they coming, Adam? Is Johnny coming?'

'No, they're not coming. But we can't wait for them.'

When all the hands, with the exception of Daly, were gathered about the fire, Adam squatted on the ground and with a broomweed stalk he drew a map of the border-thieves' camp in the dust. 'There are twenty of them,' he said. 'There's a fire here, and their horses are along the stream her, not hobbled but roped. There are no guards out.' He looked up at the faces above him but saw no change of expression in them. 'They've been drinking, particularly the big man, Docherty. Maybe to a man like him that makes no difference, and he'll still sleep light.'

'So now?' said Bridges.

'So now I'll need all of you, even Daly. We'll have to leave the herd. If it strays it won't be across the river. Dutchy can stay with Miss Norton and The Old Man, but the rest will ride with me.' He looked up at the sky. The moon had set. 'We'll get there before dawn if we ride soon.' He broke the stalk between his fingers and looked carefully at each face. 'Anyone who thinks I'm playing a hand with my eyes shut can say so. I'll not hold it against him.'

They said nothing, and he looked down to the map again. 'They'll be nothing without their horses, just men with liquor in them. You'll have to drive off their horses, Curly. Come in here from the east, through the brush, and drive them down to the mouth of the draw. They'll break the rope easily. If they don't you'll have to cut it.' He marked the brush with his finger in the dust. Then he drew a line down from the top of the map. 'Sweet Jim, you and your partner'll circle round and come down on them from the slope here. Carlisle, you and Daly from the west, but let the horses through when Curly gets them running. Sughrue and Jubilo and I will ride down the south slope.'

He stood up. 'I want a lot of noise. I don't want killing lest you have to. I want their horses running, and I want the fear of hell put in them.' He brushed a foot across the map. 'All right. Sleep while you can. I'll rouse you.'

He walked away from them, to the darkness on the far side of the wagon, and it was there that Solace, with a quick rustle, moved against him. He put his arms about her, his hands moving across her shoulders.

She said 'Years ago I tried to say this to you, and you wouldn't let me say it. You thought I was asking you to look after Johnny. Now I'll say it. Come back, Adam, come back to me.'

'I'll come back,' he said, and left her.

He rode about the herd in a circle. The steers were quiet, and he collected Daly from the river's edge and returned. The rest of the men were ready and awaiting him. Driskill, the dark man, was pushing shells into his gun and scowling. Adam saw The Old Man in the saddle, on the sorrel by the wagon, and he walked his horse across. 'You can't come, Mr Ferguson.'

'I am coming, Adam.'

'Understand me,' said Adam. 'This isn't going to be easy, and I can't afford men to look after you. Stay here.'

'This is my herd, and these men are riding my brand. I don't ask them to do what I won't do with them. You ride for me, too, Adam Carthage, so it'll be as I say.' The words were words he might have used a month ago, but now there was no harshness in them.

Adam turned his horse to face the others. 'Sughrue,' he said, 'and you, Jube, look after Mr Ferguson. Mount up!'

'Wait a minute, Adam!' The sorrel came forward on high, pretty steps at The Old Man's urging. Ferguson took off his hat and raised his head. He said *'God is our hope and strength, a very present help in trouble. Therefore we will not fear, though the earth be moved.'*

'Amen!' called Jubilo.

'Adam,' The Old Man put on his hat, tightened the thong, and pulled down the brim. 'We're ready to ride.'

*

There was a greyness along the eastern horizon when they reached the draw, touching men and horses with uneasy light. It was late. It was almost too late, and Adam was impatient. He sent Sweet Jim and Driskill away to circle the draw to the north, warning them to come down quickly on the camp when they heard his yell and a rifle shot. Carlisle and Daly and Bridges went off to the west and the east with the same instructions. When they had gone Adam climbed to the rise and lay there, looking down at the camp. He could see little. The fire was no more than a spark now, and the draw was in darkness. There was a restless movement from where the horses stood, and a man's snore, but these were the only sounds from below. In the great bowl of earth and sky about him, however, Adam could hear the plains life awakening, a rustling, a murmuring, the faint, cautious cries of birds. It was late. It was almost too late. He went back.

'Adam,' said The Old Man softly, 'Is it time?'

'It's time, sir. We'll ride to the top of the rise. Stay here. You must stay here below.'

The Old Man said 'Sughrue, are you there? Rope your pony to mine, and to Jubilo's on the other side of me. Rope me between you both.'

'Let it be, Sughrue,' said Adam. 'He stays here.'

'Hold your tongue,' said Ferguson, as if he were talking to the boy Adam had once been. 'This will be as I say.'

The light was rising quickly. To the east grey had turned to pink. Sughrue shrugged his shoulders, spat, and moved over to the sorrel. He unhitched the rope-strap on his saddle-tree, and passed the coils of the rope through his hands. He began to whistle softly.

'Sughrue,' said Adam. 'You'll not do this damn-fool thing. Do you hear me?'

Sughrue's whistle sharpened, but he did not reply. He took three dallies of the rope about the horn of his saddle and made it fast. He leant over with the free run and turned it about The Old Man's horn and tossed the slack to Jubilo. The negro silently made it fast. The horses moved restlessly. *'Sughrue!'* said Adam. 'Do you hear me?'

Sughrue looked at him with a crooked grin. 'I ride for Mr Ferguson, Adam. He's The Old Man.'

'Jubilo,' said Ferguson. 'You remember my son's face?'

'Yes, sir, I do.'

The Old Man's voice was firm. 'Then if you see it this morning you pay no mind to it. Do you understand.'

'I hear you, sir.'

'Is that rope fast, Sughrue?'

'It's fast, John.'

'Then we're ready, Adam,' said The Old Man.

Adam gathered his reins. 'All right,' he said. 'Come on!' He touched a spur against the black horse's flank and pointed it up the rise. Behind him the three horses jerked against the rope that joined them, and then followed. On the ridge Adam looked to the east. The sky was now reddened by the approaching sun, red moving to pink, moving to grey, moving to indigo as the sky arched to the west. Below, however, all was a cold grey. He could see the bottom plainly, the metallic twist of the creek. A thin strand of smoke curled up from the near-dead fire. Three men lay beside it, one on his face, the other two on their backs with arms outstretched. None of them was Docherty. By the tree was a humped group of bodies.

It was time to ride down, Adam knew this, but he waited. He waited and he watched the opposite rim of the draw where the grass moved. He looked for Sweet Jim and Driskill. The grey light below became blue and then pink. He saw Bridges' horse appear momentarily before it passed into the brush, with the cowhand bending low in the saddle, a rifle in his right hand.

In the rope corral below a mare threw up her head and whinnied. A man sat up beneath the tree, kicking aside his blanket and scratching himself. Adam looked anxiously to the far rim where there was still no sign of Sweet Jim or Driskill. Thin mist was knitted to the higher branches of the tree below. The man stood up from his bedroll, still scratching with his right hand as he shuffled towards the fire. The mare whinnied again, and behind Adam the sorrel answered. The man below quickly straightened his back, looked up, and saw Adam. He opened his mouth to shout. At the same time the Sugg riders topped the rise.

Adam yelled, pointed his rifle to the sky and fired. He put the black horse down the slope, yelled, and fired again. He saw Sweet Jim and Driskill coming down the other side, dust trickling away at ground level behind them like smoke from a windless fire. To the east there were four quick shots and a curdling Rebel yell as Bridges broke out of the brush, riding at a gallop for the border-thieves' horses.

The men who had been asleep started up from their blankets, to their feet or on their hands and knees, some stumbling, at least two running quickly towards the horses. But Bridges was there before them, his rope flailing. The horses surged to the left, to the right, broke through the corral in a wave to the west.

These things Adam saw fragmentarily as he rode down, and

heard the sharp, splintering noises, and then he was at the bottom, the black horse rising and leaping the stream, coming down on the white ash of the fire. There were shouts, shots, the scream of frightened horses and the drubbing of hooves. The horse-herd went across Adam's front with manes and tails streaming, and with Bridges hurrahing them on, a bandana across his mouth, the front brim of his hat blown up.

Adam heard Docherty's great bull-roar, and then eight shots from a rifle, one after the other quickly. A horse squealed to his right, and he heard the thud and slither of it as it went down. He turned in the choking dust and rode towards the sound of shots. Sweet Jim rolled from beneath the black horse's hooves, that extraordinary grin stupidly and miraculously still on his face. There was a gun in his hand, and he thumbed back the hammer and fired, at no apparent target.

The dust blew away, and there was Docherty, his red mouth open and his tongue yelling through his beard. He was bootless and hatless, but he was standing firmly astride and he held a rifle halfway to his shoulder. He pumped the lever and fired into the dust, swinging the barrel this way and that until the hammer clicked emptily. He threw the rifle away and tugged a gun from his waist as Adam came upon him. He fired one shot that hit the rearing black horse in the chest.

The animal coughed, and went slowly to its knees. Adam kicked his feet free and fell on his side. He saw Docherty grin and he saw the gun levelled again. Then, out of the dust came Driskill, easy in the saddle, and swinging a rifle by the barrel. Like a child lopping the head of a flower, Driskill calmly swung the butt against Docherty's head. It struck the base of the big man's skull, and there was a noise like a pumpkin being punctured. Docherty flung his arms wide, his mouth closed. He staggered forward three steps and fell on his face.

Driskill twirled the rifle in the air, looked down at Adam with his sour grin, and rode on.

The Old Man had come down the hill between Sughrue and Jubilo. He had turned the reins about the sorrel's saddle-horn and gripped this with his hands. He knew from the grey haze before his eyes that it was now daylight, and for the first time since his blindness he had no wish to see. He heard no sound from Jubilo on his right, but to his left he heard Sughrue richly profaning. He drowned this with a great cry of his own.

'Thou hast covered my head in the day of battle!'

The three horses went through the stream and into the mill beyond it. Roped together so strangely they were unmanageable, and Sughrue made no attempt to control them. Jubilo, however, yelling hysterically, gathered his reins, pulled back his horse's head, and thus swung all three of them in a wide curve.

Then Sughrue saw Johnny. In shirt and breeches, gun in his hand, the boy was running away from the camp, up the draw to the east, making for the shelter of the brush. Before he could reach it however, Carlisle rode across his path, firing at him.

'Carlisle!' yelled Sughrue. *'No!'*

Johnny ducked, turned, and ran back. He halted, rubbed at the dust in his eyes, and ran on clumsily. He ran straight into Sughrue, Jubilo and The Old Man. Sughrue instinctively pulled in his horse to the left, but Jubilo tried to turn to the right. Each horse was checked by the drag of the other two, and the three of them fell back with forelegs flailing. Jerked against the cantle of his saddle The Old Man was saved from falling only by the grip of his hands on the horn, but the spurs on his swinging boots raked the ribs of the horses on either side.

What followed then could not have taken more than a few seconds, yet to Sughrue it seemed to unfold itself slowly and leisurely. Johnny looked up at the riders, saw and recognized his father, a recognition that momentarily broke the hard tightness of his face. He straightened his back. The sorrel's right foreleg struck him on the chest, pawed and struck again, this time on his face.

'Jubilo!' shouted Sughrue. 'Cut free!' He slashed at the rope with his knife. It parted, and he felt his horse stumble forward over Johnny's body. Sughrue dropped out of the saddle.

Now the noise was dying and the dust was settling. Sughrue knelt beside Johnny, and he looked, and he swore softly and bitterly. The sorrel turned away, with The Old Man swaying, and it cantered up the draw. The Estribo hands were riding back, one by one, the border-thieves were scrambling through the brush or up the grass slopes. There was one more shot as

Adam killed the black horse. Then he went over to Docherty's body. The big man was dead.

Sughrue wiped his hands over his cheeks and was surprised to find that they were wet. 'Adam!' he called.

Adam came to him, and he looked down at Johnny's body. 'He's dead?' he asked incredulously, as if he had not, a few hours before, wished to kill Johnny himself, as if what had been fiction for so long could not now be fact.

Sughrue wiped his face again and stood up. 'It was the sorrel.'

'So be it!' said Adam.

'But, boy, it was The Old Man!'

'No,' said Adam. 'We don't know how Johnny was killed. Tell Jubilo that Sughrue, and remember it!'

Bridges came riding in, waving his hat above his head, standing in the stirrups and yelling. He shouted to Adam 'Them horses won't stop running till they reach the Salt Fork!'

'Sughrue,' said Adam. 'Burn everything. Saddles, blankets, burn it all.' He turned away and walked towards The Old Man who, brought back by Daly, had dismounted and was stroking the sorrel's neck soothingly and whispering to it.

'It's over,' said Adam. 'We've done it. We've run off their horses and we'll burn their gear. We've run them off, too. They won't bother drovers any more.'

The Old Man lifted his head and wiped his lips. He said 'Is anyone hurt?'

Adam looked about him. 'None of Estribo.'

'You know what I mean, Adam.'

'The big man, Docherty, he's dead.'

'Is he the only one?'

'No. Johnny's dead, too, Mr Ferguson. I'm sorry.'

For a long while The Old Man said nothing, and in that silence his hand continued to stroke the sorrel's neck. Then he said 'Answer me truly, Adam. Did you kill him?'

'No sir. We found him back there.'

'I'll not have a lie now, Adam. You said you'd kill him. Would you have done?'

'I can't answer that, sir. I don't know. But I can say this now ... I don't wish him dead.'

The Old Man took his hand from the sorrel's neck. He

stretched it out towards Adam and then withdrew it quickly. 'Thank you, boy.'

The jayhawkers' gear was burning. Daly and Carlisle had built up the fire, and piled on it the blankets and saddles. The smoke rose in an oily black column, pulling away to the south-west. The air was strong with the smell of scorching leather.

Two graves were dug beneath the tree, and Docherty and Johnny were buried there. The graves were covered with stones, and over Johnny's Adam placed a thick branch from the tree. With a red-hot cinch-iron held between two green sticks he burnt Johnny's name on to the branch, and below it he marked the Estribo brand.

'Is it done,' said The Old Man.

'It's done,' said Adam, and rose to his feet.

'Face me towards the boy's grave,' said Ferguson, and Sughrue took his arm and turned him gently. 'I'm going to speak the Word. None of you need join me if you haven't the feeling for it. But this was my son, and the only child of my wife, and I shall speak the Word over him.'

Nobody moved. A horse sneezed, a breath of wind moved down the draw and scurried the dust at the feet of the standing men. The Old Man cleared his throat. He took his Bible from the pocket of his duster and held it tightly between his hands, so tightly that the veins rose up against the thin brown skin.

'For as the heaven is high above the earth, so great is His mercy towards them that fear Him.'

He halted, and Jubilo called 'Amen!'

'Like as a father pitieth his children so the Lord pitieth them that fear Him, for He knoweth our frame. He remembereth that we are dust.'

'Amen!' said Jubilo again.

The Old Man put on his hat. His fingers did not tremble as he returned the Bible to his pocket. 'Adam?'

'I'm here, sir.'

'Will you ride back with me, son?'

At noon, two days after the crossing of the North Fork, Adam found Joe McCoy's plough furrow. It ran straight to the north across the plain, turning a black lip of Kansas earth.

He dismounted and sat on his heels in the shadow of his horse, making himself a cigarette and waiting for the herd to come up. His spirit was moved by the sight of it, this lowing, dust-coiling, horned snake that Estribo had driven more than eight hundred miles. The good feeling that was in him rose to his throat and demanded release. He stood up and yelled, although the point-riders were still too far away to hear him. The empty air took his cry and lost it in the grass, the long, rolling, treeless grass. He mounted, and, still yelling, rode down at a gallop towards the flank of the herd where The Old Man was riding with Solace and Sughrue.

There he turned his horse beside Ferguson's right stirrup. 'We're there,' he said. 'The furrow. A day's drive along it, Sugg said, will bring us to the railroad.' As if he did not believe he could be understood he bent forward to look into Ferguson's face. 'We've done it. We've taken Estribo through!'

The Old Man said nothing, but he lifted his head.

'Sughrue,' said Adam. 'Noon 'em.'

Sughrue whirled about and rode back down the herd, slapping his horse with his cap and shouting the news. One by one as he passed them, the hands began to call, high cries as they waved their hats.

Adam looked across The Old Man to Solace. She shook her head and placed a finger on her lips. He took Ferguson's bridle and turned the sorrel off the trail. He moved in until his knee was touching The Old Man's saddle-fender.

'Adam?'

Ferguson's hand fell on his shoulder, gripped it, released the hold and then grasped more tightly. Adam leant over and put his arm across The Old Man's back, and thus linked they rode.

Adam looked to Solace again. Her hat hung down her back and her dark hair was free. Her head was high on her neck and she was smiling. She was also crying.

The Long Hate

Martha Boyd was the first to see the rider. She was making starch from potato-water settlings. She was standing by the window at the back of The Boyd House when she looked to the west and saw the rider.

He was a long way off, perhaps four miles, maybe more, and he was like a fly on the yellow earth. Martha watched him for ten minutes, her body relaxed in her cotton dress and her brows drawn together in a frown. Now and then she pushed two fingers at her pale hair where it clung with sweat to her cheeks. The rippling heat played tricks with the rider, moving him up and down like a leaf on a creek, but at the end of ten minutes he seemed to be no further from the blue mountains and no closer to Salt Flats.

Martha thought awhile of telling her father, but in this heat it scarcely seemed worth it. In any case, the men on the veranda would see the rider soon, if they had not already seen him. She gave the bowl of settlings a twist with her hand, and then looked away from the rider to the old Hallady wind-pump on the edge of town. Boyd had ordered it from Illinois twenty-three years before, when he and the rest of Salt Flats believed that the drovers would pass through every summer on their way to Denver. Water and whisky were always important to drovers, and Boyd had set up a plank-bar and a wind-pump to supply both at a price.

Martha Boyd could not remember the drovers, but she could remember her mother talking about them. The dust of the cattle moving, said Mrs Boyd, would hang over the valley like the cloud in the Book of Exodus, with the sun rolling red inside it. The cowmen came for a season or two, and never again, finding free water and a sweeter trail along the bottom-lands of a river far to the east. But Salt Flats went on believing that they were sure to return one day. Mrs Boyd used to say that this would never be in her lifetime, and she was right. She had been dead for sixteen years.

Beyond the pump was Cemetery Hill, and when Martha looked at it from the window now and then, like this afternoon, it was her mother's grave she really saw. It was the best grave in town, with a stone marker and a white rail-fence, and a glass bowl of china flowers that had come from Illinois too.

Martha poured the water from the settlings, tested the gluey mess with her fingers, and wiped her hand on her apron. She glanced once more at the rider, and couldn't be certain that he had come any closer. Then she went through to the front of the house.

'Rider coming, Paw,' she said.

Her father did not turn his head. He was in his shirt-sleeves, leaning on the bar and staring out to the white light of the sun. Two men were playing checkers in the coolest part of the room. The batwing doors were tied back and Martha could see three more men out there on the veranda, feet on the rail, hats over their eyes. Their shirts were black with sweat.

'You see the rider, Paw?'

A chair creaked as a man on the veranda turned and squinted into the saloon. It was Mr Harvey. He always sat on the veranda to drink his beer. In the same place every day where he could keep an eye on Harvey's Corn and Feed across the street, and next to it Harvey's General Merchandise, and next to that Harvey's Ladies' Emporium. If a man wanted to annoy Nathan Harvey he had only to say that the three weatherboard buildings wouldn't make one middling-sized store back East.

He was a thin, brown man, and most of his teeth were missing, but what he had left he showed now in a yellow smile. 'We seen him,' he said.

'Who do you reckon it is, Paw?' said Martha, as if her father had answered.

Boyd looked at her and, as always, betrayed himself by the look. A man who had come West on a gamble, intending to make a fortune in a new town across a cattle trail. Brought his wife, too, like most men, and like most men he had planned raising sons along with his fortune. But there was only a daughter who looked too much like the wife who was dead. Salt Flats had remained a small town of false-fronts along one dusty street, with less than seventy people and only half a living to be made out of the sheep-farmers up in the Mogollons. It was all there in the look which Boyd gave his daughter.

'Now, how do I know?' he said. 'You done your chores?'

'Yes, Paw.'

'Then set in the shade and cool.'

Martha took a chair and put it near the door where she could see the rider coming, and where she could see the forge at the end of the street. She hoped that she would see Jason there, but there was no sign of him. There was not even the sound of his hammer on the anvil. Salt Flats brooded silently in the sun, and the dogs yawned on the boardwalk.

Her hands loose in the lap of her dress, Martha read the sign above the forge – *Jason Fletcher, Blacksmithing, Shoeing and Wagon Repairs.* She repeated the words again and again to herself, making them important.

At last Nathan Harvey eased one boot on the rail and said 'What do you figure?'

He was talking about the rider, that was plain, but it was a long while before anybody answered, before John McGill the saddler moved his back against a veranda chair and said 'He's riding a burro.'

'Ain't an Apache then,' said the third man out there. Martha knew from the wheezing voice that it was Old Reuben, the express agent.

'When *they* come,' said Harvey, 'you won't see them. Not till they're here.'

Martha suddenly wished that the Apaches would come. For as long as she could remember, that was all her remembering life, Harvey or some other man had been saying things like that. As if any day, any hour, there could be Indians in Salt Flats, whooping and riding like they did in the pictures on a seed calendar.

'And you'd see a mountain-cat sooner than an Apache,' said Harvey, his eyes on the rider.

He always said that, too, and Martha waited for his third and inevitable observation on the subject.

'Can't think what the Government's at,' he said.

She remembered that Harvey was saying these things the year she put her hair up, and that was a long time ago now. Nobody ever contradicted him, nobody ever disagreed, and Martha, remembering something more, thought that Mr Harvey could be right even now, long after.

The stranger who was playing checkers with Martin Schurmann lifted his head. 'What's that?' he said.

He was a drummer, travelling with ladies' goods. He had come in on the Lordsburg stage the day before, making a stop-over on his way to Holbrook. Nobody thought fit to tell him, until the stage had gone, that there wouldn't be another for six days. He had accepted the situation philosophically, figuring he might at least open up his pigskin bags to the owner of Harvey's Ladies' Emporium. His samples included ivory-handled curling-irons, amber hairpins, hip-bustles and bust-pads filled with swan's-down, satin drawers and petticoats embroidered with the ace of hearts. Harvey said there wasn't a woman in Salt Flats with the gall to wear those things, more's the pity, so the drummer had become a customer instead, buying a dollar's worth of Harvey's twofer cigars.

But Martha had been in the store when the pigskin bags had been opened, and the sound of the drummer's voice now made her think hotly of their contents.

'What's that about Apaches?' he said.

Harvey turned his chair to stare into the saloon. 'We said it ain't an Apache.'

'You expecting Indians?' said the drummer. He saw Martha looking at him, and he smiled at her boldly, inviting her to share his amusement. But he held the smile on his face too long for politeness, and she turned her head away quickly.

'I heard the noble savage was now on a reservation,' said the drummer. 'Surely? About ten years now, isn't it?'

Nathan Harvey spat. 'Noble savage?'

'A figure of speech, friend.'

'You weren't here,' said Harvey. 'Not in the old days. Not when Victorio was loose in the Mogollons. *You* weren't here.'

'No,' said the drummer, puzzled. 'No, that's right, of course.'

'You're damned right it's right!' said John McGill.

The drummer took his hand from a checker. 'Is there something I ought to know? About the Indians, I mean.'

Nobody answered him.

'I mean,' said the drummer. 'You aren't scared of them, not now?'

Martin Schurmann rapped a knuckle on the table. 'You touched that checker,' he said. 'You got to move it.'

'All right,' said the drummer, and he moved the piece.

It was the heat, Martha knew. The heat, and the dust, and the loneliness. And the town not being anything, and all. That kept alive the hate, like the reason for it had been yesterday.

Martin Schurmann cackled as he picked up a checker and leapfrogged across the board. 'You lose!'

'Yes,' said the drummer, and then, looking about him, 'You haven't told me ...'

'It's Keno,' said John McGill.

Harvey nodded. 'Reckoned it was.'

Boyd came from behind the bar, pulling up his shirt-sleeves where they were gripped by garters. He walked to the door, put a hand across his forehead and stared at the far rider. 'It's Keno sure enough,' he said. 'He'd better have money this time.'

Harvey looked at the drummer and sucked a tooth. 'Being from the East, you wouldn't know.'

'Know what?' asked the drummer.

'How we feel about Apaches.'

Boyd turned away from the door and walked slowly towards the bar, but the drummer caught his sleeve and held him. 'What's this about Apaches, Mr Boyd?'

Boyd looked down at the young man, frowning heavily, but before he could answer Martha spoke up lightly.

'Folk in Salt Flats are always worrying about them. Like it was years ago. But's there's only ten of them in the hills, and nobody ever sees them. They don't bother nobody.'

Boyd turned to her, his face empty. 'You shut your mouth!' he said.

He looked back at the drummer. 'They killed her Maw. You'd think she'd remember that, wouldn't you?'

'Killed my boy,' added Harvey without emotion.

'That's too bad!' In the drummer's voice there was a rush of genuine sympathy.

'Now you see?' said Boyd.

But the drummer was puzzled. 'This was a long time ago?'

'It don't seem it.' Boyd went back to the bar and poured himself a beer, drinking it sourly.

And in the heat and the silence Martha wanted to cry, because what her father had said was true, and perhaps what they all believed about the Apaches was true, and because at times like this she felt the hate in Salt Flats as if it were a blanket over her face.

Harvey pulled the palm of his right hand across the back of his neck, and then wiped it on his shirt. 'Damned heat!' he said. 'Takes the juice of kindness out of a man.'

'It's Keno, sure enough,' said John McGill.

'Who's Keno?' asked the drummer.

'He's late this year,' said John McGill.

'He'll get nothing to drink here.' Boyd eased his shoulders and put the weight of them on his elbows. 'Less he's got money this year.'

'Who's Keno?'

Nobody was going to answer the drummer, and Martha felt sorry for him. 'He's an old man. He's a prospector. He spends all the time in the hills but he's never found nothing.'

Boyd looked at his daughter. 'Girl, you got nothing to do but just set?'

Martha got up and walked through to the back of the house. Through the door she heard the drummer say 'But if it was years ago, and there's only ten of them up there . . .'

And Harvey's voice, pitched high. 'They're Apaches, ain't they?'

'Yes, but . . .'

'Man gets rid of snakes when he finds them, don't he? Burns out loco weed when he can? We ought've done that with them. When the cavalry moved out of the Mogollons.'

'When was that, Mr Harvey?'

'Twelve year ago.'

'Fifteen,' corrected John McGill.

'That's a long time to go on hating them.'

'Who asked you, Mister?'

Martha moved across the room and sat by the starch bowl. Again she wanted to cry, and she told herself that it was just the heat. But Salt Flats was always like this, every year when the heat was bad, and the land just desert dust.

Outside, Keno came down the street with the sun behind him, his legs sticking out on either side of the burro, and his skillet and panning-bowl clanking on the animal's flanks. He stopped in front of The Boyd House, wiped a hand over his dirty beard and looked up with sad eyes.

'Hot, ain't it?'

John McGill nodded a greeting. 'Hello, Keno. You're late this year.'

'I ain't. You folks is early.'

'What do you mean by that?'

'You got nothing to do in this town but count the time. You count too fast.'

Keno got down from his burro and stood by the rail, scratching himself thoroughly from groin to arm-pit. Then he stepped on to the veranda, peering into the shade of the saloon, waiting. Boyd came to the batwings and stood there, one gartered sleeve blocking the way. 'You got money this year, Keno?'

'You know I never got no money, Boyd. I'll trade you my panning-bowl for three beers.'

'No,' said Boyd, and he went back to the bar. He shouted back, 'And stay out there, Keno. You stink of that damned burro!'

Keno grinned and sat down on the boards. He was willing to wait. When he thought he had waited long enough, he said 'Mr Harvey, you gonna buy an old pocket-hunter a beer? Just one beer?'

'No.'

'How about you, Mr McGill?'

'My woman's going in your store, Nathan,' said McGill.

Harvey got up and went across the street wearily. When he came back, five minutes later, he sat inside the saloon, for the walk across the street had made him hotter still. It had made him a little angry, too, and when the drummer, setting up the checkers for another game, spoke up again about the Apaches, Harvey snarled at him. '*Mister*, you never seen them!'

'I saw some at Taos, selling blankets.'

Schurmann cackled. 'Them's Pueblos. You don't know.'

'He don't know,' agreed Keno, from outside.

'You shut up,' said Harvey. 'You desert rat!'

'Buy a desert rat a cool beer, Mr Harvey?' Keno got up from the boards and came inside the saloon.

'Keno!' said Boyd, 'I told you. Stay outside!'

Keno moved back to the door and stood there. 'Friendly town, this,' he said, and looked at the drummer. 'You going to buy me a beer, Mister?'

'Well ...' said the drummer.

'No, he ain't,' said Boyd. 'I've told you, Keno.'

Keno narrowed his eyes. 'Everybody telling me. Nobody saying Hello, Mr Keno, what you seen out there in the hills.'

'Nobody cares,' said Boyd.

'You was talking about Apaches. Every year I come you're talking about Apaches,' said Keno. 'Like they was about to call. Like in the old days.'

'Well?' said Harvey.

'Buy me a beer?'

'No.'

'Then I don't tell you nothing.'

'You got nothing to tell,' said McGill.

'Like they was coming,' said Keno, his voice quickening. 'Well, I tell you, *they is!*'

Nobody moved or spoke for a moment or two. Keno smirked, and scratched himself.

'Keno,' said Boyd at last, 'that ain't no joke.'

'It ain't no joke,' agreed Keno.

John McGill took his feet off the rail. 'What's he say?'

Keno grinned at them. 'I'm dry,' he said.

Boyd straightened his back. 'Keno, if you're just after a drink ...'

'You don't want to know. All right!' said Keno.

'Boyd,' said Harvey. 'Give him a beer.'

'And a shot of John Gideon to follow,' said Keno. 'Bad beer needs a good whisky to smarten it up.'

But Boyd brought the beer only, holding it out to Keno. 'Nathan,' he said, 'you paying for this?'

'I'll pay for it.'

Keno took the beer and poured it down his throat in one throw of his head. He wiped his beard, licked his moustache with his tongue. 'I'm obliged,' he said.

'What about the Apaches?' said Harvey.

Keno shook his head. 'I'm still dry. I got desert dust right down to my guts.'

'You'll have another beer when you've told us.' Harvey stood up. 'Now, what is it?'

'I seen 'em,' said Keno, 'whooping and killing.'

'Who?' said John McGill.

Keno thought for a moment, scratching. 'That young buck. Chiquito. And a couple of others.' He looked at Harvey and whined. 'How about that shot of John Gideon, Mr Harvey?'

Harvey looked away from him to Boyd. 'What do you figure?'

'You telling the Gospel truth, Keno?' said Boyd.

'I seen 'em. I told you, didn't I?'

'You're a liar.'

'All right. Mr Harvey, if you can't run to whisky I'll take another beer.'

'You'd better be telling the truth.'

'You know I am,' said Keno, aggrieved. 'Ain't you been talking about it, all these years? Ain't you going to believe it when it happens?'

'When what happens?'

'I sure am dry.'

'Put up another beer,' said Harvey to Boyd. He took it from the bar and held it out to Keno. The old man stretched a hand towards it, but Harvey drew the glass back.

'Any other man,' he said in anger, 'would tell a thing like this. You got to be bribed.'

'I'm dry,' said Keno. 'Can't talk when I'm dry, can I?'

'You say what you know,' said Harvey furiously, 'or I'll pour it on the boards, and you can lap it up there.'

The drummer stood up. He was suddenly and unpleasantly alarmed. 'What is it?' he asked, but he was ignored.

'What did you see?' said Boyd to Keno.

'Up in the hills. You know where Matt Bowyer and them's been herding sheep?' said Keno. 'There. They was at his place. Give me the beer now, Mr Harvey.'

'What were they doing at Bowyer's place?'

Keno sighed and wiped his mouth. 'I come over the bluff, figuring maybe Mrs Bowyer might have a bit of bacon or flour. Then I saw it.'

'*Saw what?*' Harvey tilted the glass and some of the beer struck the boards at his feet, becoming little beads powdered with dust.

'No call to do that, Mr Harvey.'

'What happened, you old fool?'

'I saw Chiquito and the others. All painted up. And yelling. You know the way it was.'

'We remember,' said Boyd heavily.

'I saw Matt Bowyer and his wife coming out of their house, and their kids with them. Matt Bowyer had a gun held in his hand, and a rag, like he'd been cleaning it. Didn't seem like he was expecting anything.' Keno looked longingly at the beer.

'Go on, damn you!'

'Well . . . This Chiquito give a yell, and he and the other two started running down through the brush at the Bowyers. They let off their guns.'

'What did you do?' asked Boyd.

'I lit out. Fast. You want I should've stayed?'

There was a silence as the men in the saloon looked at each other. Keno reached forward and took the beer from Harvey's hand, and drank it gratefully. Then he wiped his mouth.

'Like the old days again, ain't it?' he said.

Harvey's voice was slightly hysterical. 'I been telling you! All these years I been saying it. Now it's happened!'

John McGill said 'What we going to do, Boyd?'

The drummer cleared his throat cautiously. 'But can you believe the old man?'

'Now, look here . . .' began Keno resentfully.

Harvey turned on the drummer, spittle springing from his lips. 'What you talking about? What you know about it? You ever had folks killed by them?'

'No, but . . .'

'All these years hating them,' shouted Harvey, turning to Boyd, 'and doing nothing. Letting them live.'

'But there's only three,' said the drummer.

Boyd eased his neck. 'Three's enough to kill the Bowyers. Three's enough to pull the rest off the agency if they get away with it.'

'What're we going to do, Boyd,' asked McGill again.

'Keno,' said Boyd. 'You swear?'

Keno looked at them all, and thought carefully. 'I swear,' he said. 'Anyway, you go see for yourself.' The suggestion seemed to amuse him.

'All right,' said Boyd, 'it's happened.'

Harvey began to shout again. 'I always said . . .'

'We hold a Town Meeting,' interrupted Boyd. 'Here. Tonight. Nathan, you tell them. Everybody.'

The drummer sat down on his chair again, in the shade. It seemed to be hotter than ever, and blood throbbed at his temples excitedly.

'Nathan,' said Boyd as an afterthought. 'You tell Fletcher. You tell him first. He's got to do something.'

'Who's Fletcher?' asked the drummer, his voice too casual. But nobody answered him.

*

Martha Boyd sat in a corner during the Town Meeting. Now and then she looked across the room to Jason, and once he smiled to her reassuringly, and the smile was a bridge between them across the smoke and the heat and the hate in the room.

There were nigh on fifty men and women in the saloon, a whole Town Meeting, their faces sallow in the light of the Rochester hanging-lamp above the bar. They had been there an hour and done nothing but shout their fears at each other. The men were drinking whisky, sitting apart from the women whose faces showed a prim disapproval. Some of the men, like Harvey, had brought guns with them, as if they expected Chiquito to come into Salt Flats that night, and they sat with the guns across their knees and the light of the lamp winking on the metal.

Keno snored outside on the boardwalk. He was not needed any more. But the drummer sat among the other men, one of them for all his hard suit and Eastern voice. His face was flushed with excitement, his thumbs tucked into the arm-holes of his vest as he tilted back his chair. He felt he shared the hate of these people and their fear.

'What we going to do?' said John McGill for the tenth time. And, just as before when the question had been asked, the women whispered and rustled and drew together, like chickens in a run when there's a dog outside the wire.

'I told you,' said Harvey, and his face was wet with sweat, and red with the raw whisky he had been drinking. 'We go up there, all of us. In the morning, and we find them and we do what's got to be done, that's all.'

Ted Meriam, who was lay preacher as well as carpenter and undertaker, hawked in his throat. 'The Lord said vengeance is mine ...'

'What's that supposed to mean?' shouted Harvey.

'The Book says ...' began Meriam.

'The Book says an eye for an eye,' said Boyd, and he looked hard at Meriam. 'You weren't here in the old days.'

This was what everyone was told who hadn't been in Salt Flats since the beginning, and Martha saw how it shut them up, as if they were afraid of being left out of something, even though it was only hate and fear.

'You'll take us after them, that right, Jason?' asked Harvey, 'you being Town Constable.'

Martha's eyes went to Jason Fletcher, and she saw how he scuffed his boot-heels on the floor, and stared down at them. She saw the strength of his shoulders beneath the hickory shirt, and she loved him.

'You made me Town Constable, that's true,' said Fletcher at last.

'Now you got to do something,' said McGill.

'On account of nobody else wanting the job,' finished Fletcher, as if he had not heard McGill. 'I think we ought to tell the Army.'

'Army's a hundred miles away, or more,' said Harvey. 'It's up to us.'

Now Fletcher looked up. He was puzzled. 'To do what?'

'Ride out and clean up the Apaches. All of them.'

'What for?'

Harvey began to splutter. 'My boy was twelve when they took him and killed him.'

'I know, Mr Harvey,' said Fletcher gently, 'but that was eighteen, twenty years ago, wasn't it?'

Harvey stared, his blue eyes wide and his mouth open, as if he did not believe this. He looked quickly at his wife and then back to Fletcher. 'You heard what Keno told us.'

'I heard it, Mr Harvey. But I ain't heard nobody say we should find out if it's true.'

Harvey took a step towards him. 'You afraid, Fletcher?'

'No. And I ain't drunk neither.'

Harvey turned to his wife. 'Go home, Sarah,' he said, 'we don't need you. We know what to do.'

And McGill nodded to his wife, and other men to theirs. The women got up, their skirts rustling, their faces turned in hard doubt and fear towards their men. The drummer, full of the whisky's courage, saw how frightened they were, and wanted to tell them that he would be there to protect them. But his tongue was too thick in his mouth.

Boyd turned to his daughter, and looked at her. 'Get out,' he said.

She rose, and she was not angry with her father for the way he spoke to her in front of the whole Town Meeting. She saw the bitterness in his face, and she was sorry that she could not tell him that she understood. He was thinking of nothing now but her mother, of finding the body alone, and of seeing what Victorio's men had done to it.

'Yes, Paw,' she said, and she left the saloon and went to the back of the house. She sat by the window in the darkness. She heard the wind-pump creaking in the small night-breeze, and she thought of the water below the dry crust of the land, maybe gurgling and fighting to get up to the trough, and not quite making it. Yet it was so hot, even with the wind, and the heat brought anger against the men inside. She heard their voices rising now and again, angry, shouting voices.

For an hour more she sat there, listening, until she heard footsteps outside the window, and Jason's voice said 'Hello, Martha.'

'They've not finished,' she said.

'They'll be all night. They're too drunk and too frightened to be alone.'

'What are they going to do.'

'They want to go out in the morning. All of them. Even the drummer. He's buying drinks for everybody and talking about the time he put in the militia back east.'

'Are you going with them, Jason?'

He did not answer her. 'It's twenty years since there was any trouble with the Apaches.'

'Sixteen,' she said. 'Maw was killed sixteen years ago.'

'They talk like it was yesterday.' He turned his shoulder to her, looking into the darkness. 'It's the heat and the dry land, and knowing this town's nothing, and always would've been nothing. They have to hate something.'

'They remember . . .' she began to say.

'I know what they remember,' he interrupted harshly. 'We've been told it since we were kids.'

'Are you going with them?'

'They're all drunk in there. I don't know them. That drummer acts like everything he ever read about the West has come true. And your father . . .'

'It's on account of Maw.'

'I know,' he said.

'Is Mr Harvey going?'

'He's going,' said Fletcher. 'He's talking big about going. He's talking like his boy was just killed. And John McGill, he's never talked about his brother for years, but he is now. But it's your father that scares me.'

'Everything he's got is here.'

'He's only got one thing I crave,' said Fletcher. 'Martha, you leave here with me. When this is over. You promise that, now, will you?'

'Paw . . .' she began.

'What holds you to him? The way he treats you . . .'

'He's alone, Jason. And grieving still.'

'You don't owe him your life, just because your Maw's gone. Anyway, it's sixteen years.'

'I ain't going to leave him, Jason.'

He went so silently that she was not aware that he had gone until she called his name softly three or four times. Only the wind-pump creaked an answer. So she went to her room and sat on her bed, listening to the arguing and the shouting in the saloon. Once she heard her father come to the back of the house to get more bottles. She heard the clink of them beneath his arm, his uncertain step and his heavy breathing. She thought she could not sleep, and even though her eyes were closed she could see Salt Flats like it was day, with the sun hot on the dust and the grey boardwalks.

But she did sleep, for when she next opened her eyes it was really day, and the dawn was rosy on the far wall. She stared at the old Currier and Ives print that hung there, people skating on a river somewhere in New England, and the sun was so strong on it that morning that it did not make her feel cool as it did most days. She got up, and she threw cold water on her face. She dressed, tying back her hair with a ribbon because she was too much in a hurry to put it up with pins. Then she went through the house.

The saloon was stale with the smell of liquor and tobacco. Her father was lying on his back behind the bar, with his mouth open and his shirt unbuttoned to the waist.

'Paw, do you want some coffee?'

He opened his eyes and sat up slowly, knuckling his right hand and rubbing his skull with it. Then he looked at her. 'No,' he said, and reached for a bottle.

She walked across the room. The drummer was sitting upright on a chair against the wall, and his eyes followed her without expression. She went outside to the day, squinting at the light, and looking down towards the forge.

Jason was coming, leading his apron-faced roan, and its hooves and his feet kicked up little spurts of dust. He had a pistol stuck into his waist-band and he was carrying a rifle in his hand. He came to the hitching-rail and he looked up to her with a faint smile. Then, slowly, he looked about the empty street, and the smile became twisted.

'Well ...' he said, but he did not seem surprised to find nobody there but Martha.

The drummer came out on to the veranda. His face was very pale and he put a hand against the wall to steady himself. He said 'Where are the others?'

'What others?' Fletcher pushed the rifle into the saddle-boot.

'All of them ... They said they were going.'

Fletcher swung himself into the saddle, the leather creaking, and he looked down at Martha. 'Good-bye,' he said.

'Wait a minute,' said the drummer hoarsely, 'you're not going alone?'

'You see anybody else?'

'There's me. I said I'd go.'

'It don't need nobody but me.'

'You need everybody you can get!' Boyd had come to the door. He had put a black vest over his shirt, and a soft hat on his head. He had strapped on a gunbelt.

'I don't need nobody to ride with me to the Bowyers,' said Fletcher, and then after a pause. 'Thank you, Mr Boyd.'

'Get inside!' said Boyd to Martha, but she did not move.

'Where can I get a horse?' asked the drummer.

Fletcher sighed, and leant forward in the saddle. 'You want to come? Everybody else is scared. No call for you to come.'

Martha looked across the street and, for a moment, she saw Harvey's white face at a gap in the curtain above the Emporium.

'There's a mule down at the forge,' said Fletcher. 'It's John McGill's. I saddled it for him, but I guess he ain't wanting it.'

'Will I need a gun?'

'No.'

'You know everything?' asked Boyd thickly. 'Give him a gun. You got two yourself.'

Fletcher took the pistol from his waist and handed it to the drummer silently.

'A mule you said? At the forge?'

Fletcher nodded, and watched as the drummer walked down the street with the gun held self-consciously in his hand.

'Get inside, Martha!' said Boyd again. 'What do you want out here? Do you want to see how the town's shaming its dead?'

'No, Paw.'

'Never had no mind for your Maw's memory, all these years.'

'Mr Boyd . . .' said Fletcher quietly.

But Boyd ignored him. 'You close up everything, you hear, Martha? Don't sell nothing.'

'No, Paw.' She looked at Fletcher and went inside.

Boyd put a hand into his waist-band and stared up and down the street, his eyes hot and sad. '*You damned cowards!*' he suddenly shouted.

He listened, and waited, as if expecting a reply, and then he shouted again. 'Ain't one of you thinking what they did? Ain't one of you?'

Fletcher straightened his back. 'You coming, Mr Boyd?'

Boyd licked his lips and took his eyes from the empty street. 'All right,' he said, 'I'll get my horse.'

Martha watched from the door of The Boyd House as the three men rode out. Fletcher first, then her father, and then the drummer straddled uncomfortably on the mule, his derby hat bobbing and his collarless neck very red. She watched them, her hand held across her brows, and she felt the growing heat of the morning thicken about her. She did not turn her eyes from the riders until she heard a scuffling in the dirt.

There were Nathan Harvey and John McGill, and Martin Schurmann the barber, and Old Reuben, all of them red-eyed and the night's beard rough on their cheeks. They looked towards the distant riders and then at each other.

Harvey was the first to speak. He swallowed the spittle in his throat and brought a hand down the stubble on his jaw. 'Mrs Harvey was against it,' he said, as if somebody had asked him.

'And Mrs McGill,' said John McGill.

They looked at Schurmann. 'She's been on about it for two, three hours,' he said, 'saying some of us should stay, lessen the Apaches come down here.'

Old Reuben grinned at them. 'Having no woman,' he said, 'I got to say it. I'm too scared. Or too old. Or both.'

They looked up to Martha. 'You opening up today, Martha?' asked Harvey.

'No,' she said, and went inside.

It was a long way to the sheep pastures. First, the desert floor on which Salt Flats stood like a skeleton of sun-whitened wood. Then the rise of raddled hills, stippled with viper cactus and Spanish bayonet. And above them, still to come, the high valleys rich with blue-spiked grama grass. The drummer had not known there was such country, nor yet how long it could take a man to cross it. Before noon the loping stride of the mule had galled his thighs and knotted his back with pain. No one spoke, the heat was dry in their mouths. The only time there was talk was when the drummer asked Fletcher how far they had to go. Fletcher looked from the shadow of his hat and smiled a little.

'Twenty, thirty miles. Maybe more.'

'That far? How close is the Bowyer's place?'

'Twenty, thirty miles. Maybe more.'

'We won't get back today?'

'Did you figure we would, mister? There's a blanket on your saddle. Gets cold at nights up there.'

'But I thought . . .'

'Can't you shut up?' said Boyd, as if the conversation had lasted an hour instead of less than a minute. The drummer fell back into silence, enduring the sweating grip of his derby, the iron press of the pistol at his waist, the jerking agony of the mule.

At noon they dismounted and took shade in a ravine. Fletcher uncinched his saddle, laid it carefully on the ground so that the skirts picked up no dust, and then went to sleep against it, or seemed to, for he pulled his hat over his eyes and lay still. Boyd walked a way up the ravine, his gun in his hand, and he stood for a long time on a rock, looking at the country about him. The drummer moving with difficulty and with pain, came to Fletcher's side.

'Mr Fletcher,' he said, 'what is Mr Boyd looking for?'

Fletcher pushed back the brim of his hat and looked. There was no expression on his face. 'For Apaches, I guess.'

The drummer's sudden alarm was in his voice. 'Are they here? Are they about us, then?'

'Boyd figures they might be!'

'But you, Mr Fletcher, what do you think?'

'I think you ought to sit down, rest a mite, Mister.'

'Thank you.' The drummer sat down, but he was not at ease.

'This Chiquito, Mr Fletcher, do you know him?' And, when Fletcher nodded shortly, 'What's he like?'

'Young. Maybe nineteen. Kind of short, like Apaches are. Speaks English good. Bit of Spanish, too. I'd say that was pretty good for a noble savage, wouldn't you?' There was no smile on Fletcher's face, but the drummer felt he was being laughed at. He took off his hat and wiped his forehead. The pain in his back made him wince.

'I told you not to come,' said Fletcher unsympathetically, and pulled his hat over his eyes again.

After half an hour Boyd came back from the top of the ravine. He thrust his toe into Fletcher's ribs. Fletcher opened his eyes, but he did not move. 'Ain't no sign of them,' said Boyd, 'but that don't prove nothing. You going to lie there all day?'

'Just so long as it takes the stock to freshen up, Mr Boyd.'

'You never had no drive, no push.'

'Mighty useless things to have in Salt Flats,' agreed Fletcher.

The drummer sat forward, sensing the undercurrent of hostility between the two men.

Boyd said 'Always lazing, no sand to raise a bit of hell. You reckon I'd give Martha to a man like you?'

Fletcher stood up, taking his time. 'I'll let Martha make up her own mind, Mr Boyd.'

'She ain't got no mind on this. It's my say-so.'

'You come out here to fight with me, Mr Boyd?'

'I come out here to catch them Apache murderers. Now, are we moving on, or do I go alone?'

Fletcher looked at the sun and then at the horses and the mule. 'We move on,' he said. 'Should be up in grass by nightfall. Then we'll make the Bowyers by mid-morning.'

'What do you expect to find there?'

'The Bowyers, I hope,' said Fletcher.

They mounted. Boyd pulled his horse about viciously and faced Fletcher. 'I said there ain't no sign of them. There ain't, not here. But you saw them birds go up couple of hours back?'

'I saw them.'

'Well, then?' said Boyd, inviting comment.

'Could've been nothing,' said Fletcher., 'Let's ride.' And he moved his horse forward and upward, one hand holding the leathers high.

The drummer kicked his mule up to Boyd as they rode. 'Is it true, Mr Boyd? Do you mean they're watching us?'

Boyd looked at him with disgust. 'What did you come for? What good you figure to be?'

The drummer's face tightened. 'There was no one else. I mean ...'

'You're a fool.'

'No, sir, I'm not!'

'We'll see. Ain't over yet. You ever fired a gun?'

The drummer straightened his back. 'I took a little practice before coming West, sir. I was advised by ...'

'I'll tell you,' said Boyd. 'You see an Apache, if only his back, you point that thing and fire. Then you ride that mule back and over him. Then you let me come and kill him.'

'Yes, sir,' said the drummer earnestly. He looked about him. The heat played fantastic games with the blue hills and the red land, as if the drummer saw them through a rippling film of water. 'I had no idea ...' he began.

'Just shut up!' said Boyd, and pushed his horse forward.

By dusk they reached the high tableland. The drummer felt the cool air, and breathed in the scent of grass, and watched the day pass in a colour that made him homesick. As the sun went down they unsaddled in a gully where there was water and a knotted tangle of oak. The drummer took off his hard hat and climbed up to the rim of the gully, welcoming the mountain wind on his face.

'You're a fool all right,' called Boyd from below. 'You *want* to be seen?'

'No, sir,' said the drummer, and he slid hastily down into the gully. 'I didn't know.'

'And that's a fact!' Boyd turned to where Fletcher was building a fire. He went across and kicked the sticks apart angrily. 'You sending up a calling-card, Fletcher?'

Fletcher looked at the scattered sticks and he stood up, slipping the matches into his pocket. 'Have it your way, Mr Boyd.'

Boyd looked at the gathering darkness and was silent for a

while. He turned then to the drummer. 'It was a night like this,' he said, 'time they took my wife. She was coming home in the buckboard.'

'Yes, Mr Boyd,' said the drummer sincerely. 'I understand.'

'You don't understand nothing,' said Boyd, the confidence quickly regretted. He picked up his rifle. 'I'll take first watch,' he said to Fletcher. 'You and me'll have to go turn and turn about.'

'There's me . . .' began the drummer.

'Not you,' said Boyd shortly.

'All right, Mr Boyd,' said Fletcher. 'If you want it that way.' And he turned his body into his blanket.

The drummer lay on the ground, his eyes open, staring up to the stars and the sky. He heard Fletcher's steady, untroubled breathing, and once the clink of a spur against a stone from where Boyd stood in the darkness. It was a long time before he slept, nor would have said that he slept at all except that one moment there was darkness, and the next moment Fletcher was pulling at his shoulder. The sun was up.

'All right,' said Fletcher, 'rouse out.'

They drank brackish water, ate dried beef and sour bread, because once more Boyd insisted on no fire. It seemed to the drummer that the big man had now taken command, and that although Fletcher had allowed him to do this it was not in fear. They rode on with Boyd in the lead, his face hard and his eyes swinging from side to side. He breathed between his clenched teeth, his lips drawn back.

'Mr Fletcher,' said the drummer, pushing to the young man's side. 'Will I be of any use to you? I mean . . .'

'You came, didn't you?' said Fletcher shortly. 'Don't see none of the other loudmouths here except Mr Boyd, do you?'

'What is it between you two? Forgive me for asking.'

'Nothing. There's nothing.'

An hour later, Boyd suddenly halted his horse, looking over his shoulder as the others came up with him. *'Listen!'* he said, and held up his hand.

They heard laughter, voices and laughter mingled, and they smelt the sharp scent of burning wood. Then there was a high, throbbing yell that bounced back and forth across the walls of the little valley. The drummer looked at Fletcher in alarm. The young man's face was quite still.

'You hear that, Fletcher?' said Boyd in a thick voice.

'I hear it.'

'It don't mean nothing to you?'

'It's Apaches, if that's what you mean,' agreed Fletcher.

His face red with anger, Boyd opened his mouth to speak again, but instead he kicked his feet into his horse and pushed it up the rise. Fletcher sighed and followed. The drummer tried to say 'Wait for me!', but the words were dry and soundless in his mouth. The mule moved after the horses of its own accord.

At the top of the rise the drummer put a hand across his brows to break the glare of the sun. Below, a wood fire smoked lazily, grey-white threads climbing about a tripod of green sticks. There were three young men by the first, two of them not much more than boys. When they heard the riders they turned, looking up, and for a moment white men and Apaches stared at each other.

The Indians were butchering a sheep. The dirty fleece lay on the earth, and the carcass was slit open. The knives in the hands of the Apaches were red with blood, and there was blood on their arms too. They wore thick blue shirts and skirts of gaudy calico. Their legs were gaitered in buckskin to the knees, and their harsh black hair was held back from their eyes by sweat-bands. The drummer saw all this momentarily only, and if anything held his attention longer it was a woman's sun-bonnet, pale blue and with starched wings, that lay on the ground near the fire.

The oldest Apache, a muscular young man with short arms and heavy shoulders, frowned up at the white men. Then he saw and recognized Fletcher. He smiled and stepped forward.

'*Sikisn!*' he said. 'Brother!'

'Hello, Chiquito,' said Fletcher.

A strange sound came from Boyd's throat, a desperate intake of air like a sob, and he lifted his rifle, pumping the lever. Sudden alarm erased the smile on Chiquito's face and he cried a warning '*Ugashé!*'

The two boys behind him obeyed immediately, but as they

turned to run the valley thundered with the discharge of Boyd's rifle. One of the boys slid down into the fire silently, a red stain expanding across the back of his shirt. The other boy ran on into the bush like an animal. Chiquito did not move, but he looked hard at Fletcher.

Boyd swore again, and he pumped the rifle. He stood in his stirrups, taking careful aim at Chiquito.

Still looking at Fletcher, the Apache said, *'Sikisn?'* And Fletcher leant over and pulled the rifle from Boyd's hands. For a moment the drummer thought that the Town Constable was about to strike the older man with it.

'Fletcher!' yelled Boyd wildly.

'Chiquito,' said Fletcher, 'look to your friend.'

The Apache pulled the body from the fire, and knelt beside it, slapping out the smouldering shirt with his hands. Then he stood up.

'He is dead,' he said, without expression.

'I'm sorry.'

'Why you come, *sikisn*?'

'Chiquito, it's said that you and your friends have killed Mr Bowyer and his family.'

'Give me that gun, Fletcher!' Boyd stretched out a hand, but Fletcher backed his horse away, still looking at the Apache.

'Are you going to kill me too, *sikisn*?'

'No. How about the Bowyers, Chiquito?'

The Apache's face was cold. 'We have killed nobody' He looked at the dead boy and he looked at Boyd. 'But he kill Pa-nayo-tishn. You see. You take *him*, Fletcher.'

'I want that gun!' yelled Boyd.

Again Fletcher moved his horse from Boyd's reach. He said 'Chiquito, you come with us to the Bowyers. We'll see what this is all about.'

The Apache nodded towards Boyd. 'You will hang him for Pa-nayo-tishn?'

Fletcher breathed in deeply. 'Chiquito, don't make trouble.'

The Apache sneered. 'Kill deer, kill Apache. All the same.' He looked at Fletcher. 'If I run now, you shoot me?'

Fletcher leant forward wearily. 'Chiquito, if you run you know what that'll mean.'

'If I stay, he will shoot me.'

'Chiquito, don't make trouble. We've got enough.'

'I make trouble nowhere.' The Apache folded his arms. 'No kill.'

'He's a damned liar!' shouted Boyd. 'You lying snake, where'd you get that sheep? Where'd you get that sun-bonnet?'

'From Bowyer –'

'You're damned right you did!'

'Chiquito,' said Fletcher sadly, 'we've got no spade. We can't bury your friend. You want to pile rocks over him?'

Chiquito looked down at the dead boy impassively. He shook his head. 'My people come soon.'

'He's right there,' said Boyd. 'Fletcher, you want to stay to be butchered?' He looked about him wildly.

'All right,' said Fletcher, 'let's get on to the Bowyers.'

'You!' said Boyd suddenly to the drummer. 'Give me that pistol!' Before the drummer had understood the words the big man had pulled the weapon from his waistband and cocked it.

'Fletcher,' said Boyd, 'we ain't going anywhere but back to Salt Flats. That one you let get away will have the whole bunch of 'em down on us if we go further.'

'We're going on to the Bowyers,' said Fletcher calmly.

'You try that,' said Boyd, 'you just try that and I'll shoot him down before you go a foot. We're taking him back to Salt Flats, which is more of a chance than he gave the Bowyers.'

'You're a damn fool, Boyd!'

'Maybe so, maybe not. But I aim to stay a live one. Now, I mean it. We go back to Salt Flats or he's a dead Indian right now!' He put the gun on the Indian, who looked up to him calmly.

'*Sikisn*, he is a bad one.'

'You shut up, you hear?' shouted Boyd. 'You just shut up right now or maybe I won't even bother to take you back.'

'We've got no reason to take him yet,' said Fletcher.

'We got Keno's story of what he seen. We got them with one of Matt Bowyer's sheep and Mrs Bowyer's sun-bonnet. Now, how about it? You want him dead right here or not?'

'Chiquito,' said Fletcher, 'will you give me your word not to run?'

The Apache glanced at Boyd before answering. 'I can trust you, *sikisn?*'

'You know that, Chiquito.'

'Then I will come.'

Boyd took a rope from his saddle and dismounted, walking towards the Apache with the pistol still pointed. 'Turn around, damn you!' he said. 'And put your hands behind your back.'

Chiquito looked at Fletcher, who leant forward sharply. 'There's no need for that, Boyd. He gave his word.'

'He gave his word to you, not me. And I wouldn't believe it if he had.' He jerked the gun. 'Turn around, like I said!'

'Mr Fletcher,' said the drummer cautiously, 'surely it's wiser. I mean, on account of ...'

But Fletcher interrupted him. 'Boyd, let him be!'

Boyd pulled back the hammer of the pistol and pointed it at Chiquito's head. He grinned. 'How's it going to be, Fletcher? I'd as lief it was this way.'

The Apache looked into the pistol for a moment, then calmly turned his back, putting his wrists together behind him. Boyd tied them brutally, then returned to his horse with the free end which he turned about his saddle-horn. He mounted, jerked his horse about, and the Apache fell. Boyd laughed.

Chiquito rose with dignity, one side of his face white with wood-ash.

Boyd laughed again. 'Got his war-paint on, ain't he?'

'Boyd,' said Fletcher, 'I'll not forget this.'

'You coming back to Salt Flats with him, or you going to stand jawing here all day?'

'Chiquito ...' said Fletcher.

'It is all right, *sikisn*.'

'I want to know. What happened at the Bowyers?'

The Apache's face became cold, and he did not answer.

'Let's go!' yelled Boyd, and he heeled his horse forward suddenly. The Apache was jerked to the ground again, and dragged over the dead body of the boy. Fletcher rode forward, grasping the bridle of Boyd's horse and pulling it to a halt. The Apache got up.

'Boyd ... You do that again and I'll kill you!'

Boyd grinned. 'You kill Martha's paw? Not you.' But he

moved forward gently this time, the Indian running after, to keep the rope slack.

Fletcher turned a hard face to the drummer. 'I want you as a witness of this.'

'Of what, Mr Fletcher?'

'Of what you've seen. Don't you understand?'

'If you wish, Mr Fletcher.'

'All right!' Fletcher lifted the reins and moved his horse on after Boyd. And the drummer, following them, thought that he must be dreaming.

Martha Boyd sat in darkness at the back of The Boyd House, but outside the window, down the length of the street, there were lights everywhere. The sound of voices in the saloon had started at dusk and grown in volume since. She heard the deep baying of her father's voice and she shivered. He began drinking four hours ago, just after he had brought the Indian into town. Everybody had come to their doors to watch, and the children had danced and yelled. At first Martha had wanted to laugh, and then only to cry. The Apache had been covered with dust and dried blood. There had been nothing frightening, nothing dignified about him. Her father had pulled him the whole length of the street, like he was taking a calf to the slaughter-pen, yelling and jeering. Then Jason had cut the rope and taken the Indian to the forge.

Martha remembered it all very clearly.

She rose suddenly and went to the door, opening it a piece, and she listened to the voices on the other side. She heard Mr Harvey and she heard John McGill. She heard Martin Schurmann's whine. And they were all talking about the same thing.

They wanted to hang the Indian.

Now and then the talk broke away from the Apache, when someone spoke of the heat and the dust and the loneliness of Salt Flats. But Martha knew that even when they spoke of these things they were really thinking of the Indian. Or perhaps it was that when they spoke of the Apache it was the heat and the desert-land only they were hating.

She shut the door on her father's voice and she went to the

window again and sat down. She looked along the street to the forge. The dust on the street was white in the moon, patched with yellow where the oil-lamps threw their glow. There was enough light, from the moon and the lamps, for her to read the signs, and she read them, again and again, without knowing why – *Harvey's General Merchandise, McGill's Leather, Saddlery and Harness, Schurmann's Tonsorial Parlour*. The only building without lights was the old *Bella Union*, its sign almost faded, its windows boarded up for sixteen years now. And, always, after she had read the signs, her eyes came back to the black, open mouth of the forge, and the thought of Jason there with his Indian prisoner.

Fletcher heard the voices, too. He stood just inside the forge, with his back against Harvey's spring-wagon which still wanted new wheel-rims. Now and then the fire collapsed a little more, rustling, sending up a spinning spark. And now and then Fletcher heard a deep and regular breathing in the darkness, from where Chiquito lay with his back against the wall, his hands and feet tied. But most of all Fletcher listened to the sound of talk in the saloon of The Boyd House. He could not hear the words, but he sensed the anger and the passion of them. Since dusk he had counted the men going in, and he reckoned there must be thirty in there now, almost all the grown men in the town.

Once Mrs Harvey had gone across from the store, to fetch her husband home, Fletcher guessed, and this had made him smile a little. But he saw no humour in it when she came out alone, walking stiff-legged in pride and indignation, her skirts lifted from the dust. From somewhere, from the bottle or from the men about him, Harvey had found enough courage to defy his wife.

Sometimes other women had come and stood in the lamp-light outside The Boyd House, but none of them had brought their husbands out, and they had gone back home and kept their lights burning.

When he saw this Fletcher went to his bunk at the back of the forge, and he took down his rifle. For the first time in his life, since he was a boy, the feel of the weapon was strange and ugly. He had never seen a lynching, but he had heard men talk of it. Sometimes the stories had begun like this, on a hot night when there was hate and anger and failure in a town. And too much for men to drink while they thought. Other stories had begun a different way. So Fletcher did not know what to think or what to expect, except that whatever was to happen he would probably be alone.

Behind him the Indian stirred. '*Sikisn?*'

'What is it, Chiquito?'

'It is hot.'

Fletcher walked to the water-barrel, scooping some out with a dipper and carrying it across to the Apache. He caught a flash of white eyes and teeth. The Indian's roped hands came out of the darkness to steady the dipper as he drank.

'Thank you, *sikisn*.'

Fletcher was unreasonably angry. 'Why do you call me brother? We've met two, three times, that's all.'

'A man knows his brother.'

'Maybe so,' said Fletcher emptily. He allowed the remaining water to dribble from the dipper. Then he went back to the barrel and scooped some for himself. He drank, took another scoop and poured it over his head. It cooled him a little. He went back to the door of the forge, and once more the Apache's hoarse, insistent voice attacked him.

'*Sikisn?*'

'What is it now, Chiquito?'

'Let me go.'

Fletcher breathed in deeply. 'No, you know that's ...'

'You hear men talk.'

'That's all it is, Chiquito. It's just talk.'

'Will they hang me, *sikisn*?'

But Fletcher would not reply. He looked angrily at The Boyd House and saw how white it was in the moon, and the high veranda which was a manifestation of Boyd's pride and ambition because he had refused to have a boardwalk porch. The voices were louder now, mixed with violent laughter, and there was the crash of a glass or a bottle breaking. The rifle was wet with sweat in Fletcher's hand, and he untied his neck-cloth and wiped the weapon carefully.

'They will kill, *sikisn*.'

'No, Chiquito.'

'I know. You know.'

'You're wrong. It'll be all right tomorrow. I can take you out to the Bowyers' then.'

'Maybe Bowyer dead.'

Fletcher paused before speaking. 'Is he, Chiquito?'

The Indian did not reply. Fletcher stood away from the spring-wagon and walked to the door of the forge where he could see down the whole length of the street. He saw a woman approaching, and at first he thought it was Mrs Harvey coming to ask him to get her husband out of the saloon. But even as he thought this he saw that it was Martha. He watched her as she came closer, the lightness of her body, and the sad, tired way she held her head. She stopped a few yards from the forge, and Fletcher moved out of the shadows so that she could see he was there.

'Jason?'

'I'm here.'

'Is it all right to come?'

'You can come closer,' he said, a little bitterly. 'He's tied up, like your father wanted.'

She came up to him, her heart-shaped face lifted. 'I didn't mean that. I meant that being Town Constable you might have rules.'

'I ain't got no rules,' he said. 'I know nothing about being Town Constable, 'cept you do the work other folk ain't got the sand to do for themselves.'

She said nothing for a moment, then took her eyes from him and looked into the darkness of the forge. The fire was a pin-prick of scarlet and almost dead, but the forge smelt as always of hot iron. 'What is he doing, Jason?'

'He's tied up, feet and hands. What could he do?'

Again a pause, and then, 'Did he kill the Bowyers?'

'He ain't said. I guess he figures it don't matter one way or the other. Listening to your father and the others over there.'

Now she spoke quickly. 'They're talking of hanging him. Harvey, and John McGill I mean. Even Old Reuben.'

'Not your father?'

He heard the hiss of her breath. 'Him too. Most of all. He's putting them on to it.'

'I should have taken you away,' said Fletcher, 'two years ago. When my folks died. When I spoke for you and your father took a whip to me.'

'Jason . . . !' she pleaded.

'Lot of things I should've done,' he went on. 'I should've stopped your father up there, before he shot the other Indian. I should've –'

'Try and understand him.'

'He runs this town. Like it was his.'

'He was one of the first here. Understand him, Jason.'

'I understand him. There's your Maw, and you're all he's got to remind him of her, and every time he looks at you he remembers he ain't got her any more. But now it's different.'

'How's it different, Jason.'

'Now he's got an Indian, don't you see? Now's he got an Indian he can hang, and he ain't thinking it's on account of the Bowyers. It's your Maw.'

'It's the town, being nothing and all, Jason.'

'It'll be like that for us, if we stay. You've got to come with me.'

'I can't.'

'Do you want to grow old here?' asked Fletcher passionately. 'You want to be dried up with the town?'

'I can't leave him, Jason.'

'You owe him nothing. Will you leave with me?'

'Not yet.'

'When? When, Martha?'

'I don't know.'

She stood outside the door, with her hands clasped before her, and the moonlight dropping her shadow gently. She could scarcely see Jason, where he stood in the darkness, but as he moved, in anger or in weariness, the moonlight was held for a second on the breechplate of his rifle.

'You do understand, Jason? You understand?'

She waited for him to answer, and when he did not she turned and walked slowly back to The Boyd House. Fletcher watched her go.

'Sikisn?'

Fletcher swung about quickly, and shouted angrily into the darkness beyond. 'Now, you shut your damned mouth, Chiquito! You hear me? I'm not your brother!'

He heard the creak of rawhide as the Indian moved arms and legs against the thongs. And then there was silence. He turned back to face the empty street, the pools of yellow light from the watching windows, the laughter and the shouting that had no recognizable tongues. He waited.

An hour later Boyd came through the batwings. He burst out of them and stood there swaying, his big body a black silhouette against the light. He yelled like a cowboy and then plunged down the steps to the dirt of the street. There he swayed again and yelled. The others came out of The Boyd House in a crowd, pushing and fighting. The crowd broke into fragments on the street, with arms waving bottles, or fists clenched. Fletcher saw the drummer, his city coat off and his derby hat twirling in his hand. He was shouting and singing, and he was very drunk.

Then the crowd, instinctively almost, came together in a tight knot, and moved down the street towards the forge. Twenty or thirty men when they shout, thought Fletcher, do not sound like men at all. He stood away from the wall and took a pace into the street with his feet astride and the rifle held across his body by both hands. He knew they must see him, but they did not stop. They came in a great hurry, their feet kicking at the dust, and in front of them walked Boyd, his shoulders very broad, his shirt white and the sleeves gartered. A coil of rope hung from one hand.

When they were twenty yards from him Fletcher shouted. 'Mr Boyd!'

They halted, and for a moment they were silent, eyes shining, stupid grins held lop-sided on sweating faces. He tried to put names to the faces, but could not, yet he knew them all.

The drummer pushed his way to the front, standing at Boyd's side. 'Mr Fletcher,' he began, 'for the safety of the West and its brave womenfolk . . .'

There was an ironic cheer, and the drummer turned to the crowd and bowed from the waist. Then he turned back and opened his mouth, but before he could speak Boyd grasped his shoulder and threw him in the dirt.

'Fletcher!' he shouted.

'What do you want, Mr Boyd?'

'You know what we want!'

'You'd better put it into words, Mr Boyd, so's the rest can hear and remember.'

Boyd stepped a pace forward and slapped the rope against his legs. Then he held it up. 'Why, we figure on hanging ourselves an Indian.' He looked back. 'That right?'

There was another cheer, and Old Reuben broke away from the crowd and began to stomp, his bald head bobbing and his knees going up and down in a war-dance. He hooted and flapped his hand over his mouth, until somebody pushed him and he fell down. He got up angrily, flailing his fists. The crowd moved forward, jostling against Boyd.

Fletcher pumped the lever of the rifle and brought it up to his chest. The crowd stopped and was silent again.

'Fletcher,' said Boyd at last, 'boy, you hear me now!'

'I can hear all of you. Go on back to your homes.'

'Well, now,' said Nathan Harvey. He stepped out of the crowd, swaggering a little, his thumbs stuck into his vest-pockets. 'Well now, look what we got here.'

'You go home, too, Mr Harvey,' said Fletcher. 'I saw your wife looking for you.'

The crowd laughed, enraging Harvey. 'Who the hell do you think you are?'

'I'm the Town Constable, Mr Harvey. Elected by all of you.'

'Then, by Jupiter, we hereby unelect you!' shouted Old Reuben, and he hit his thigh. The crowd laughed and pushed forward again.

'You hear that?' shouted Boyd. 'You're no longer Town Constable. Now get out of the way.'

'I'll hand in the job,' said Fletcher, 'when it's taken from me by a proper Town Meeting, which you ain't.'

'Don't you tell us –'

'I'm sorry, Mr Boyd. But you're all drunk and you don't know what you're doing.'

'What you going to do about it, eh?' shrieked Schurmann. 'You going to shoot us all down with that pop-gun?'

Fletcher did not answer. From behind him came a soft and urgent voice.

'Sikisn!'

'We're wasting time!' yelled Boyd, 'he ain't going to shoot nobody!' He lurched forward, only to halt as Fletcher brought the rifle to his shoulder. Boyd looked at the gun in astonishment, and then began to laugh.

'Put it down,' he said, 'I told you, you ain't going to shoot nobody.'

'I will if I have to, Mr Boyd.'

For a moment Boyd stared at him, then turned to the others. 'Now you listen to me . . .' he began.

'Let's get on with it,' shouted Harvey.

'Listen to me! Hear this first. Because if he fires that gun at me you ought to know why.'

'Why?' The drummer collided with Boyd, pulling at his shirt. 'Why, Mr Boyd? You tell us why?'

Boyd pushed him away. 'Because he figures with me dead he can get Martha. He ain't protecting no Indian. He's figuring on killing me legal.'

He turned on Fletcher, his face contorted. 'Ain't that right. You been wanting Martha all these years. Only me stopped you. Stopped you with a whip once, didn't I? You going to shoot me, boy, you'd better be mighty certain why.'

Fletcher let the rifle slip from his shoulder a fraction, and in that second Boyd brought up an arm in a throw. The coils of the rope struck Fletcher across the face, blinding him, wrapping themselves about the rifle.

He staggered back, and felt the rush of men grapple with him as he fell to the ground. Somebody pulled the rifle from his hands. Another fell heavily on his chest, driving the breath from it. Arms fought with his legs, hands gripped his wrists, and a fist thudded and thudded again at his temple.

He heard the sound of unnatural voices, screaming, laughing, calling, and although his eyes were open he could see little in the darkness as he fought and struggled with the men upon him. For a moment, when he was able to force his body upright, he saw the open gap of the forge door, and the moonlit street beyond. Boyd and two other men, one was Harvey and the other was the drummer, were dragging Chiquito out by the feet, and the Indian's head was bouncing on the rough earth.

Then Fletcher was thrust down again. He heard a voice yelling '*No . . . ! No . . . !*', without realizing that it was his own. He smelt the raw whisky on the breaths of the men above him, the harsh odour of the earth below. The smell of liquor, and iron, and sweat, the smell of men and the smell of horses . . . Then he could no longer move. There were men sitting on his arms, lying across his legs, and Martin Schurmann and Old Reuben were sitting on his body yelling at each other.

But he could stretch out his neck and see the door. He saw the rope go up, snaking, and then the noose swinging as it passed over the beam of the hay-loft. It seemed to swing and swing a long time before an arm reached out and grasped it, an arm in a white, gartered sleeve.

Then Chiquito was there, held upright by Harvey, and the noose was going round his neck.

There was a shriek of protest, and suddenly the drunken drummer was clawing at Boyd like a woman. Boyd laughed, and the drummer next tried to take the Apache's head from the noose. But Boyd took him by the throat and threw him away.

The unexpected interruption caught the attention of the men on top of Fletcher, and he pulled himself free of them, standing up, swinging his fists. He lurched towards the door, and saw the taut, tight rope slanting, and at the bottom of it the tilted head of Chiquito, the knot behind his ear.

The Apache stared at Fletcher. '*Sikisn!*' he said, and his eyes were like an animal's.

Fletcher yelled and leapt at Boyd. The big man swung up his arm and brought the butt of the rifle against Fletcher's head. There was nothing more then, nothing to see but darkness, nothing to hear but a rushing like winter rain.

He came out of the darkness slowly, feeling, smelling, hearing things before he could endure the pain of opening his eyes. He felt a coldness on his face, and tickling threads of sensation running down his cheeks to his neck at the back of his ears. He smelt the dust and the iron smell of the earth. And he heard a rhythmic, remorseless creak of a rope swinging.

At last he opened his eyes, and above him was the night sky, clear and clean in the moon with the stars bright. He saw this until a shadow came between them and him, and a face looked down. It was Martha, and her hand was on his forehead. He closed his eyes again against the pain, but he knew that he was really taking shelter in the darkness because he was afraid of what he might see if he opened his eyes and looked about him, instead of up to the sky. He heard the rustle of Martha's skirt, the ring of a dipper against a bucket, a cloth being wrung, and then there was the gentle coolness on his face again.

At last he sat up on his elbow, despite the restraining pressure of Martha's hand. He forced himself to look up. There hung Chiquito at the end of a rope, and the body moved and the rope sang.

'*Damn them!*' shouted Fletcher.

'Jason ...' said Martha unhappily.

He pushed her away and stood up, staggering against the wall of the forge, supporting himself there as he looked up and stared, and stared.

Something moved at his feet, a hand clutched at his leg and he looked down. The white face of the drummer below was wet with tears.

'I helped ...' he said. 'I tried to stop them. God pity me!'

Fletcher looked down the street. Salt Flats was now in darkness except for one light burning in The Boyd House. But it was a dying darkness. All along the eastern rim a new day's heat was beginning in rose-grey and yellow. And still the body of Chiquito creaked on the rope.

'God pity me!' said the drummer, and repeated it again and again in a dying whisper, until his lips were moving soundlessly.

'Jason ...'

Fletcher turned to Martha. 'Where are they? Where's your father?'

'In his room. He just sits there, looking at Maw's picture.'

'I hope he never sleeps. I hope none of them can sleep again.' Fletcher staggered into the middle of the street yelling wildly.

'Do you hear? I hope you can't sleep! I hope you never sleep! *None of you!*'

'God pity me!' moaned the drummer.

Fletcher went back to the forge, leaning his arm on the wall and his head against it. Martha came to him and stood by him, and at last put an arm about him.

'Shall we take him down, Jason?'

He lifted his head and looked at her. 'Take him down?'

'The Indian.'

'No,' he said. 'Let him hang there. Let them see him. Let their wives see him. Let their kids. They were drunk enough to hang him, let's see if they can bury him when they're sober.'

'What are we going to do, Jason?'

'We?'

'You and me.'

He began to understand. 'Just you and me?'

'There's nothing to hold us here.'

He looked up at Chiquito. 'There'll always be something to hold us here.' Then he looked back to her. 'Your father ... ?'

'When he came back ... Afterwards ...' she said, 'He sat awhile, just looking. Then he told me to come and help you. Then he kissed me. He hasn't done that, Jason, not since Maw died.'

'Chiquito would be glad to know,' said Fletcher bitterly.

'I've got my things,' she said. 'I ain't got much, but what I've got is in Maw's old carpet-bag over there. Take me away, Jason. Now.'

'God pity me!' said the drummer softly.

The sun was up a handsbreadth above the horizon when they drove out of Salt Flats. By this time, on other days, there would have been folk in the street already, getting chores done before the day grew too hot. By this time Martin Schurmann would have been sweeping the walk before his Parlour, and Harvey would have been putting bags of meal outside his store. But there was nobody in the street when Fletcher drove the buckboard down, his apron-faced roan clopping behind.

They did not look to left or right, and they left Salt Flats behind, and they did not look back.

Five miles out of town they met a wagon coming down the

trail from the Mogollons, and Fletcher pulled up and waited for it.

There was a man sitting on the front seat with a woman. On the seat behind were four young children, their faces bright and scrubbed. In the wagon itself, and staring over the side-boards, was an Apache, the boy who had run into the brush when Boyd shot down Pa-nayo-tishn.

The wagon halted, and the man put his whip into the socket, nodded to Fletcher and flipped the brim of his hat to Martha. He did not smile, and his face was hard.

'Good-morning, Jason. Good-morning, Miss Boyd.'

They returned his greeting and he looked at them for a while and then jerked a thumb towards the Indian. 'Is what he says true, Jason?'

'It's true.'

'This is a bad business.'

'It's worse than you think.'

The man looked curiously at the bags in the back of the buckboard. 'You leaving Salt Flats?'

'We're leaving.'

The man nodded, and then he said 'Where's Chiquito? Is he in town?'

'He's in town.'

'I want to talk to your father about this, Miss Boyd.'

'He'll listen to you, I reckon,' said Fletcher in a hard voice. He lifted the reins.

'Well ...' said the man.

Fletcher touched the brim of his hat. 'Good-bye, Mr Bowyer,' he said. 'Good-bye, Mrs Bowyer.'

He clicked his tongue, slapped the reins and drove on, with Martha beside him.

More about Penguins and Pelicans

Penguinews, which appears every month, contains details of all the new books issued by Penguins as they are published. From time to time it is supplemented by *Penguins in Print*, which is a complete list of all titles available. (There are some five thousand of these.)

A specimen copy of *Penguinews* will be sent to you free on request. For a year's issues (including the complete lists) please send 50p if you live in the British Isles, or 75p if you live elsewhere. Just write to Dept EP, Penguin Books Ltd, Harmondsworth, Middlesex, enclosing a cheque or postal order, and your name will be added to the mailing list.

In the U.S.A.: For a complete list of books available from Penguin in the United States write to Dept CS, Penguin Books Inc., 7110 Ambassador Road, Baltimore, Maryland 21207.

In Canada: For a complete list of books available from Penguin in Canada write to Penguin Books Canada Ltd, 41 Steelcase Road West, Markham, Ontario.